About the Author

Vanessa was born and raised in the suburbs of the Midwest until her entry into the Juvenile Justice system and her years spent in the Troubled Teen industry. After leaving the Troubled Teen Industry, Vanessa went to college for Psychology, where she met her husband. Vanessa worked in the Naval Reserves, got her Masters in English, and made her career as a computer programmer, all while raising two daughters, both of whom are now in their own undergraduate degree programs.

While Vanessa published a few articles and short stories in college, and more recently published two technical papers in her field of specialty, this is Vanessa's first semi-fiction novel and the first time Vanessa has written publicly about her life on the Island of Troubled Teens.

Fall of the Guardians

VANGUARD PAPERBACK

© Copyright 2024
Vanessa White

The right of Vanessa White to be identified as author of
this work has been asserted by her in accordance with the
Copyright, Designs and Patents Act 1988.

All Rights Reserved

No reproduction, copy or transmission of this publication
may be made without written permission.
No paragraph of this publication may be reproduced,
copied or transmitted save with the written permission of the
publisher, or in accordance with the provisions
of the Copyright Act 1956 (as amended).

Any person who commits any unauthorised act in relation to
this publication may be liable to criminal
prosecution and civil claims for damages.

A CIP catalogue record for this title is
available from the British Library.

ISBN 978 1 80016 702 5

This is a work of fiction. Names, characters, businesses, places, events and
incidents are either the product of the author's imagination or used in a
fictitious manner. Any resemblance to actual persons, living or dead, or
actual events is purely coincidental.

*Vanguard Press is an imprint of
Pegasus Elliot Mackenzie Publishers Ltd.*
www.pegasuspublishers.com
First Published in 2024

**Vanguard Press
Sheraton House Castle Park
Cambridge England**

Printed & Bound in Great Britain

Vanessa White

Fall of the Guardians

Vanguard Press

Dedication

I dedicate this book to the four people who were my saviors during my time on the Island of Troubled Teens.

First, to Jess, the young girl who showed me unconditional love from the moment we met. You brought me love and luck; I don't know how my life would have gone without you. I miss you and I love you.

Second, I dedicate this book to the most important man in my life, my Dad, without whom I would have never survived my time in the Troubled Teen Industry. I wouldn't be the person I am today without you. I love you and I miss you with all of my heart.

Third, I dedicate this book to the memory of my aunt Beth. You changed my life and became family. I wouldn't have started this project without you, I just wish you lived long enough to see it completed. You will forever be in my heart.

Last, I dedicate this book to my Uncle Matt. Your support over the years was often the difference between life and death, for both me and my daughters. I love you more than words can ever say.

Thanks

I want to give special thanks to my teacher, friend, and co-author, Steven Santos (one of the only two real names in this book). I gave you a hot mess of haikus, college kid writings, and teenage diary entries as if it were an actual book. Instead of telling me to file it in the round receptacle, as you should have, you helped me to process my experiences and turn that steaming pile of crap into the powerful story it has become. Without you, I would never have truly processed my experiences, let alone have produced a work that tells my story, and for that, I will forever be in your debt.

I would like to thank my second co-author, Noah LeFlore (the only other real name in this book), a recent TTI survivor. Your work on this project has been immeasurably valuable. Where I struggle with expressing emotions, somehow you were able to translate my feeling into words. While I know I didn't make this project easy for you, this would not have happened without you. You really earned that whole big case of brownie points.

I want to thank the 127 survivors of TTI programs who suffered through interviews with my co-authors. Your interviews provided them with questions and insights that made this process work, and I thank you with all my heart.

A note to my readers

Writing this book was the most difficult project of my life. I did a lot to repress these memories, especially the brutality of it. Reliving these experiences through this process was not easy, but I think it was worthwhile.

I publish this book under a pen name, first because even my husband and my children do not know most of the horrors I went through that are contained in this book, nor do I want them to know. Secondly, the church involved is a cult that has a history of serious violence towards its detractors, and I will not risk my, or my family's safety for a book.

I have changed the names, dates, and other identifying details of everyone and every place in this book to protect the innocent (and the guilty). While I am sure many people will be able to figure out what the program was, and a few may even figure out who I am, I ask you to respect my privacy.

There are places in this book where my memory wasn't as clear as I would have liked it to be. In those places, I took artistic license to fill in those gaps. As such, I present this as a work of fiction that is informed by my life experiences.

I hope this book spurs our society to take a closer look at how we treat troubled teens. I think there are many lessons to be learned from my experiences.

But I feel I must warn you; this is not an easy read. It deals with a lot of sadness, dark truths, and uncomfortable situations. You have been warned.

-Vanessa White-

About the Pictures

I don't have very many pictures from the Island, but in this book I will share with you the photos I can share. All of the pictures I have from my time on the Island, including almost all of the pictures used in this book, came from an album I inherited from a former staff member (you can find out who in Chapter 14).

One of the things that really limits what I can show you is that the vast majority of pictures we have contain the every-day nudity of our life on the Island. While that was our everyday normal, that kind of teenage nudity is just not the accepted norm in the Western world, and that greatly limits what I can show you. Most of the pictures we used were just small corners of larger photos, though the punishment pictures in Chapter 2 are of an adult model I hired.

With the exception of a single picture of Jess from when she was 4 years old, we made a conscious choice not to include any pictures with faces in order to protect everyone's anonymity.

I ran all of the pictures I used in this book through an artistic pencil sketch filter to make them printable, but also because I like the effect.

-Vanessa White-

Table of Contents

Chapter 1:	17
Beginnings	
Chapter 2:	28
The Island Handbook	
Chapter 3:	62
Life in Bunk 7	
Chapter 4:	84
Mr. S	
Chapter 5:	117
Birth of the Guardians	
Chapter 6:	133
Learning to Fly	
Chapter 7:	157
And the Jedi Moved The Mountain	
Chapter 8:	177
New Responsibilities	
Chapter 9:	193
Gulliver on the Island of the Amazons	
Chapter 10:	207
School Begins Anew	
Chapter 11:	231
Fall of the Guardians	
Chapter 12:	246
An Angel Takes Flight	
Chapter 13:	261
Letters from Home	
Chapter 14:	294
Afterthoughts	

Chapter 1: Beginnings

If you are like most people, you have never heard of the Troubled Teen Industry. For your sake, that's probably a good thing. The Troubled Teen Industry is made up of groups and individuals that profit from the troubles of teenagers. While I have heard of a handful of programs that have actually helped kids, the vast majority leave kids battered and broken people. Most of us that did well after one of these programs did so despite them. We are the lucky few.

No one ever asks to grow up, but you also can't stop it. I came of age in the Troubled Teen Industry. My experiences in this industry are some of the most defining of my life. Unlike most, I had enough adults in the program that actually cared that I am not completely screwed up by it. But I also saw and experienced horrors no human should ever face.

My name is Vanessa. In late September of 1989, my parents were killed in a car accident. I was twelve at the time, the only child of two very loving parents, and I was a Daddy's girl. Their death devastated me in ways

I can't explain. After they died, I went to live with my Aunt Marsha, my only living relative and I went more than a little off the deep end. I quickly got involved with the wrong crowd. I drank heavily; I smoked pot. I did some skittling, all to try to make the pain go away. And I sometimes performed oral sex to get what I wanted.

My Aunt Marsha tried, but she had never had kids before, let alone one that was as self-destructive as I was. She tried really hard, but she couldn't get me under control. I didn't listen to her. And I wouldn't go to therapy. I went to school when I felt like it, and even then, I skipped most of my classes. After I lost my parents, I just didn't care.

In January of 1990, about three months before I turned 13, I got busted for stealing a car and joyriding (yes, I crashed the car). We went to court in March, just before my 13th birthday. The lawyer had a plea deal set up. The judge was going to let me off with community service and sending me to see a shrink when my lawyer told him about losing my parents, but I was drunk. So, instead of apologizing to the court and promising to see the shrink, I mouthed off and told the judge what I thought of him and his therapy. In so doing, my smart mouth wrote a check my ass would have to cash for the next five years.

But the judge gave me a choice: Juvi with a record, or a teen program without a record. My aunt and lawyer chose the teen program. I was sentenced till my 18th birthday.

My aunt threw a big party for my 13th birthday and invited everyone I knew. I was in the middle of a bender; I didn't understand that it would be my last party at home. I was an ass to her and mostly drank her liquor and treated her like shit.

Two days later, at four a.m. on April 1st, just before the sun came up, two large men woke me up from a drunken sleep. They said they were my escorts and that I was being transported to the teen program. They said that if I didn't cooperate, they would restrain me.

I was drunk, but I got it that I was being kidnapped. I tried to fight my way free, but I couldn't. I didn't even weigh seventy pounds. They put me face down on my bed and handcuffed me. Next thing I knew I was pulled up and out of my room. I kicked one and spit in the other's face. I started to run, but the first one got my foot, and down I went. The second one was on top of me. The last thing I saw was my Aunt Marsha crying and then everything went black as a hood was put over my head and my feet were shackled.

I was thrown over a shoulder and carried outside. I remember hearing the sliding door of a van, then felt the wind knocked out of me as I landed face-first on the floor. I heard one of them get in next to me as I struggled to break free, then the door closed. The rest of the van ride is a blur of being hungover, feeling fear, terror, anger, desperation, exhaustion, hate, hunger, thirst, and sleep.

It was night when we got to our destination. I remember the sounds of a propeller plane as I was carried from the van inside a building and then stood on my feet. The goons each had an arm, and then my hood was yanked off. I remember squinting at how bright it was. We were in a small, private airport with a single terminal (if you can call it that).

I was one of about twenty-two girls here. We were in two lines facing each other. Most of the girls looked to be between fourteen and sixteen, but one girl looked to be about four. I think everyone but the littlest one was in handcuffs. About half of us were in leg shackles and a few were gagged. Most of us were dressed only in pajamas. I only had on a nightshirt. Several only had underwear on and one was completely naked, and no one seemed to care about that.

Then the woman in charge, Sister Lisa, started barking at us. I was too hungover; I didn't catch a word of it until she told the goons to load us up. We were taken to a bathroom where the goon pulled up my nightshirt, sat me on the toilet, and told me to pee if I knew what was good for me. I was so humiliated, but I had been holding it so long by that point that I peed.

I was then taken out and loaded on the plane. Turns out I was the first girl loaded. My hands were re-cuffed in front of me, then the goon locked the cuffs to the armrest using another set of cuffs and then belted me in. We were all locked to our seats that way. I had never been on a plane before.

I cried a lot. The four-year-old was sitting next to me. She was the only girl not cuffed and chained to her seat, but I don't think she had a chance of escaping that car seat contraption. Her name was Jess, and we tried to comfort each other the whole trip. We nuzzled our heads together and despite the noise of the plane, we both fell asleep.

We flew for a long time. I don't know how long, but it felt like forever. I think girls sobbed the entire time. I slept a lot. I woke up when the voice overhead told us we would be landing. Out the window, you could see the Island. It looked so peaceful from the window, almost like it was a tropical paradise, the kind my mom and I always dreamed of going to. I remember the butterflies in my stomach as we descended for landing. Jess held on tightly as soon as the butterflies started.

The goons pulled us out of our seats and lined us up outside the plane. Jess and I held onto each other for all we were worth. They took all of us into this building and put us in some big holding room; they sat us on benches and locked our hands to these ring things. The goons took the two girls that had been in the seats across the aisle from us and dragged them out. We heard the girls scream and then cry and then scream and then cry again. We didn't know what they did to those girls, but we knew it wasn't good. Then everything was silent. You couldn't hear those girls crying anymore, and nobody in the holding room made a single sound.

A minute later, the goons came back in. They were headed directly for Jess and me. I can't describe to you the fear and anxiety I felt as they walked over to us, nor the terror I felt as they dragged Jess and me out of the room and into that smaller room. They took my nightshirt away and chained my hands to the wall. They took away Jess' clothes and then they tried to chain her hands to the wall too, but the cuffs were too large and her arms didn't reach that high. Jess ran over and hugged my leg and one of the goons said to let her stay there. Then they hosed us down with cold salty water and threw some powder on us.

I thought it was over, but instead, it got worse. The goon raked his fingers through my hair, tearing hairs out when they hit knots and leaving my scalp sore. He told me to shut up when I screamed and said to keep quiet if I didn't want to get hit. It's a weirdly intimate feeling having a goon run his hands through your hair like that, and not in a good way, a feeling made worse by the confusion and having no idea what was going on.

It was such a jarring feeling when the other goon came up and squeezed his finger and thumb into my cheeks, forcing my mouth open. He then shoved his fingers in my mouth; I gagged horribly at the gross, oily taste. I felt like a slab of meat at a butcher's shop. Then I was uncuffed and forced to the ground. The first goon forced my legs apart and shoved his finger into my vagina. No one had ever touched me down there! Every alarm bell in my brain was now going off and I was panicking. Then my brain registered the pain and I started bawling. The feeling of his finger moving inside of me like that was one of the worst feelings of my life. The goon took his finger out and I felt such a deep shame and humiliation at what was just done to me. I felt dirty and violated in a way I had never in my life felt before.

Then it got even worse. The next thing I knew, they flipped me over and I felt the goon poke my butt. I didn't understand why he was poking my butt. But it didn't stop at poking my butt; it really hurt! He was pushing his finger into my butthole! I screamed and he just pushed in more! I panicked even more and screamed for help, but the other goon just held me down.

I was humiliated, panicked, violated, and scared. It hurt. When they let me go, I sat up and hugged my knees close to my chest, shivering from both cold and shock, and sobbing. Then they grabbed Jess. Thankfully, though, they only searched her hair and mouth. Jess ran over to me, but I was so upset that I couldn't even comfort her in that moment.

After that horror was over, they took us to a hallway with a bunch of 10-by-10 cells and put us in one. They were empty except for a couple of blankets and a metal sink/toilet thing, like in a jail cell.

The concrete floor was cold. Jess and I were allowed to sit together, but the other girls were not allowed to touch each other in any way. If a goon saw them do it, they would first give a warning, then yell, then hit and beat them. It was terrifying to see a goon go into a cell and beat a girl like that. We hid under the blanket a lot.

One set of girls was chained to different sides of the cell after being beaten for it several times. They locked one end of the chain to the first girl's ankle, ran the chain out the bars, across the cell, and then into the other girl's ankle so that only one could get to the toilet at a time and they couldn't touch each other.

I would say about half of us were detoxing during that time, including me. We all tried begging, bargaining, throwing tantrums, offering the goons sexual favors, making promises, and anything else we could think of to get out, but the goons just laughed at us, or worse, ignored us. At least a laugh was an acknowledgment that we were alive. After a while, you just kind of give up hope. At least I had Jess.

They fed us soup three times a day. Chicken broth in the morning, beef soup in the afternoon, and tomato soup in the evening. I had diarrhea, as did most of the girls. Jess was also given a bottle of Pedialyte and some bread and cheese every day. Unlike the rest of us, she didn't have diarrhea.

On day four, the staff started coming in. Male and female staff would make us stand in front of them and answer questions while they filled out forms. You knew immediately which ones were just doing their jobs and which ones just liked looking at or humiliating naked girls.

We were told we would be required to learn a number of commands before we would be allowed to leave processing and join our bunks. At first, I resisted, but at that point, I didn't have much fight left in me. If it was only me, I think I would have fought this indignity more, but it wasn't just me—I had to think about Jess. I quickly gave in and learned the commands.

Some of them were the standard responses, about the only words we were allowed to say. Some of them were military-type commands: Attention, Parade rest, Rest, At Ease, Fall In, Fall Out, and Sound Off. Some were the lesser punishment commands: Wait on the wall, Watch the wall, Nose-tits-n-toes, Mongra. Some of them were the moderate punishment commands: Lap, Bend-over, and Assume the Position. Strip was another common command, and they were clear that it didn't matter where you were or who was watching.

By day six, I had them all memorized. Jess didn't, but she did what I did, and they let us go to the bunk area. I was so relieved to be able to get us out of that cell.

It was Saturday, April 6th, 1990. It would have been my Mom's 37th birthday. We were taken to a storage room at the back of the shower building and given a bag with uniforms, a towel, sheets, and a blanket. I started to put on clothes and was yelled at. The goon made me take them off because nobody gave me permission to get dressed. I remember thinking how gross it was that I needed permission to get dressed and even grosser that I had to thank the goon for 'correcting me'. The goon made me carry both of our bags on my head to our bunk, Bunk 7.

Bunk 7 looked a lot like the cabins we had at the Girl Scout camp I went to back home, front porch and all. It was even painted the same white with blue trim. We walked up the front steps and through the door. We had to take off our shoes and put them on a shelf that the goon locked again as soon as we put our shoes in. He then had us put on flip-flops. Jess's flip-flops were the same size as mine, way too big for her feet. She had a lot of trouble keeping them on her feet.

Inside, you had three rooms, two rooms for the bunk parents, and a large dormitory room for the girls. In the dormitory was a wood stove for heat (not that we used it very often) and fourteen sets of bunkbeds lined up along the wall, seven on each side. Between each of them was a shelf where girls' socks and underwear were stored. Underneath each shelf was a hanging rod, with uniforms hung on hangers that didn't come off the rods.

When the goon that escorted us to the bunk left, we were surrounded by the other girls, who taunted us for having flat chests and being hairless (I was a late bloomer). Then they beat me to a pulp and made Jess watch. I was glad they didn't hurt Jess; I know I couldn't have protected her.

I was then left bloody on the floor while the bunk went to dinner, Jess trying to comfort me. Jess was hungry, so despite the beating, I got us dressed and went to chow.

While I don't have any pictures of Bunk 7 that I can share, this is a picture of Bunk 2, the bunk closest to the main office. All of the bunks on the Island were built in this general style, though Bunk 2 was the smallest of the bunkhouses. The rest were wider and longer, with the door at the center and a window on either side of the door and windows along the side walls. Bunk 2 was one of the only bunks that sat on taller stilts like this, and while every bunk had a front porch, only a few bunks had steps and porch rails like Bunk 2 did. Bunk 2 only had one staff room, where the other bunks had 2.

Chapter 2:
The Island Handbook

We didn't have any kind of handbook for the Island, we had to learn these things by being punished when we broke a rule we didn't even know existed, but this chapter is what I imagine an Island Handbook would have looked like when I arrived. It is mostly taken from my memories and my diary. The handwritten notes are my thoughts on each one.

I promise you that we didn't see the logic in the chores that are presented here. To us, they were mostly random tortures with very little reason. It wasn't until writing this book that I was able to piece together the logic. While I suspect this may have once been used to help girls build real-world skills, that's not how it was during my time on the Island

-Vanessa-.

Welcome to the Island.

This handbook is designed to give you an overview of our program and help you make the most of your time here.

We are a Christian Military school, with a focus on reaching God through hard work and discipline. We have many programs and traditions here to help you make the most of your time here.

The headmaster is the final authority on the Island. The assistant headmaster is Brother Sam. The Dean of Students is Sister Lisa. They are supported by a full-time secretary and a medical provider. The Island maintains a full-time staff that includes a head counselor, headteacher, farm manager, construction manager, and boiler operator as well as maintenance staff.

The school is divided into pods, with each pod having a Head Bunk Parent. Each bunk within the pod has a bunk mother and a bunk father. These Brothers and Sisters are missionaries from the church and spend an average of three years on the Island, but some stay on much longer.

The Brothers and Sisters of our order will administer discipline; they are encouraged to apply it liberally. We are strong believers in the power of discipline to set girls on the right path.

The Point System

Each level has a required number of points you must earn throughout your daily activities in order to advance. Points are cumulative and are tracked daily by your bunk parents and counselors. They get added to your score for completing tasks and fulfilling requirements and taken away when you fail to meet expectations. You may earn extra points for going above and beyond the requirements.

Points are assigned by your bunk parents, counselors, and upper-level girls.

The Level System

We utilize a comprehensive level system on the Island. Girls who are not court-ordered must reach level 10 to graduate.

With levels come privileges and responsibilities. You are responsible for following any orders given to you by any staff or any girl two levels your senior, and you must always answer them with a 'sir'.

Level 0: Everyone arrives on Level 0. You will remain in the intake center until you have detoxed, answered all the assigned questionnaires, and passed the basic commands test, at which point you will have earned the 50 points needed to be promoted to Level 1 and go to the bunks. This usually lasts about a week.

Level 1: Level 1 is about learning our system. Your primary responsibility is to watch and listen. While on Level 1, you are not permitted to speak unless given permission. You will take your weekly bath as a sponge bath at the slop sink behind the shower-house. You are to silently watch and observe what goes on. You are "tagged in" to a staff member or a Level 5+ at all times and must not be more than ten feet away from them at any given moment. It is your responsibility to follow them. You must earn 500 points to be promoted to Level 2.

Level 2: Level 2 is about learning the basic chores and uniform marching in formations. You will join your bunk for your weekly shower instead of a sponge bath in the slop sink. You are allowed to speak to other girls during your free time after dinner. You are no longer tagged in, but you must remain within the eyesight of a 5+, or staff member at all times. You must earn 1,000 points to be promoted to Level 3.

Level 3: Level 3 is about gaining proficiency with the basic tools used on the Island. This includes bow drills, yokes, saws and farm tools. On Level 3, you get permission to write letters home and to receive postcards from home. You also get permission to speak to other girls during bunk time, parade rest, transitions, and during some work assignments. You are still on eyesight. You must earn 2,100 points to be promoted to Level 4.

Level 4: Being promoted to Level 4 is an accomplishment. It earns you the privilege of being eligible for meals #4 and #5 a lot more of the time and you are now allowed to ask a limited number of questions of the staff. On Level 4 you are now allowed to look Level 4 and lower girls in the eye when you speak to them. You may be out of eyesight briefly in pairs or small groups with permission from a staff member or Level 6+ (i.e., go to the bathroom, grab a spare tool, etc.). Level 4 is where you begin meeting with the counselors in small groups. You must earn 3,200 points and complete all learning assignments to be promoted to Level 5.

Level 5: Level 5 is the first trusted level and is a major accomplishment. You may now use the latrines with stall doors. As a Level 5, you may get the privilege of being a "water girl" during chores. For older girls, it also earns you the privilege of disposable menstrual products instead of using your washcloth. Level 5 girls may be assigned to be the guides for new girls and can give out lesser punishments for Level 3s and below except for NTNT or Mongra (covered later). On Level 5 you may be out of eyesight with permission from a 7+ or staff member. Besides earning 4,500 points and all learning assignments, you must be nominated by a higher-level girl (7+) to be eligible for Level 6. Once the nomination is received, it will be evaluated by the high-level council for your pod.

Level 6: Level 6 is about beginning to lead others. Being on Level 6 makes you eligible for some reward tasks. Level 6s are expected to lead up to 8 lower levels in small chore tasks. You get the power to give out lesser punishments for Level 4s and below except for NTNT or Mongra. You are expected to report all infractions.

Level 6 allows longer letters from home. You must earn 5,600 points, be nominated by an upper-level girl, get a positive vote at council, and complete all learning assignments to be promoted to Level 7.

Level 7: Level 7 is another major level. As a Level 7 girl, you may use the bathroom in pairs outside of the designated shit times and run errands for the staff unaccompanied as well as lead half a bunk (12) of lower levels in chores. Level 7 girls are now eligible to do better domestic chores. As a Level 7, you can give out all of the lesser punishments to Level 5s and below and you can now lead a circle correction. Level 7+ girls must participate in the pod peer council. You must earn 6,700 points, be nominated by an upper-level girl, get a positive vote at council, and complete all learning assignments to be promoted to Level 8.

Level 8: As a Level 8, you may lead groups of up to 16 lower levels in chore tasks and are expected to run them with efficiency. You get the privilege to shower in private stalls with shower curtains. You have the authority to assign punishments to Level 6s and below. You must earn 7,800 points, be nominated by an upper-level girl, get a positive vote at council, and complete all learning assignments to be promoted to Level 9.

Level 9: As a Level 9, you are on the most trusted long-term level. You can lead an entire bunk in chores and can lead some therapeutic groups. Level 9 makes you eligible for the most sought-after domestic chores, such as babysitting. Level 9 girls have the authority to punish Level 7s or below and, in some cases, may refer girls for office punishments. You must earn 8,900 points, be nominated by staff, get a positive vote at council, and complete all learning assignments to be promoted to Level 10.

Level 10: Level 10 is the highest level achievable on the Island. This level is the precursor to graduation and comes with many privileges. You must earn 10,000 points, get a positive vote at council, and complete all learning assignments to be eligible to graduate. You will work with your counselor to develop a plan for when you return home, but just because this plan is complete does not mean you will graduate right then. Your counselor, bunk parents, and the headmaster will decide together when you will go home based on your continued good behavior, and you will be escorted back. Congratulations!

Basic Punishments and Commands

As a student at this school, you will need to learn the basic punishments and commands. These range from the basic responses to the lesser punishments to major punishments to office punishments.

The Nine Basic Responses

As a girl in the program, you will be required to know and use the following basic responses. Unless answering a direct question or if you have been given permission to speak freely, these are the only words you are allowed to say. Please note that some responses are restricted to upper-level girls.

Level 1-3

Sir/Ma'am, yes sir/ma'am.

Sir/Ma'am, no sir/ma'am.

Sir/Ma'am, thank you for _____ sir/ma'am.

Sir/Ma'am, permission to _____ sir/ma'am?

Level 4

Sir/Ma'am, I will find out sir/ma'am.

Sir/Ma'am, I do not understand sir/ma'am.

Sir/Ma'am, may I ask a question, sir/ma'am?

Levels 5 and up:

Sir/Ma'am, may I make a request, sir/ma'am?

Sir/Ma'am, may I make a statement, sir/ma'am?

The lesser punishments:

Chewing out: Staff and upper-level girls can stand you at attention and then chew you out for any infraction of any rule.

Do you have to chew out every girl, every day? Do you really have to chew out lower levels ten times a day?

Wait on the wall: Waiting on the wall is the mildest punishment. When given this command, you will immediately stand at attention facing a wall, your nose no more than 8 inches from the wall. Typically, you can expect to wait on a wall for between 10 and 20 minutes.

Watch the wall: Watching a wall is a little more serious a punishment than waiting on a wall. You will stand at Parade Rest facing a wall with your nose pressing up against the wall. Girls given this punishment can typically expect to have to Watch the wall for between 30 minutes and an hour.

I hate waiting and watchin the walls! Especially when Sister Mary makes me hold up that coin with my nose!

Nose-tits-n-toes: This is one of the most serious of the lesser punishments. When given this command, you will strip naked and stand at Parade Rest, with your nose, tits, and toes touching the wall, your hands on your head with your fingers interlocked. Girls given this punishment can expect to have to stand nose-tits-n-toes for between 30 minutes and several hours. When called out from the wall, you will keep your hands on your head while you got chewed out. You will stay naked, hands on your head until given permission to take them down and/or dress.

They let the other girls torment you during this punishment! So humiliating! Especially when they make you do it outside for the other bunks to see! About the meanest variant of Nose-tits-n-toes is the dreaded Nose-tits-n-knees. This is when they make you do it kneeling! Minutes feel like hours, especially when they make you kneel on dry grains of rice or gravel.

Mongra: This is a serious punishment. When given this command, you will bend over with your knees bent. You will reach your arms around your knees, and you will hold your ears. This stress position is hard to hold; it is the most severe of the lesser 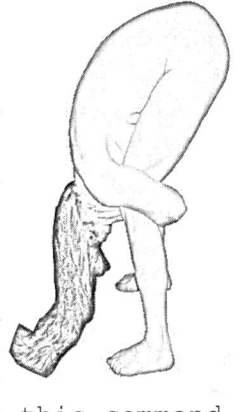 punishments. When given this command, you can expect to hold this as long as the staff member wants, but usually for 10 to 30 minutes.

This position is pure torture! Everything hurts after 5 minutes; 30 minutes just sucks!

Strip: While not exactly a punishment command, this command is used whenever a staff member requires you to remove your clothes. This could include getting ready for laundry and shower ("strip and pack"), getting ready for bed ("strip and bunk"), getting ready for a search ("strip and attention"), getting ready for a body cavity search ("strip & Mongra") or any other reason staff may have.

Gross! Yuck!

Moderate Punishments & Commands

Moderate punishments are the mid-level physical punishments girls may be given. These include:

Lap: This command is given by staff that preferred to spank you over their knee. While staff may use this for girls of any age, most girls under 14 are spanked this way. When given this command, you will pull down your pants and underwear and bend over the staff person's knee for a spanking. Kicking, struggling, or in any way resisting is not permitted. Staff will use a hand, wooden hairbrush, small paddle, or even a belt to spank you. They will spank you until you are crying *and* they think you have learned your lesson. When let up, you will immediately watch the wall, but your pants will stay down.

I hate being spanked over Sister Mary's knee!
It's so humiliating!

Bend Over: Most staff prefer to spank with girls bent over. This is usually, but not always, more severe than a lap spanking. If this command is given by itself, you will drop your pants and underwear and touch your toes. If it is given with an object (such as "bend over the chair") you will bend over that object. Staff may use medium paddles, leather belts, riding crops, and switches to spank the butt and thighs. When allowed up, you will either watch a wall with your pants down or nose-tits-n-toes.

Brother Mark and his crop are even worse than Sister Mary's knee!

Privilege removal: Staff can take away anything they chose as a short-term punishment. This could include the privilege of speaking ("muting"); looking people in the eyes; walking (you will have to crawl); having any peer interaction ("shunning"); having use of your hands (cuffing); taking full steps (shackling the feet); sleeping on a bed; going through doors without permission or anything else the staff may think of to punish you with.

This is psychological warfare! These really screw you up!

Meal Restriction: Staff can downgrade your meal level as a punishment (for example, from #5 to #1), reducing your calories for the meal. They may also make you "eat raw", which means eating uncooked rice and beans that had been soaked in water, some raw vegetables, and maybe the calorie-neutral salad. Staff can even take away meals if they want to, but not more than 3 in a row.

No! It means you are just hungry all the time!

Major Punishments

Major punishments are serious punishments designed to reign in willfulness.

Level Removal: Any adult is empowered to drop your level as they see fit. Losing the level means a loss of the associated privileges. When you have dropped levels, your point count is dropped to match entry to that level.

So, they can just take away years of work on a whim? So not fair!

Punishment Tasks: Punishment tasks must be completed during free time on Sundays, after dinner, or if the staff pull you from your normal routine to do them. Minor punishment tasks include things like having to count the grains of rice in a container or moving and restacking the small pile of bricks. Larger tasks include crushing a whole boulder with only a sledgehammer, moving the large brick stack, doing shit chores by yourself, or using a toothbrush instead of a scrub brush or other difficult chores.

In other words, this is to break you!

Wear you down until nothing else matters! Gross!

Paddling: Paddling is a punishment dished out by the head bunk parents. Large wooden paddles with holes drilled in them are used for correction. You can expect these to leave significant bruising on the buttocks and thighs. "The paddling hasn't begun until the tears run". Staff will not start counting the whacks until they feel you are truly crying, and real tears are flowing.

Starvation Diet: This is a serious punishment. You will be fed raw once a day.

So, you are going to starve us to death?

Circle Corrections: One of the most severe punishments given in bunk is Circle Corrections. When given, your entire bunk will participate in administering this physical punishment to you. At the conclusion of this, you can expect to be caged at the office.

Do you mean Circle beatings?

And if you don't participate, you are the next one to get beaten!

Office Punishments

These are the punishments that break you!

No one comes back well from these!

Major punishments given out by the office are the most severe ones you can get on the Island. You will be ordered to report to the main office, where you will stand nose-tits-n-toes to wait from Brother Sam to be ready for you. When called in, he will pass sentence and deliver your punishment. Common office punishments include:

Caging: When given this punishment, you will be put in a dog-kennel-type cage that is just big enough to be curled up in a ball in and left outside. The cages come in small, medium, and large for different size girls. You will usually spend a few hours like this, then be dropped a level and returned to your bunk. You could also spend as long as two or even three full days caged like this (even in the storms), which usually means a return to intake, restarting the program at Level 1, and being assigned to a new bunk.

God, I hate being caged! You can't move, your body hurts, it's just so gross!

Whippings: Whippings are given with a leather strap. This is about the most common of the office punishments. You will be bent or tied over a sawhorse and whipped on the legs, butt, and back until Brother Sam feels you have really learned your lesson. You will be dropped a level or more and returned to your bunk most of the time. Defiant girls will be caged for the night, then get it again the next day till they have stopped being defiant. Those girls will then have to start the program over again.

Whippings are just bad! But they are so much worse when they give you one in front of the whole school!

Solitary: Solitary is a rarely given punishment, but a very severe one. Girls sentenced to solitary are placed in one of 4 cells under the Main Office, where you are left naked and alone for anywhere from a week up to a month. Girls in solitary are usually fed raw twice a day. After solitary, you can be expected to be whipped and then sent back to intake to start the program over again. Solitary is not used except in the most extreme cases, like assaulting a staff member.

No one comes out of solitary well. At least when you are caged, girls sometimes talk to you.

Public Whipping: Public whippings are done at Parade for all the girls to see. This is both painful and humiliating, and it is designed to both punish you and to send a message to all other girls to follow the rules.

And terrifying to watch!

Creative Punishments: The office may make use of other more creative means of punishing girls as they see fit. Office staff can be extremely creative in devising punishments when they need to be.

These are often the most inhumane punishments...

Bunk 22: For girls that cannot get with the program, they may be sent to the segregated unit known as Bunk 22. This is a severe and long-lasting punishment; one we strongly advise you to avoid at all costs.

A few hours in Bunk 22 is enough for most girls to do anything, even unspeakable things, to get out!

Parade Commands

The most commonly used parade commands you will have to learn are as follows:

Attention: When standing at Attention, you are required to silently stand upright, heels together, toes apart (feet at 45 degrees), chin up, chest out, shoulders back, and stomach in. Your arms must be fixed at the side, your middle finger parallel to your pants or skirt seam. Your head and eyes must be in a fixed forward posture. You are not allowed to move from this position until given an order to do so, or until you are dismissed.

Parade Rest: From Attention, you will raise the left foot from the hip (knee straight) so it barely clears the ground and move it quickly to the left, so your heels are 12 inches apart on the inside of the heels. Your legs are straight, with the knees slightly bent (not locked) and heels are in line. At the same time as the left foot moves, the arms are brought to the back of the body while fully extended. Once your arms are behind you, your fingers are extended and joined, pointing towards the ground, palms facing outward. The right hand is in the palm of the left hand. The right thumb is over the left thumb, so they form a letter X. You must remain still and silent with your head up and your eyes straight ahead until given an order to, or until you were dismissed.

At Ease: From Attention, you keep your right foot in place and remain silent, but you can otherwise relax in a standing position.

Rest: This is the same posture as in at ease, but you are allowed to speak quietly to those next to you if you are on a level that allows it.

Fall In: You will line up in the basic formation. This means standing at attention in rows of 6 girls, spaced roughly an arms-length apart, both front and to the side, unless you are in bunk, then you will stand shoulder to shoulder. If Double-wide is called, you will line up 12 across.

March: Walking in formation. Every step has to be exactly 24 inches and exactly in step with the other girls. When marching you must raise your knee to waist height every step. Marching always starts with the left foot.

Fall Out: When given this command, you may either relax while standing in formation, or if on an appropriate level, you may break ranks, but you must remain in the immediate area.

Dismissed: When given this command, you are released from the immediate control of the staff person or upper-level girl.

Cleanliness

Maintaining cleanliness is important on the Island.

Dry brush stations. Dry-brush stations can be found at the farm and shit-pads. Girls on these chores will use these stations to remove the majority of mud before use of a sand station.

Dying Stations. Drying stations are decks built in sunny areas. These decks are used to allow girls to dry off in the sun. The use of these stations is at the discretion of bunk parents.

Sand Stations. Sand stations can be found in several places around the Island, including the large station outside the Chow Hall. These stations are used daily to scrub off mud. All girls are to do a sand scrub of their hands before any meal.

Slop Sink. The slop sink's running water is only used for maintenance. Girls on level 1 will have water to wash up with added by staff.

Showers. Shower use is strictly controlled. The water will be turned on and off by the bunk parents at the control station. Lower-level girls will use group showers. Upper-level girls may use the stalls. For control of foot fungus, girls are advised to Is wear their flip-flops in the shower area.

Laundry. All laundry is done in the large machines in the laundry building next to the shower building.

Meals

All girls on the Island are kept on a low-calorie, high-nutrient, mostly vegetarian diet. You will get chicken and beef stock in some foods, but meat is only served in Meal #6. This helps promote a healthy weight and a thin physique. This diet also helps to naturally control periods and reduce their frequency.

You will be measured and weighed once a week and the meals you get that week are in relation to if we want you to lose weight (meals #1 or #2), maintain weight (meal #3), or gain weight (meals #4 and #5).

You are generally allowed to eat as much salad from the salad bar as you want.

Eating "raw" is a punishment meal. Chow hut staff will soak your beans and rice in water overnight, and then serve you that along with some raw vegetables. If you are eating raw, you may not be allowed to have the salad.

Meal #6 are staff meals and generally not for girls, except as a major reward. Meal #6 always includes real meat and not just a meat stock. If meal #5 is a vegetable soup in chicken broth, Meal #6 will usually include actual chicken soup with real chicken in it. Meal #6 always comes with bread and a cup of coffee with milk and sugar. At dinner, Meal #6 usually includes a small dessert.

Most girls would do just about anything for a #6 meal, especially a #6 dinner with its dessert! It is almost twice the calories of a #5 meal and tastes a lot better!

Some girls, especially those 13 and under, will be given milk with meals, while older girls will usually get water or sometimes bug juice.

Staff that live in the houses (teachers, counselors, paid or long-term staff) will usually do family meals, where they cook home-style meals themselves. Girls on certain domestic chores, such as babysitting, may be invited to join a house for family meals. That is the biggest food reward girls can earn on the Island.

Chores

We believe hard work builds character. You can expect to spend a lot of time on chores. Chores are generally done by bunk, with the whole bunk working on one or two chores at a time. Reward and punishment chores are usually given to individual girls, and not generally to a group, though there are exceptions to this rule.

Farm Chores

Much of the Island's food is produced on the farm, including almost all of the fruits and vegetables. Food is grown here year-round. Talking is generally not allowed during these chores, with harsh punishments for disobeying that rule. All the chores involved in food production come with strict quotas that you must meet each day, with various punishments for falling behind.

Plowing: Up to 24 girls will be strapped to a metal yoke, which is then connected to a manual plow to turn the soil  or a box plow to flatten the soil. When not needed for farming, the girls assigned to plow may plow and grade the roads of the Island or just plow a gravel field. Yoked girls can also be used to pull the cart. This is used to transport goods from the boat dock to the storehouse or other locations as needed.

This is backbreaking work!

They treat us like pack animals!

Planting: Girls assigned this chore will plant seeds or seedlings in the plowed fields. Girls assigned to this task are required to stay kneeling/walk on their knees the whole time.

This chore leaves your knees all scraped up!

Weeding: Girls assigned this chore must pull weeds in the crop rows. Girls assigned to this task are required to crawl the whole time.

If you thought planting for 8 hours was hard, this is worse! Backaches and God help you if you miss a weed!

Harvesting: Girls assigned this chore will harvest the ripe crops. How you harvest depended on the individual crop. Breaking the plants in any way is cause for harsh punishments, especially any of the trees in the orchard.

If you dare to taste what you harvest, it's a beating!

Seedlings: Girls on this chore will work in the greenhouse to plant seeds in paper containers and otherwise care for seedlings that will later be planted on the farm or traded with the ship. You will also make various sprouts for the chow hall. While you have quotas, compared to the other farm chores, this is an easy and clean job. This is a reward task on the Island, as you are allowed to talk to other girls.

This is actually a nice chore.

Rock Chore Tasks

Rock chores involve the building and repairing of stone walls used around the Island, as well as most road maintenance. All of these chores come with strict quotas you must meet each day, with various punishments for falling behind.

Boulders: You will use the bow drills (unpowered hand drills) to make space for the feathers and wedges we put in large boulders. Then you will use large hammers on the wedges to break the stones into slabs, and slabs into the rock chunks used in walls, roads, crushing, and baking.

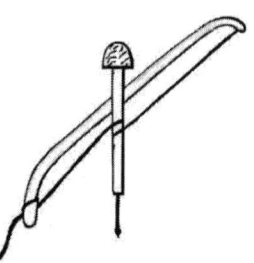

Crushing: You will use a sledgehammer to crush rock chunks into gravel. This is hard work, with strict quotas depending on the kind of rock. *This is <u>back-breaking work</u>! Sandstone is easy. If you get granite, you knew you are not making quota, and the question is how much you were short. Your beating is always based on that.*

Sand: When given this chore, you will dig sand out of a hole and put piles of it where you are told to, or you will put it in burlap sacks. You could also be made to dig out clay the same way.

Baking: When given this chore, you will cook rocks over a fire, maintaining the proper heat. This is used to make concrete and mortar.

Digging: When assigned this task, you will use shovels and digging bars to make drainage ditches, foundations for roads, building foundations, or other such excavations as needed.

Masonry: Older girls (fifteen and up) given this task will stack rocks with mortar to make stone walls or roads. While not a reward task, it is a skilled task and earns girls a #6 lunch.

Horse Chore Tasks

The school has a horse therapy program. Girls are not allowed to touch the horses if not part of this program, with severe consequences for doing so.

No, they don't, but we still have to clean up after them!

Mucking: When assigned this chore, you will shovel the hay and horse dung out of the 12 horse stalls into carts and then pull the carts to the compost piles where you will shovel it into those piles. Do not drop any horse dung along the lane.

Drains: When assigned this chore, you will re-dig and clean out the trenches that keep the horse fields from flooding.

Seeding: When assigned this chore, you will either collect or spread grass seed by hand in the horse fields.

Shit Chore Tasks

Shit chores are a necessary part of life on the Island. Shit chores must be completed before you can get dinner that day (and dinner will be eaten outside).

Shit chores are the worst chores on the Island. You smell like shit until your next shower and it takes at least a week for your bunk to stop smelling like shit after you rotate off.

Shitters: When assigned this chore, you will scrub down the two latrine buildings, including inside the latrines. If this is given as a punishment task, it will be done with toothbrushes.

Third worst chore on the Island! Disgusting!

Showers: When assigned this chore, you will scrub down the shower building. Like with shitters, if this is given as a punishment task, it must be done with toothbrushes.

Emptying: When assigned this chore, you will take the 350-gallon carts full of human waste out from under the latrine and pull it to either the shit pads for it to dry out in the sun, or to the compost piles to be turned in. If you are assigned this chore, you may also have to shovel the dried shit off the concrete shit pads and take them to compost.

Second worst chore on the Island. Especially if you can't reach over the side of the cart and they make you climb in to shovel out the shit!

Turning: Turning compost is the process of turning wet or dry latrine waste into the compost with shovels. As a punishment, you may be made to do it on your knees with only your hands.

Worst chore on the Island! It sucks as a punishment, because you always throw up and then they make you turn your own vomit in. Disgusting!

Firewood Chores

Firewood is the primary source of energy on the Island. It feeds the boiler that produces the electricity and hot water for the Island. It is also used for cooking and other energy needs. All of the chores involved in firewood production come with strict quotas you must meet each day, with various punishments for falling behind.

Trees: When assigned this chore, you will cut down the three-year-old trees, then make them into logs by removing the branches using an axe. You will then drag the trees to the cutting area using a chain with a pull rope. Felling trees is a skilled task and earns a #6 lunch.

Rounds: When assigned this chore, you will cut the logs into rounds using hand saws.

Splitting: When assigned this chore, you will split rounds using a maul axe. The resulting wood is stacked by other girls at the hopper. Girls assigned to splitting also have to feed the hopper for the boiler.

Stumps: When assigned this chore, you will dig the old tree stumps out of the ground using only a shovel and a hand saw. While daily quotas are not possible, girls are expected to work at this until all assigned stumps have been removed.

I hate this chore!

I hate stumps!

Hate! Hate! Hate! Hate!

Planting: When assigned this chore, you will hand plant seedlings to replace the trees that were cut down. These seedlings would be planted where the previous stump was. This was a reward task on the Island.

While you have quotas, compared to the other firewood chores, it was easy to meet. I don't mind this chore.

Domestic Chores

Domestic chores are only for trusted upper-level girls. These chores often involve crossing the staff fence line over to the staff side. These are assigned to individual girls, not to a whole bunk. These chores come with rewards such as not being nearly as dirty as other chores, being easier than other chores, Meal #6, using flush toilets, extra showers, and being able to speak freely with the girls you were working with. Common Domestic chores included:

Compost: When assigned this chore, you will take all of the food scraps and food waste from the chow hall and staff residences to the compost piles, then scrub out the cans.

Trash: When assigned this chore, you will pull a cart around and collect the cans of trash staff put out in front of their houses. This will then be taken to the boiler to be incinerated.

Kitchens and Baths: When assigned this chore, you will clean and tidy the kitchens and bathrooms of the various staff houses. You will often assist with cooking staff meals, and as a reward, you may be invited for a family meal doing this.

Flowers: When assigned this chore, you will maintain the flowers that grow in planters around the staff area.

Chow Hut: When assigned duty in the Chow Hut (kitchen) you will work cooking food all day. You will get to drink a cup of coffee each day, showers every other day and may be rewarded with Meal #6 up to two days a week.

Chow Hall: When assigned this chore, you will work the Chow Hall (large dining room) serving food in the chow lines, cleaning up, and doing dishes. You will get to drink a cup of coffee each day, showers every other day, and may be rewarded with Meal #6 one day a week.

Laundry: When assigned this chore, you will work in the laundry washing, drying, and folding laundry. You may be rewarded with Meal #6 one day a week.

Babysitting: Off and on, young children may be on the Island. When assigned this chore, you will babysit while the staff work. This is a highly trusted job and as such, it comes with many rewards. Babysitters usually get as many as 3 family meals a day or at least a #6 dinner. Babysitting is widely considered the best possible job on the Island, restricted to older Level 8, 9, and 10 girls.

Mantras

The school has a number of mantras you must learn. The most important ones are:
"Intentions are irrelevant."
"It is no one's fault but my own."
"You can't control others, only your reaction to them."
"If you can't trust yourself, you need to trust us."
"Be patient and tough; someday this pain will be useful to you."
"Punishment is your salvation."
"Better a pink bottom than a black soul."
"The paddling hasn't begun until the tears run."
"You must embrace your mistakes to ever heal."
"Hard work is good for the soul."
"Idle hands are the devil's tools."
"'It's not happening to you'; it's happening for you."
"My choices got me here; I must accept the consequences of my actions."
"God will only save those who have truly repented."
"Focus on the task at hand, not what comes after."
"Obedience above all things."
"Slow obedience is disobedience."

Chapter 3:
Life in Bunk 7

April 6th, 1990. Sleeping in bunk that first night was terrifying. Jess and I were by far the youngest and smallest girls in the place. They made two girls change beds so that Jess and I got lower bunks right next to each other. The Goon said that Jess was too little to climb, and he got an order to keep us together.

The bed smelled musty; it was hard and lumpy, and they made us sleep naked. I had been naked in the cell, but at home, I always slept in underwear and a nightshirt or at least a nightshirt. Sleeping naked just felt wrong, but the goon made us do it, I had no choice. Jess climbed into my bed in the middle of the night.

The next day, we were woken up at six a.m. by the goon from last night (Brother Mark, one of our "bunk parents") and his riding crop. He used it liberally on anyone he thought wasn't moving fast enough. Even Jess felt the sting of that fucking crop, just for having climbed into bed with me.

Someone yelled 'Fall-in!' and we were lined up, shoulder to shoulder, all still naked. Brother Mark ordered us to attention, then walked up the front of the line, his crop running across each girl's breast (or in the case of Jess and I, our flat chests), lifting the tits of the more developed girls. Then he walked down the back of the line, his crop running across our asses or running up or down our butt crack. Then he ordered Parade Rest and walked down the front of the line. This time the crop was applied to the crotch, though thankfully he skipped this part with Jess. Last, he walked back, the crop to each of our cheeks (we had to open our mouths when he did this).

Any girl that flinched got hit *hard* by that crop wherever he was running it, including Jess. The indignity of this was infuriating. But you didn't have a choice, you had to hold it all in and you quickly learned not to flinch.

As he walked, he told us what our day was to be. Breakfast, exercise ("you will work out till I am tired!"), Tree stumps (one of the Firewood chores), lunch, class (stupid packets) or "groups" (where they tried to mentally break you), stumps, drill (marching), dinner, bunk time, bed. Brother Mark told us we had exactly 3 minutes to be dressed in our work uniform and ready for breakfast.

Only the Level 5 girl assigned to us, Debbie, spoke to us for a whole week. And she only spoke to us to give orders, we couldn't ask her any questions, even when we didn't understand what she meant.

One of the weird rules they made us follow was that we weren't allowed to look anybody in the eye, especially not the staff. I guess this was different for the higher-level girls, but for us lowly low-level girls, it really made forming relationships hard, though they turned a blind eye to it with me and Jess. Having to look down all the time also meant it was almost impossible to assert yourself in any meaningful way. I think it was one of the ways they kept us all submissive.

Another weird rule was that we weren't allowed to touch each other without permission, and to get permission you generally had to be on an upper level. They completely ignored this rule with Jess and me, even letting Jess sleep in my bed with me, but they enforced it if we ever wanted to touch anybody else. Unless you've been through it, you have no idea how much this screws you up over the long term. Humans need touch for our own psychiatric health, but here it was just another way they controlled us.

Chores were hard work. You had to do the work, it wasn't a choice. It wasn't uncommon for new girls to refuse to work at first. If they were lucky, a staff member just beat them. If they were unlucky, it was a circle beating.

The first time we were at stumps, a new girl from another bunk, she was maybe fifteen, was being supervised by a Level 7 girl. I think she was newly Level 7 because she said it a lot. This new girl just refused to work. She sat down and just refused to work. The Level 7 girl told her that if she didn't work, the whole bunk would be punished, and the Level 7 girl said she wasn't going to take a beating because the new girl wouldn't work. The new girl refused.

The Level 7 girl asked if she really wanted this. The new girl said she wasn't working. The Level 7 girl told the other girls that they knew what to do. One of the bigger girls threw the new girl to the ground. The other girls formed a circle and beat the new girl to a pulp.

They hit, kicked, and stomped her relentlessly. The new girl begged them to stop, promising to do her work. They didn't care. They kept beating her and beating her until she was a bloody mess on the floor. They only stopped when the Level 7 girl said she had had enough. Then two girls dragged her away; she couldn't even walk. I was scared as hell by this, especially when Debbie told me to let that be a lesson for me, that this is what happens to girls that are too stupid to follow the rules. I could only give the required 'Ma'am, thank you, ma'am' response.

I saw that girl again later that day, as we were rushing back to bunk before the storm hit. She was naked in a cage outside the main office. They left her in that cage in the storm the whole night.

It was worse for the girls that refused to do the shit chores. I saw one group hold a new girl's head underwater in the shit and piss latrine water after they beat her for refusing to empty a latrine. They held her head under so long I thought they were going to kill her. She too was then dragged off and caged for a night, her head still covered in shit. That scene played out more often than I want to remember, even in my bunk, where Jess and I were required to participate in the circle beatings. It always seemed to play out the same way.

The thing about a circle beating is that the worst part isn't the beating itself, although that's still really bad. No, the worst part is that it's the other girls that do it to you. You have to live with them, knowing it could happen again at any time. The mental torment of that lasts far longer than the physical effects of the beating itself.

You quickly learned to do the work, no matter how tired you are. It was far better to be seen trying and take Brother Mark's crop or even his belt for being behind on your quota than get the circle beatings and an office punishment.

As bad as Brother Mark was, he was better than a lot of them. He was mostly consistent; his rules didn't change every 2 minutes like most of the bunk parents. That lets you feel a tiny bit in control. Most of the older girls preferred Brother Mark to the other bunk parents and even thought he was fun. Many girls tried hard to transfer into Bunk 7.

At least Brother Mark hadn't been kicked out of 2 other missionary assignments before coming to the Island, like many of the missionaries. The Bunk 18 guy, I don't know his real name, but we called him 'Brother Roid', as in "Roid Rage"; he had been kicked out of three places before coming to the Island. He liked to "restrain" girls. He would force their arms up behind them, forcing them to bend over. He would then drive the girls' faces into the ground, then say they were resisting so he could pick them up and slam their faces into the ground again. When that was over, he beat them with a belt, and it was far worse than anything I ever got.

While the daily chore changed every week or few weeks (shoveling shit, pulling the plow, splitting and stacking wood, etc.) and Sunday was church, laundry, and our weekly shower. This was the format of our days for a long time.

Sundays were our weekly shower and laundry. The routine was that we would pack all of our laundry into the pillowcase, then we would line up at the shower wearing only our flip-flops. Brother Mark would stand in the shower at the control station to turn on the water and watch us all shower in the group shower. I would have to help Jess wash, then I was allowed to get my own shower on the next turn. It was so embarrassing being in the group shower that first time but having to shower with Brother Mark watching us was just humiliating. I mean, he had seen me naked many times already, I was used to that, but somehow having him watch me shower, watching me do something that was so intimate was just way worse, especially when I washed down there.

The Showers

You get used to the humiliation, brutality, and monotony of it all. I mean, what else can you do? You sneak in talking to the other girls and other small acts of rebellion where you can without getting caught. While I had Jess to love and care for, I otherwise shut down my emotions just to survive.

Jess was always my helper or a water girl. Older upper-level girls (17 and up) could "buy" a day off chore by blowing Brother Mark and getting to be a water girl, but only if you were pretty, had perky tits for him to play with, and was one of the first two. I never got to be a water girl; I was only thirteen and I didn't have perky tits for him to play with, only a flat chest.

Once or twice a week we were subjected to a body cavity search. You get used to it. The feeling of being violated goes away after a while. The trick is that you try to be somewhere else in your head while they do it to you. I would think about this one time being on the swing set with my mom and dad at the park by my house and by the end of the memory, it was over.

You had to earn everything on the Island. Showers, permission to speak, cooked food, the right to shit in a closed stall or shower with a modicum of privacy. Everything had to be earned and it was all tied to the level system.

Sister Mary was our House Mother, but mostly the cook (they were not married). She was protective of Jess, but she didn't really help to care for her. So, Jess was left mostly to me. I was punished anytime Jess got in trouble. I got punished a lot, maybe four or five times a day, sometimes a lot more, mostly for Jess. I spent a lot of time standing nose-n-toes (and tormented for not yet having tits to do the punishment properly) or bent over to take a beating just for her basically being four. I mean, it's not my fault her flip-flops were way too big and she would walk out of them. It wasn't my fault that Jess couldn't hold her bladder for 8 hours at a time. It wasn't my fault she wouldn't give the required responses, but I still got beaten for it. It's also why I never got past Level 3.

After our first week, one of the upper-level older girls in bunk, Gretta, came in with a pair of scissors and some rope. Gretta certainly wasn't the friendliest girl to us, she yelled at me a lot about Jess, and she gave me a lot of wall time for Jess being 4. It was scary seeing her walk over to us with that stuff, but instead of hurting us, she remade Jess's flip-flops to fit her feet. This made a huge difference in terms of caring for Jess – we no longer got in trouble for her walking out of her flip-flops!

The next month, we had two new girls join us. Brother Mark made us beat them up the same way I was. He even made Jess kick them both in the face when they were on the ground. Then we were not allowed to talk to them until the next week. That's how every new girl was greeted, and we got new girls once or twice a month. And very often, they thought they could just refuse to work and had to learn that the hard way.

Bunk 7, along with Bunks 6, 8, 9, and 11 were the bunks of Pod 2. We shared a Head Bunk parent, Brother Thomas. We went to meals together (we were in the second group for breakfast, lunch, and dinner), we were next to each other in Parade and sometimes we saw each other at the same chore. Other than your own bunk, those in your pod were the only other girls you would ever interact with. No matter which bunk you were in though, yours was obviously the best bunk and the others were below you. Every bunk in a pod was a rival to every other bunk in the same pod.

From the first day on the Island, Jess didn't eat well. They didn't exactly serve kid-friendly food. But it was getting worse. Jess was losing weight and by the end of the second week, everybody was concerned about it. You could see her bones pushing through the skin everywhere. Jess would only eat a few of the things that they served. She definitely wasn't eating enough. They called it "failure to thrive".

They tried giving her Meal #6 (staff food), but she wouldn't eat almost anything that was on the plate. The only thing I could do to get her to eat was to get her to eat exactly what I ate off my plate. Sister Mary started giving us a special plate. It was basically Meal #6, but it was portioned out so that she could eat exactly what I ate. It worked and I was able to get Jess to eat a lot more.

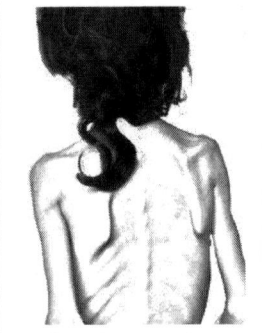

This picture shows Jess's back and how thin she was. It was taken in the first month or so we were on the Island.
~Vanessa~

After the second day of getting this special meal, one of the older girls from Bunk 11 started to take this plate from us. It meant we didn't eat anything. I started to sneak a few things from this plate into my shirt before we got back to the table. At least that way we had a little bit to eat.

The third special breakfast that we got was Cheerios. Everybody else was being served that disgusting corn grits mush they made. The older bully took our bowl of cereal from us. Sister Mary saw this and got really upset by it. She came over with a big guy who was working doing some maintenance thing. She yelled at the Bunk 11 girl. The Bunk 11 girl told her we gave her the cereal because we weren't going to eat it. But sister Mary had watched what happened and wasn't buying any of it.

Sister Mary literally had the guy take out his thing and piss in her Cheerios right there at the table! The look of disgust on that girl's face was priceless.

who PISSED in your CHEERIOS

Then the girl refused to eat the food, so sister Mary grabbed her hair and shoved her face into the bowl. Then Sister Mary yanked her head back and threw her off the bench and onto the floor. She picked up the bowl and poured it all over the girl.

Then Sister Mary announced very loudly that anybody else trying to steal the four-year-old's food wouldn't ever be allowed to eat again and would learn the hard way what starving to death felt like. Chow hall went dead silent. The maintenance guy then dragged that girl to the office by her hair.

Sister Mary then had us sit at a staff table, one of those little tables that could only seat two people instead of at the big round tables, and she brought us two pieces of apple pie for breakfast. No one tried to steal our plate again after that, though Jess kept asking me how we could get apple pie for breakfast again.

We weren't allowed to own any stuff on the Island. A common hobby was to make a rubbing stone. Mine was a little piece of white stone. When I got it, it was all rough. But every day I would rub it a little more with my fingers and other rocks and before too long it was all smooth and shiny. Like the other girls, I would tuck it into the waistband of my pants every morning and hide it by the stairs of our bunk before going inside for the night. If Brother Mark found your stone, he would throw it far into the woods and you would have to start over.

Jess had a rubbing stone too. Hers was grey. She spent a lot more time rubbing hers than I did rubbing mine, but mine got smoother and shinier a lot faster. For most of us, these rubbing stones were the closest things we had to owning something in bunk, and they were supremely precious to us, it was a major part of your identiy, of who you were.

But they did make a couple of exceptions for Jess. It started with two sticks that she used as dolls. Every time we found a little something to scavenge, both I and the other girls in bunk would add to her dolls. A piece of thread scavenged from a sheet was used to tie on another stick to be the arms of her doll. One of the other girls used some thread and some grass to fashion hair for her dolls. Abby even found a way to make a dress for one of her dolls out of a plastic envelope kind of thing that we found one day.

Brother Mark and Sister Mary fought a lot about her dolls. In the end, Sister Mary won, and Jess got to keep them, but Brother Mark definitely wasn't happy about it. Jess ended up with three stick dolls. She almost always had one of them with her unless we were going to Parade. In Bunk 7 Jess only ever talked to me and those dolls. She never would even speak to the other girls or even the bunk parents, only nod to them.

The other exception they would make for Jess had to do with singing. In general, singing wasn't allowed on the Island. They said it was an "unauthorized celebration". But if we weren't disturbing anybody else, it was OK to sing some children's songs with her. Sometimes it was even OK for some of the other girls to sing children's songs to her, but she would only sing with me. We sang 'Where is Thump kin', 'Frère Jacques', 'The Green Grass', and 'Twinkle, Twinkle' a lot.

For almost my first three months in Bunk 7, Jess and I were by far the youngest and smallest kids in the bunk. I was thirteen and the next youngest kid was fifteen. It meant that both Jess and I really were not part of the bunk's social scene. In some ways that made it easier, but in many ways, it made it a lot harder. I mean some of the girls were friendly to us, but I'm not sure I could say they were really my friends. That got better when we got a few younger girls in bunk.

The only thing we were allowed to do to differentiate was braiding our hair. Our uniforms all had to be exactly the same. Our bunks all had to be made exactly the same way. The only thing we were allowed to do differently from each other was to have slightly fancy braids in our hair. But standing out was dangerous, so you didn't want to stand out. Mostly we tried really hard to blend in. The girls that stood out were the girls that were singled out in groups or were singled out by the bunk parents for special attention, and that was never good.

Rebellion is kind of a funny thing. While any serious rebellion was impossible, little acts of rebellion were everywhere. They made you feel like you had some modicum of control in a world where you really had almost no control.

Swearing of any kind would get your mouth washed out with soap or worse. Even just the word "damn". We were always so very careful of who we said it around, but it made you feel a little bit powerful to say it, even if nobody else heard it. If you were daring, you used a stick to write the word in the dirt where someone might see it, and you always got excited to see someone else's word written in the dirt.

Jokes were the same way, especially jokes that were even a little bit dirty. You would get in trouble if the adults or even some of the upper-level girls heard you saying them, but it made you feel just a little bit powerful to say them. So, you sometimes took the risk.

Why did the ketchup blush?
Because he saw the salad dressing.
What happened to the fly on the toilet seat?
It got peed-off.
If you're American in the living room, what are you in the bathroom? *European.*

Why did the baker have smelly hands?
Because she kneaded a poo!
Why did the cop sit on the toilet?
To do her duty.
Why didn't the toilet paper make it past Jennifer?
It got stuck in her crack.
What did one butt cheek say to the other?
Together we can stop this shit.

These jokes may seem tame, but to us, they were huge acts of rebellion, and that was really important, it helped keep you sane and keep a glimmer of hope in your heart.

About 3 months into my stay, we got a new Headmaster. I don't remember her name, but when she took over, she made things a *lot* harder on all the girls. It was July. She instituted a weekly Sunday "parade" instead of the monthly ones we had before, where we all had to line up in formations for her to inspect us. Then we had to listen to her drone on about who knows what with the hot sun beating down on us while we stood at attention. She had an umbrella for shade. She lasted almost 2 months as Headmaster.

More than a few times I got punished after the parade for Jess melting down—she just couldn't stand at attention for all that time in the hot sun. Those were the worst. Those were mean beatings. They always used a leather belt on me for those.

Then in October 1990, we got another woman, who introduced the public punishments. Girls were brought in front of the whole school at Parade, stripped naked, and whipped for all to see. Sometimes they tied girls down for these whippings. This was scary, especially the thought that they could do this to Jess. This woman also introduced a new major punishment, the hotbox, a steel box in the sun girls were put in to bake for as long as a few days at a time.

I got one public whipping, but I never got the hot box; I saw enough to never want to. The mere thought of being hotboxed was terrifying and the thought of them doing it to Jess still gives me nightmares.

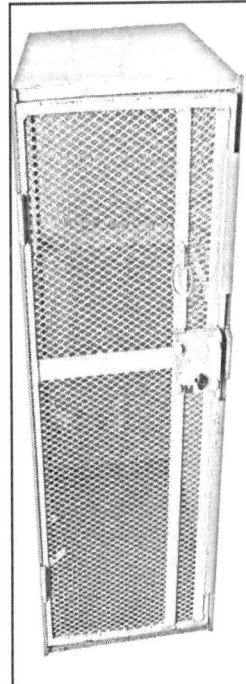

We had three hotboxes on the Island. This is a picture of the first hotbox, the hotbox that woman Headmaster brought with her. While the door was a grate, it faced right towards the sun, the other 5 sides were solid steel with grates on the inside. You could only stand, it was impossible to sit. Girls often had to try and keep from touching sides so as not to burn themselves. When staff was really mean, they put something over the door to further restrict airflow, or used a hammer to "ring the bell". That sucked.

This is a picture of Hotboxes #2 and 3. These cells were about 2 feet by 3 feet by 10 feet high and had a section of chainlink at the ceiling so you couldn't climb out. The cells had padlocks and two dark wooden beams that held the doors shut. On the back, each cell had a small feeding window. If girls were really lucky, the window was sometimes left open and it would only be about 115 degrees. This hotbox structure was pure evil, as the exhaust of both the Main Office and medical huts' AC units could be directed into this box, heating it to 130 degrees or more. If they really wanted a girl to suffer, they would put a piece of wood over the chainlink at the top, and then you had no real airflow. Unlike hotbox #1, these two wooden hotboxes were built on-site by maintenance.

~Vanessa~

I remember the first big storm we had was terrifying! We were at the farm as the storm hit. Brother Mark ran us back to Bunk 7, where we all huddled together in the center of the bunk, away from the windows. The light went out and the bunk shook as the wind hit, it was one of the most terrifying experiences of my life! Jess and I eventually fell asleep on the floor. The next day really sucked. Being covered in that wet disgusting-smelling mud was just horrible. The best you could do was dry in the sun and then try to use a sand station to get as much of the mud off as you could. It just sucked. I learned to hate the storms, no matter what chore you were on, it was much worse when it was wet.

At this point, groups changed. Groups were twice a week, and they were bad from the start. They often involved reliving bad events and being blamed for them, or making you sing the praises of the Church for saving you, or the stupid obedience class. At first, you think they are trying to help you. After your first week, you learn to lie just to protect yourself as much as you can, but that only helps so much. It's hard to keep track of the lies you have told. You try to keep your head low, you try not to be noticed so that you don't become the focus of the group.

In one group, they made me talk about my parents' car accident, then they blamed me for the accident. The counselor said that the accident was my fault, that if I had actually loved them, they wouldn't have died. She said I was a murderer, then the other girls chanted

"Murderer, Murderer!" at me until I broke down in tears and said I did it. Then she had all the girls hug me. That really screws you up.

But I knew it wasn't my fault. They were hit by a truck sliding on ice after a work event. How could my loving them more have changed that? How could twelve-year-old me, home fast asleep with a babysitter, have done anything to change that?

In one group, the counselor, Sister Jean, told Abby – a fifteen-year-old Level 4 girl who was only here about a month longer than I was – that her five-year-old sister died, killed by her mother's boyfriend. Sister Jean didn't even tell her in private, she did it in front of the whole bunk. Sister Jean said it was because Abby wasn't home to protect her little sister. Sister Jean said all of these horrible things were done to her little sister before she died.

Then, when Abby didn't react like Sister Jean wanted, she made us give Abby a circle beating for killing her little sister, and then hug her after she confessed it was her fault and said that she should have been the one those terrible things were done to. Two weeks later, Abby got a letter from home. Her sister was fine, it was all a lie. Sister Jean said it was part of her "therapy" and was "to see how she reacted". Really, it was just to break her.

Jess had just discovered herself – a huge sin on the Island. Sister Jean found her rubbing herself as we waited for a group session to start. This put four-year-old Jess in Sister Jean's crosshairs. But Jess wouldn't talk to anyone but me. This just made Sister Jean angrier, as she couldn't play her mind games on someone that wouldn't speak! When Brother Mark was in group, Sister Jean left Jess alone. When he didn't stay for group, sometimes Sister Jean would do things, really mean things, to Jess. I did everything I could to get Brother Mark to stay for groups, but it didn't always work.

In most groups, someone was getting physically or mentally beaten up like that. Sometimes they forced girls to fight until one was unconscious. For a few weeks, they made us fight almost every group. I think the staff was taking bets on the fights. We always had a lot of staff around for the fights and Sister Jean always said "Pay the winners" at the end of every fight.

We had a new fourteen-year-old, Barb, in our bunk. She was ruthless and violent and had no qualms about hitting Jess. Brother Mark didn't stay for this group. For her sin of discovery, Sister Jean put four-year-old Jess in the fight circle with fourteen-year-old Barb. Jess was 3 feet tall and 30 pounds, whereas Barb was almost 5 feet tall and over 100 pounds. How is that even remotely a fair fight? So, 4-foot tall 66 pound me did the only thing I could do to protect Jess, I hit Barb in the head from behind with a metal folding chair and then I beat Barb's head into the ground until she was unconscious and clear stuff came out of her ear.

She went to the infirmary, then got caged and dropped a level for losing the fight. She was never the same again after that, but she never went near Jess again either. This is what got me promoted to Level 3. Sister Jean said it was "a breakthrough". I think she just won the bet.

And if we didn't participate, they said "we weren't working our program", which was another reason for taking away points, not giving you points, dropping you a level, stopping you from gaining a level, or for some other punishment. They claimed it was to try to help us, but groups were just another way they tried to break us.

But under this woman, they introduced "Confessions", where we were forced to confess past sins. The counselor, Sister Jean, did things to Jess to make me talk that I still can't talk about. I mean, they could do what they wanted to me, I could take it, but she was only four, you know? Why did they need to do those awful things to Jess? They wrote these confessions down and later used them against us. It made the other groups way worse. She lasted less than 2 months, but the things she introduced lasted much longer.

This picture of Jess was taken about 6 months after the fight circle, when she was 38lbs. As small as she is in this picture, she was even smaller, only about 30lbs, at the time of the fight circle.

This is a picture of a girl caged outside of the main office, by the stone wall. Unlike the hotboxes, the cages were relatively cool in the shade. Because I can't see the face, I'm not really sure who she is. So that I could include it in the book, I altered this picture by having an artist draw on underwear.

~Vanessa~

Chapter 4:
Mr. S

It was December of 1990 when Mr. S. came in as the new headmaster. He was former military, like he had actually been a real senior officer, unlike any of the other headmasters or staff. In his first parade, he was walking down the rows of girls, and instead of just calling out each failing, he gave instructions on how to fix issues and told us why we did things the way we did, and he also complimented us on things we did right.

It was such a departure from the norm that everyone noticed it. Don't get me wrong, he really chewed out a few girls, but it wasn't just to chew them out – he did it because they deserved it! But he didn't have anybody whipped or beaten. It was just such a major change from what we had known.

Brother Mark had threatened me and Jess with the hotbox if I couldn't get Jess to stay at attention for this parade. But Jess had a really bad confessions group the day before and had not slept well, she was starting to melt down as Mr. S approached our bunk. As Mr. S got to the bunk ahead of us, Jess was now crying on the floor, but I had to stay at attention. I tried everything I could to cajole her into getting up before he got to us, but she was in full meltdown.

When Mr. S got to us, he asked how old Jess was. He was stern and authoritative in a way the other staff was not. I was truly scared of him and deathly afraid I was going to get my ass whipped or a circle beating or maybe even hotboxed for Jess's meltdown. I told him she was going to turn five. He asked me to repeat myself, a little surprise in his voice. I told him she was four and would be five in March.

Mr. S's voice became a lot gentler as he asked me for her name. I remember the terror I felt as I said, "Sir, Jess, Sir." When Brother Mark's voice got gentle, you knew the beating would be particularly mean.

Mr. S kneeled down and asked Jess if she needed a hug. She nodded and he picked her up into his massive arms and held her for a minute as she calmed down. I remember being so relieved that I didn't get hotboxed that day.

Mr. S then took her hand and had her walk with him as he inspected the rest of the parade. When he dismissed the parade, he kept Jess with him. I remember thinking her guardian angel was looking out for her.

Brother Mark did give me a particularly mean session with the belt for Jess's meltdown when we got back to bunk. Usually, when they stand you on the wall the beating is over. This time I got it again and again standing on the wall. The upwards crotch shots with that belt were the worst. But it was the last beating I got for what Jess did.

I both relished in not having to constantly look after Jess (and not having to take all the punishments I got just for her being four), but I also missed her terribly. It felt like a part of me, a very important part of me, had been ripped away. A few times I got a glimpse of her in the Head's yard. She seemed happy. I was happy for her, but also missed her a *lot* and I was more than slightly jealous of her.

The day after Jess left Bunk 7, we were at drill and Mr. S was with another bunk. He had made a contraption with old milk crates and was having girls try marching, stepping in the creates. They all fell over. I remember being floored when he put on a blindfold and marched right through, never even touching a create. Even the drill instructor couldn't do that! He said it's easy if you have perfect 24-inch marching steps. When it was our turn, I fell over a lot. My legs were only about 20 inches long, so 24-inch steps were giant steps for me!

During that next week, we had a class taught by Mr. S. Unlike every other teacher, he didn't just make us sit silently and do stupid packets or drill the mantras or try to mentally break us for our failings. He asked us to investigate a pile of dirt. But he made it fun and interesting. He had us look, touch, smell, and even taste it. He had us look at the texture, think about what its makeup was, what we thought would grow in it, if we thought it was healthy and other stuff like that. He got us to really think about it.

It was the first time I (and the other girls in bunk) could remember being excited about anything other than the monthly Sunday ice cream. He kept us more than twice as long as we had been scheduled for. He seemed to be having fun and in turn, so did we. His giving us more than a days' worth of points for that class wasn't bad either.

I learned more in that one class on a pile of dirt than I did in every Earth Sciences class I had had in Middle school. Or maybe it was just that he got me to pay attention, I don't know.

A few days later, on January 4th, 1991, I was ordered to report to the Office. Reporting to the Office typically meant a severe punishment from the top goon, Brother Sam. I had seen other girls come back from sessions in his office after they tried to rebel in one way or another. These were not the over-the-knee spankings of Sister Mary or the assume the position for the crop of Brother Mark or even the sessions with the belt, but the kind of beatings that left your ass bruised for weeks, or the leather strap that left rips in your skin or the hotbox or other "creative" punishments I wouldn't wish on my worst enemy. I had never heard of anyone below Level 7 going for any other reason. I was more scared than I had ever been in my life.

I reported as ordered and the secretary told me I was not on her list, but to strip and stand nose-tits-n-toes with the other girls, and Brother Sam would be with me shortly. I did as I was told, not knowing what I did to deserve this and not wanting to make it worse.

After a little while, I was told to report to Mr. S's office. Naked me walked into his office, hands still on my head (no one had given me permission to take them down). He was working on something on his computer and as he worked, he started to ask me about Jess. I answered his questions. Then he asked me if I would be interested in helping with Jess as my chore. I said the most excited, *"Sir, yes sir!"* I think I have ever said.

Mr. S, still looking at his computer, said, "Great, you will start-" He had finally looked up. "Why are you naked?" he asked. I felt my face go red with embarrassment, wishing the floor would just swallow me up. I told him that I had been stripped in the outer office and no one had given me permission to get dressed. He ordered me to go get dressed and then report back. A wave of shame I had not felt since my first week crashed over me, and I ran to get dressed.

When I returned, Mr. S clearly didn't like the aroma of my uniform (we had been shoveling shit out of the latrines after a cart spilled). Had he known, I think I would have been kept naked. His nose was all crinkled and he told me I was to report to the shower and draw a clean uniform before coming to his house and then said I was dismissed.

Brother Mark really wasn't happy when he learned I was given such a highly coveted domestic chore. He said that lost me over 800 points and my upcoming level 4 promotion. He said that I now had to start Level 3 all over again. He was so angry about it! I was only a Level 3 girl, and those tasks were supposed to be for the Level 7+ girls, of which our bunk had two, both of whom were usually water girls and highly favored by Brother Mark.

Level 3s like me were not supposed to be out of eyesight, we shouldn't be anywhere near the staff fence line (a 4-foot fence separating the staff compound from the bunk compound), let alone going into the headmasters' house. And being left alone to babysit? That just shouldn't happen! Even bunk parents were rarely allowed into the headmaster's house! My going all day, every day? According to Brother Mark, that job should have been given to an older level 9, or 10 girl, certainly not to me. But none of them had the history I did caring for Jess, so I got it despite my age and low level. To Brother Mark, this was somehow a personal insult.

The next day, we were woken up as usual. Fall-in was called and Brother Mark did his usual walk. He obviously still didn't like that I had gotten the "cushy" babysitting job and told the bunk that because I was missing the work, they all had to shovel more shit to make up for my share. You can guess how popular that made me.

I got whacked a bunch of times every time he walked past me in morning line. I don't think anything is more infuriating than 30 whacks of the riding crop applied to the sensitive area of the crotch, which I now got every day.

After breakfast, I reported to the shower. Sister Carol had her bunk in for their weekly shower. She obviously knew I was coming and cut me to the front of the line. She let me shower in a stall with a shower curtain! She told me to take 10 minutes (twice the time normally allotted) and to wash well. When you are used to a 5-minute shower in an open group shower, 10 minutes in a stall with a shower curtain, where you don't even have to share the soap, is a luxury!

After my shower, Sister Carol had me stand Mongra to do a body cavity search, starting with my hair, then my mouth, then my vagina, and finally my butthole. Standing Mongra let her do the search much more quickly and efficiently than other staff did them, though it is harder to be somewhere else in your head when you are struggling to balance, and your crotch already hurts.

After the search, Sister Carol got me a new, *clean* school uniform and ordered me to dress and report to the headmaster's house. I quickly dressed and went to report as ordered. I was so terrified crossing that staff fence for the first time. I felt like I didn't belong, and I was sure that a punishment for crossing it was just moments away. Normally, a Level 3 girl just being close enough to touch that fence would earn a major punishment! That terror continued to build as I approached the door of Mr. S's house. It took everything I had to knock on that door.

Mr. S had moved Jess into his residence. He brought me up to her room. She had her own room(!), books, some toys, and even a stuffy. By normal standards the room was sparse. By Island standards, she was living a life of luxury. Jess was looking at a book when we walked in. I remember the book was *One Fish, Two Fish*. I have fond memories of my mother reading that book to me as a small child.

Mr. S explained that Jess was great for him, but others had difficulty with her, she wouldn't even talk to them. I was her third babysitter. Jess's eyes lit up when she saw me. We hugged for a long time. Mr. S said she needed love, not the tough love the school used, and he thought I would be perfect to help with that. He gave me a schedule and told me to generally stick to it. He said I was to take her to the bathroom at the first sign she needed it. Jess and I had the best day.

When Mr. S came home for lunch, Jess and I were making mac and cheese in the kitchen (one of the few things I knew how to make). Mr. S had lunch with us, and Jess told him all about our morning. I felt like I could have been at home with my own dad and sister. It was the first feeling of real normalcy I had felt since arriving on the Island. I mean, I had gotten used to life on the Island, but that's not the same as feeling normal.

Mr. S did scold me for forgetting my 'sirs', and he made sure I knew he would not hesitate to spank me if I forgot them again. Then he hugged both of us and went back to the office.

It was the first real, honest hug I had gotten from an adult since I got here and the feeling of being loved again almost made my head explode. I tried to hide my emotions from him, but the truth is I was latching on to him hard. I wanted his approval more than anything in the world. I made sure never to forget my 'sir's' again!

I squirreled away the rest of the Mac and cheese in a tin I found in the trash and I hid it outside by the back door.

Dinner with my bunk was rough. I was clean, they were not. I had more food at family lunch than they had all day and to top it off, I got Meal #6 with real meat and a slice of cherry pie, and they did not – they all got meal #3. They all had to work an extra hour after dinner, I did not – I was not to get dirty or soil my new uniform and Brother Mark made sure they all knew it. You can guess how popular that made me.

But being with Jess again was worth it. My crotch took thirty whacks each morning before I went to take care of Jess. Brother Mark always made sure I felt that last whack. You can't even rub yourself for relief at night when your crotch is that bruised.

One of the hardest parts of babysitting was getting used to not having the super structured routines of bunk. In bunk, we had detailed routines for everything. A

routine for waking up, one for morning lines, one to march, one for PT, one for meals, one for chore, we had one for literally everything we did. In bunk, you always knew what you were supposed to be doing. Babysitting, I had 8 checkboxes and only two things that had a time:
```
1. Read a story
2. Play outside
3. Make and do lunch at mid-day bell
4. Nap
5. Clean 2 rooms of the house
6. Play a board game
7. Dig in the dirt
8. Wash up at evening bell
```
Without that structure, I constantly felt like I was in the wrong. I had this fear that I should be doing something that I wasn't all the time and just waiting for the punishment to come. Talk about anxiety! I kept going back to that list and making sure we did each item.

On the third day of babysitting, Jess and I played with her dollhouse all morning, totally losing track of time. When I heard the mid-day bell, I panicked. We had not read a story or played outside at all and to top it off, Mr. S said he would bring home bagged lunches for the three of us. I glanced out the window and saw Mr. S coming home with lunch. I was so sure I was going to be in such serious trouble!

Right through lunch, I kept expecting the punishment to come. Jess told Mr. S all about her doll's adventures during lunch. As she talked, my anxiety just kept building and building. By the time she told him the whole adventure, I figured I was due for a public whipping or the hotbox. But Mr. S didn't care that we were playing with the dolls and didn't do the things on the list, he cared that Jess was happy.

I still expected to be whipped, or at the very least get wall time and a good chewing out for not doing what I was supposed to be doing. But he said nothing. He was enthralled with Jess telling him all about her doll's adventures that morning. After lunch, we got our hugs, and he went back to work.

I figured he must not have had time, and I would get it at the end of the day. I made sure we did everything on the list that afternoon! But the end of the day came and no punishment. I got a hug and was sent back to bunk for dinner. So, I figured I would get it back at bunk. But Brother Mark didn't punish me for it either. I even got an extra-large piece of pie at dinner (I shared that pie with Nancy and Britney). I spent days waiting for that punishment, but it never came.

During my second week of babysitting, Mr. S kept me for Thursday night family dinner. After dinner, he told us a story about a great man who turned a magical grey stone as black as night and how that stone was a symbol of family love. He said Jess's rubbing stone was the magical stone. Then he put her stone in a cup and poured something on it as he told us more of the story. Then he put the stone in the fire and told us that we were to dig it out in the morning. When we dug it out the next day, her rubbing stone was jet black, even after we washed it in water. I still don't know how he did that, but there was no mistaking that Jess's rubbing stone had completely changed color.

The third week of babysitting the girls gave me a blanket party for having to work so much extra while I was off babysitting. While I was sleeping, they threw a blanket over me and 4 girls held it down, trapping me on my bunk. The other girls put bars of soap in their socks and used them to beat me to a pulp. I screamed and screamed, but no one came to help. Long after I stopped screaming, the beating ended, and they just went back to bed, like nothing happened. I never got to sleep that night.

I had two black eyes, a broken nose, 2 cracked ribs a sprained knee, and who knows how many bruises my body was covered in. Brother Mark told me I could stay in bed for the day, but then I would be off babysitting. I remember wanting to tell him to fuck himself as got up, took my whacks, and defiantly went in to babysit anyways.

When Mr. S saw me limp in, he demanded to know what happened. I tried to pretend everything was fine, but he didn't even pretend to buy it. I was thirteen, and I knew what happened to rats – the blanket party would look like a love tap in comparison. I saw a group just about kill a girl for being a rat. I told him that I would take whatever punishment he chose to give me for not answering, but that I wasn't a rat, and I wasn't going to die for being a rat.

He took me to the infirmary, then I was sent to a hospital on the mainland where they reset my nose, took x-rays, taped my ribs, wrapped my knee, gave me pills, and put on lots of ice. I stayed for several days and then another week in the infirmary. Jess visited almost every day at the infirmary. I heard the 4th babysitter didn't work out.

When I was let out, I had to report to Mr. S. He told me he was disappointed in me. This was more crushing to me than any beating. So, I told him what happened and why, but I refused to give up any names – I still wasn't a rat. He had me sleep with Jess that night.

The weekly parade was the next day, and thirteen-year-old naked me got my first and only public whipping. After my public beating by Brother Sam and his leather strap, I had to stand naked in front of the whole school while it was announced that as part of my punishment for disobedience and for *not* giving up who did this to me, I was being removed from my bunk and placed in another setting. I figured I would be sent to processing and transferred to another bunk, I saw that happen to another girl after a public whipping.

I was returned to my bunk for the remainder of that Sunday. To my surprise, everyone talked to me. None of the girls were mad at me. I was welcomed more as a hero for not being a rat than anything. Later that day, I was taken to the office, then much to my surprise, I was moved into Mr. S's house, in the room next to Jess.

I was still recovering from the blanket party, and I had trouble sitting for a week, but even so, life was a lot better. Gone were the morning lines of Brother Mark, in was making breakfast for the three of us.

Out were the 5 minutes to get showered once a week. In were daily showers where it was OK to spend 20 minutes to shower Jess and me if we turned off the water to soap us up. It was even sometimes OK for Jess and me to take a bubble bath!

Out were groups, where they tried to break you. On most nights, we would sit in Mr. S's lap, and he would read to us, mostly from the Bible or Greek mythology. I really liked snuggling into his chest as he read to us, and I grew to love those Greek myths.

Out were meals in the chow hall, in were making and eating real family meals. Mr. S even taught me to cook! Out was the shoveling of shit, in was keeping the house clean. Out were stumps, in was tending to the garden Jess and I were growing. Out were the stupid packets, in were daily classes with Mr. S.

But most importantly, gone was the cold brutality of bunk life, in were lots of love, hugs, and affection. Mr. S hugged us every day at least 5 or 6 times, sometimes a lot more. It really makes a difference as a kid having an adult actually love you, especially after living in Bunk 7.

Mr. S was strict but fair. His decisions were final, but unlike every other adult I had ever known, he always listened first. He was quick to reason, and not punitive unless he felt you were not trying or if you went against something that was already settled or if you disobeyed. Those earned you wall time or occasionally a spanking.

I got my share of spankings from Mr. S over the years (7 over the next 3 years). I will be the first to say that, unlike the beatings I got in my time in Bunk 7, I earned every single spanking I got from Mr. S, if not many more. And while I always knew I could get them from him, the reality is that I got fewer spankings from him in the years I lived with him than I got beatings during any given week in Bunk 7. Hell, I know I had days in Bunk 7 where I got more beatings than I got spankings over the years I lived with Mr. S!

While those spankings were far fewer in number, and far less brutal than those I took in Bunk 7 (mostly, there was the Nikki incident...) because they came with Mr. S's disapproval and sometimes his disappointment, they had a much larger impact on me.

But most of the time, Mr. S would do that sigh of his and I would just crumble to pieces. I still don't know why that sigh hit me so hard, but it did. Very often, I would have rather he had spanked me or even sent me for a whipping than given me that devastating, 'cut to your very core' sigh of his.

Mr. S was the first person to give me a real education. We had 2 hours of class each weekday after dinner and before lap time. We covered math, science, literature, psychology, electronics, HAM radio, critical thinking (this was the hardest, but also the most rewarding subject), outdoor skills and so much more. Over time, I had to read every book in his library, and we talked about them until I understood them.

Mr. S was firm in that I *was* going to college, and I just accepted that as fact. For the first time since my parents died, I felt like I had a future.

The only food I knew how to make when I came to the Island was mac and cheese, hot dogs, burgers, and grilled cheese. I guess those got old fast. He taught me the obvious dishes, like French toast and Alfredo pasta, but I also learned to make some more interesting foods.

One of the first big dishes he taught me to make was chicken fingers. It started with me making mac and cheese for the 900th time. Mr. S saw me start to make it and he said it was time for something else. When I asked him what, he looked in the refrigerator, and then told us to come with him. We went to the Chow Hut where we picked up some chicken, eggs, milk, flour, and some summer squash. We took those things back to the house. Mr. S had me cut the chicken into strips while he and Jess made the wet and dry mixes. Then I dipped the chicken in the wet mix, Jess dipped it in the dry mix and Mr. S deep-fried it. The smell of that chicken cooking was out of this world! We had extra mix, so Mr. S had us slice up the zucchini and dip them the same way.

You should have seen the look on Jess's face the first time we had those chicken fingers! She was so excited she was literally bouncing up and down! It wasn't exactly the healthiest dinner, but boy did it taste good! After two or three times making it, Jess and I could do the whole thing without any help! We made that dish a *lot*, even though I think Mr. S got as sick of it as he did mac and cheese.

The first real adult dish I learned to make was stuffed mushrooms and peppers. This was another of Mr. S's secret family recipes, one that was passed to him and his sisters by his grandmother. As he often did, he just said he had a surprise and we followed right behind him. We went to the farm and he had us pick out the 12 biggest mushrooms we could find and the 12 biggest bell peppers we could find. Then he had us pick two whole sunflowers, two big onions, a head of celery, some fresh parsley, and some fresh rosemary. Finding the 12 biggest with Mr. S is a lot more fun than harvesting ever was in Bunk 7! Then we stopped at the Chow Hut for some chicken broth, and we took two loaves of stale bread, and then he led us home.

Jess and I had no idea what we were making, but Mr. S was excited and so were we! He had Jess start shelling seeds and he had me cut the bread into cubes, then chop up all the vegetables. He had me sauté the vegetables while he and Jess whisked the egg and then mixed in the chicken broth. Then they crushed the sunflower seeds. Mr. S had me mix the bread and vegetables into a big bowl with the sunflower seeds. He poured the egg stuff in and had Jess and I mix that mix using our bare hands! It was like playing with playdough! Mr. S even made a stuffing snowman! After it was all really well mixed, we put stuffing into the hollowed-out mushrooms and peppers and baked it in the oven. The smell was just out of this world!

As we were making this, a Chow Hut girl delivered a tray of roast rabbit and vegetables. That usually meant a staff dinner, where Jess and I had to stay in our rooms, but this time he had us join them at the table for dinner! Brother Sam, Sister Lisa (the Dean of Students) the head bunk parents, the headteacher, and the new councilor, Miss Thompson all came. We got to hear all about the changes at the Island during dinner!

I found out that it wasn't just my life that changed. Brother Sam talked about how office punishments were way down. The head bunk parents talked about how kids were generally beaten far less and reasoned with a lot more. They talked about how the new girl beatings were gone, the circle beatings were mostly gone, caging was mostly gone, upper-level girls were no longer allowed to stand girls Nose-Tits-n-Toes or Mongra, and other such changes.

Miss Thompson, who had gone to a real college for psychology, talked about how she had changed groups. They no longer beat girls up in them. They sounded a lot nicer, but I still didn't want to do them, though for a while, Mr. S made Jess and I meet with her anyway.

I learned that while the searches continued, and staff would strip girls for cause, the naked lines were no longer part of every morning routine, maybe only two or three times a week for most girls. For most bunks, the new routine was standing at attention at the foot of the bunkbed, waiting for the order to make bed and dress.

I thought about how Jess and I only very occasionally were called to do a morning line. I liked those days. With Mr. S it was a game, not like it was in Bunk 7. Mr. S would come in and wake us up, we would jump to attention, then Mr. S would put on his funny voice and walk back and forth, making us open our mouths and stuff. He tried to get us to laugh, and we tried really hard to keep a serious face. He always won in the end, but I wouldn't ever break before he told us what our day would be. Those usually ended in a big hug when he dismissed us, usually because Mr. S would have to leave early. When it was a normal day, Jess and I would just get up, get dressed and make family breakfast. But I did like it when Mr. S called us for those lines, with him, I got all tingly down below.

The roast rabbit we had for dinner had a honey glaze that was just amazing! Mr. S and the staff talked about maybe making this part of meal #5 once a month, though I don't think it ever happened. But bread was now a regular part of meals #4 and #5 and not just Meal #6.

The stuffed mushrooms and peppers were to die for! Jess and I didn't like the mushroom part, but we *loved* the stuffing! I didn't like mushrooms until I was fifteen (it's funny how your tastes in food change so much at that age...). Mr. S made those stuffed mushrooms with us a few times before Jess and I got the hang of making them by ourselves. Mr. S *loved* them, so we made them for him as often as we got sunflowers from the garden or the farm. It would take us all morning for Jess and me to shell all of those seeds! I think we ate as many as we shelled for the stuffing mix!

Even though I had the run of the kitchen, I was still squirreling away food. I don't know why I was doing it, we had plenty to eat. But I was. Mr. S found my squirrel stash. We came in from playing outside and he had that tin of rotting food on the table. I thought I was in deep trouble.

Mr. S made me sit down at the table, and he started telling me a story about being a child and how his family was very poor. He talked about his big sister Beth squirreling away food for both of them. He said he knew how it felt to rather be a little bit hungry today so you're not a very hungry tomorrow. He promised that so long as he was around, we would always have enough food and that I didn't have to worry about that.

Mr. S said he understood how scary this place could be, and how I was clearly trying to provide for Jess as his sister had for him. He gave me a crate of these things called MREs, he said the crate had enough food for Jess and me to eat for almost two full weeks, a month if we stretched it. He told me that I was to go and hide those someplace safe so that I always knew I had at least that much food to provide for Jess if I needed to. I buried them under a big pine tree we liked to play under.

Mr. S said it was perfectly fine for us to keep leftovers and have them as snacks when we wanted, but they had to be kept in the refrigerator because of the rats. I would still tuck food from our meals into my shirt. It's just not as easy to break that habit as you would think.

For the next week, we ate MREs almost every meal, Mr. S did that just to make sure I knew how to use them. He even talked about how to stretch them if you really needed to, like how to make soup out of some of them so you can feed two people with one MRE. MREs are not always as good as Meal #6 and not nearly as good as family meals, but they are a lot better than most of the meals at the chow hall.

Jess and I lived in our own little world those months, almost completely separate from the life of those living in the bunks. We played in the grass, threw stones over the cliff (Mr. S even had a pile of stones delivered for us to throw), played in the sandbox, did a lot of make-believe games, made a pile of rubbing stones, and basically lived a carefree, almost ideal life.

While the big storms were still terrifying (Jess and I would usually hide under the kitchen table or sometimes in Mr. S's bed when they hit), we liked watching the lighter rains out the living room windows or sometimes from the front porch. Those light rains sucked when we lived in Bunk 7 and still had to do chore in them, but now we liked it, it made building sandcastles in the sandbox so much better after the rain stopped.

One night we were watching the rain after dinner and Jess fell asleep. I carried her to bed, then I went back to the porch. The rain had stopped, and the clouds had cleared. The stars were now visible. I sat and stared at the stars. After a while, Mr. S came out and sat next to me on the porch swing. We spent the rest of the evening looking at the stars together. Mr. S started teaching me the constellations and telling me about the Greek stories behind them. I loved those stories and our time staring at the stars together. We did that often. Sometime that was our evening lesson.

Mr. S occasionally took us to the chow hall for dinner (sometimes just for dessert), and we sometimes saw girls doing domestic chores. We sometimes got a kitchen and bath girl and we talked to the trash girls every week. Ericka, an upper-level older girl was often one of the trash girls, we liked talking to her, she always called us "Chickee", and she was really fun to talk to. But other than that, we really lived in our own little world.

In February 1991, the flu hit our little world. I guess it went through the school first, but Mr. S got it first in our little world. He was in bad shape, and I did everything I could to care for him. I hugged him, I sat with him, I changed the cool cloth on his head, I cleaned up when he got sick, I got him chicken soup from the chow hut (they even made it for him when it wasn't on the menu), I got him to drink water. I did everything that thirteen-year-old me could possibly do to make him better.

Then on the third day of flu, Jess came down with it. She was miserable. I did everything I could to care for her. Taking care of both of them was a *lot*! Then I started to come down with it on day 4.

On day 5, Mr. S wasn't doing well and had asked for soup. His head was still burning, but he had not asked for anything since getting sick and I so badly wanted to make him better. I remember being in the house kitchen and feeling the world spinning. But I just had to make him better and to do that, I had to get him his soup. That meant a trek to the chow hut. I remember how far away that felt at that moment, but I wasn't about to let him down in his hour of need, no matter how badly I was feeling.

I made my way outside, I got partway to the staff fence and threw up. Moments later, down I went. Ericka, who was working some domestic chore, probably trash duty, must have seen me fall. She came running. She said I was burning up. I told her Mr. S wasn't doing well and I needed to get the soup. I tried to get up. She told me not to worry about the soup and to stay put. I tried to get up, but my body wasn't letting me get up.

It must have been bad because Ericka went running (girls were not allowed to run on the Island without permission). I saw her burst through the staff gate, past a bunch of staff, and disappear towards the office and infirmary. I closed my eyes, shivering at how cold I felt. A few minutes later, Ericka came running back, followed by Brother Sam and the nurse.

I told Brother Sam I had to get the soup for Mr. S and I tried really hard to get up, but as hard as I tried, I couldn't get up. Brother Sam told Ericka to take care of the soup, then he carried me to bed and covered me in blankets.

I know the nurse checked us all out, but all I remember is being told to stay in bed. At some point, I woke up and tried to get up to check on Jess and Mr. S. Ericka wouldn't let me up, she told me she was taking care of Mr. S and Jess while I was sick and if I tried to get up without permission again for anything other than the bathroom, this little Chickee would be watching the wall. This little Chickee stayed in bed.

I guess Jess wasn't as easy for her as she was for me. I could hear Jess asking (screaming) for me from my room and eventually, Ericka brought Jess to me. We slept a long time and Jess stayed with me in my bed until the flu was gone.

Ericka stayed with us while we were sick. She changed the damp cloth on our heads, she brought me a bucket to be sick in (Jess and I were both sick in that bucket a bunch of times). She cleaned up after us and brought us bread, soup, and water every time we woke up and she even helped us to the bathroom. I remember waking up to Ericka reading Jess a story, then us falling back asleep.

Mr. S was the first one to recover from that nasty flu, but even for him, it was day-by-day. It wasn't one of those flus where it's just over, it was the kind that lingered. The kind that got better and worse.

Mr. S kept Ericka to care for all of us while we were sick. I think she was with us for 2 weeks, but it's all kind of foggy. I remember thinking that the babysitter (me!) shouldn't need a babysitter, and I was worried that I might lose my babysitting job over it. But I wasn't in any shape to do anything about it.

I remember that when I first got up from being sick, Jess was sleeping, and the house was a disaster. I tried to clean it, but my body just wouldn't go as it should. Mr. S wasn't feeling much better, and he said to let it go till I was feeling better, but I was stubborn and kept trying to clean. I told him it was part of my job, and I needed to do my job. I was really worried about losing this job and having to go back to Bunk 7. He told me he wasn't going to fight with me, so just take it easy and make sure to rest when I needed to.

I was trying to do the dishes, then I needed to sit down. I guess I fell asleep for a while at the kitchen table. When I woke up, Ericka and two other upper-level older girls, Kate, and Michelle, were in the kitchen with Mr. S. They were trying to figure out where the strainers were kept (last cabinet on the left in the pantry, bottom shelf).

Mr. S told me that since I wasn't feeling so hot and since I was perhaps the only one who actually knew where things went in this house, it was my job to sit and direct these girls on where things went and what to do to clean the house. I was grumpy, but Ericka, Kate, and Michelle were really nice the whole time. They did all the work cleaning up the kitchen. I think they mostly humored me, but at least I felt useful.

At some point, Jess came down and we fell asleep on the couch together. I guess the older girls washed the bathroom and floors and took all the sheets and blankets and stuff to the laundry while we slept.

I remember waking up to the smell of roast chicken and butter rice. My mom used to make roast chicken and butter rice, it had been one of my favorite meals, one mom would serve when we were recovering from being sick, but I didn't know how to make it.

I remember crying when I saw what they had made. I said it was just from the flu and that I was fine, but at that moment, I really missed my mom something awful. Kate sat with me and Jess and hugged me for a while. It was really nice to have them for family dinner

It took us 3 days to get the house back in order. While Ericka stayed with us, the other two girls came every morning and made breakfast, then helped clean, make lunch, help clean, make dinner, and cleaned up after. They even read Jess and I a story when Mr. S wasn't up to it.

Ericka, Kate, and Michelle never once complained about how grumpy I was (and I was a real grouch!), or about how little of the work I was doing, or about helping me with Jess or even about cleaning up after Jess or I were sick (it happened more than it should have…). They were just really nice to us. It was so nice having them for as long as we did.

After we all got better from that nasty flu, Jess and I went back into our own little world. We built a fort under a pine tree out of big sticks and other things we scavenged and had some wonderful adventures.

And we delighted in telling Mr. S all about our adventures! When he would come home for lunch or dinner, we would race to hug him and tell him all about our wondrous days. He was always excited to hear what we had done and always greeted us with a big hug. He almost never told us about the school, I think he liked hearing about our world more than thinking about the school world.

Two days a week, Ericka came over to help cook family dinner with us Chickee's. Those were usually the nights Mr. S was working late. She taught me to make a lot of dishes, including roast chicken and butter rice. It wasn't exactly the same as what my mom made, but it was close.

Since Jess and I both had March birthdays (I turned fourteen, she turned five), Mr. S had chocolate cupcakes for us. If you were to compare my fourteenth birthday to my thirteenth, the fourteenth should have been a disappointment. But since except for Christmas we never had any celebrations on the Island, and because I felt like I had family, this small celebration is one I remember much more fondly. Mr. S gave Jess a new doll and gave me a fancy bible and a leather journal as birthday presents. I still have them to this day.

Sundays were the best days. While we had to go to church after lunch, we spent the whole morning with Mr. S. We would sing, dance, wrestle, make things, play games, and otherwise have our very own "family time". The best part was that during those 3 hours, no one was allowed to bother any of us, including Mr. S. It was the only time during the week where "island business" wasn't allowed to interrupt. That was our special time, and I cherished every moment of it.

Our first Sunday family time was about a week after our birthday party. Mr. S really liked having a big breakfast on Sundays, so Jess and I made a breakfast quiche and fruit. We all sat down for breakfast and Mr. S told us that he had set aside the time from now until church just for the three of us. He said he wanted to show us something after breakfast, but he wouldn't tell us what it was, only that it was a surprise. We were very excited! Normally we took a lot of time eating these fancy Sunday breakfasts, but on this day, we rushed through. We didn't even wash the dishes, just left them in the sink! Mr. S said we didn't have time to waste, a Kitchen and Bath girl would take care of them!

Mr. S took us for a hike in the woods of the Island. He carried Jess on his back for a lot of it. We ended up in a grassy field over by the farm. Mr. S's soccer ball was already there. I never really played soccer. I'd kick the ball around, but that's not the same as actually playing soccer. Mr. S, however, did all sorts of fancy tricks with that soccer ball! We must have spent hours passing that soccer ball back and forth between the three of us.

At one point Mr. S played keep away. Jess and I did everything we possibly could to get that soccer ball from him. He was just way better with that ball than I was! Jess and I came up with a plan. Jess wrapped herself around one of his legs so I could get the ball. Even with Jess wrapped completely around his left leg, getting that ball from him was really, really hard. I went running to try to kick it from him and suddenly the ball just wasn't there! My foot kicked the air so hard I fell on my butt.

When I looked back, he was bouncing the ball between his foot and his knee. I mean, who does that? I got up and I threw my whole body at the ball and somehow managed to knock it away from him. We both chased after the ball, but he had Jess on his leg, so I was able to get it first. I tried keeping it away from him and it worked for a little while, but only because Jess was on his leg!

I teased Mr. S with the classic, "Na-na-na-na-na, you can't get it," and then suddenly he scooped a giggling me up into his arms, spun me around and we all collapsed into the grass. We laid on the grass for a while. Mr. S lay on his back, Jess on his chest and I laid my head on his shoulder, snuggling in as one of his huge arms wrapped around each of us. We could have stayed like that all day, but after a little while, we heard the midday bell and very reluctantly we headed back to Chow Hall for church.

These were some of the best days of my life, I was almost as happy as I was before my parents died.

Mr. S's Chicken Fingers

Ingredients:
- Egg mix: 2 eggs, 1/4 cup of milk, 4 Tbs Canola oil
- Flour Mix: 1 cup of flour, 2 Tbs Italian Seasoning, 1 tsp cayenne pepper, 1 tsp of salt and pepper mix
- Chicken cut into strips (dark or white meat)

Directions:
1. In a large bowl, mix the egg mix ingredients as you would to make scrambled eggs and set aside.
2. In a second large bowl, mix the dry ingredients, blending them well.
3. Dip the chicken strips in the egg mix, then coat in the dry mix.
4. For the healthy version, cook in an air fryer or pan fry. For Mr. S's version (the tastier version), deep fry in oil.

Mr. S's Stuffed Mushrooms

Ingredients:
- 12 large mushrooms.
- 1/8 cup of shelled sunflower seeds (about 1 sunflower).
- 1/4 loaf of stale bread cut into cubes (or toasted in the oven).
- 1/4 cup of butter.
- 1 chopped large yellow onion.
- 3 sticks of chopped celery.
- 1/8 cup chopped parsley.
- 1 tsp of minced fresh rosemary
- 1 tsp of salt and pepper blend.
- 1 large egg.
- 3/4 cup of chicken broth.

Directions:
1. Crush the sunflower seeds in a plastic bag with a rolling pin and set aside.
2. In a large bowl, whisk the eggs and chicken broth and set aside.
3. In a skillet, melt the butter and add the onion and celery. Sautee until vegetables are soft then set aside.
4. In a large bowl, put in the bread cubes, sunflower seeds and the veggies. Add the wet mixture and mix together. Add the seasonings and mix well. Bake this on a cookie sheet for 35 minutes.

5. Take the stems out of the mushrooms (this can be added to the mix if you choose to). Fill the mushrooms with the stuffing mix and bake for 15 minutes. Serve hot.

The adult trick method
for college students or parents with time constraints

Ingredients:

- 12 large mushrooms
- 1 box of stuffing mix
- 1/8 cup of shelled sunflower seeds (about 1 sunflower).
- Chicken broth.

Directions:

1. Crush the sunflower seeds using a food processor.
2. Mix the crushed sunflower seeds in with the dry stuffing mix.
3. Replace the boiling water the mix calls for with hot chicken broth and use 1/2 cup more broth than the mix calls for.
4. Then cook as directed.
5. Stuff and bake your mushrooms.

This stuffing is good without the mushrooms too! My family uses this for our Thanksgiving stuffing.

Chapter 5:
Birth of the Guardians

In May of 1991, Mr. S started adding a second daily class to each bunk. By July, every group had a daily philosophy/religion class, an academic class (rotated between math, science, and English), and either Phys ed or wilderness.

Mr. S was my house parent and teacher. But I also had a major crush on him. I liked it when he took complete control of me. It felt safe and loving, especially when I would feel out of control (that happens a lot when you are thirteen and fourteen, and even sixteen and seventeen). Mr. S had a few peculiarities. One of them was how the silverware was put away. Not a big deal, just stack them neatly in the caddy, putting like with like. Salad forks in one place, dinner forks in another, that sort of thing. I rushed putting away the silverware. It wasn't a big deal, but after dinner, Mr. S made me fix it. He made a playful threat about making me watch a wall if I didn't put them away correctly.

We both knew he wasn't really serious, I mean, in all reality he was more likely to do that sigh of his and watch me crumble. But I was fourteen and suddenly found that I had a way to get him to take control when I wanted him to. That was a major discovery for me, it felt like a superpower.

A few days later, I purposely just dumped the silverware all over the drawer. Jess tried to fix it, but I wouldn't let her. I wanted to be in trouble with Mr. S. Not enough trouble to be spanked or earn another serious punishment, but enough that he would take control of me.

When he saw the drawer, he looked at me and asked if we were really going to do this or if I wanted to come and fix it. I remember looking right at him as I nodded my head and said, "Yeah, I guess we are". He shook his head and did that sigh of his. I was so close to crumbling and just fixing the drawer and asking him to forgive me when he told me to go to the living room and watch the wall. The authority in his voice made me feel safe and warm.

I don't know why, but I got undressed and stood nose-tits-n-toes (I now had tits, well, little ones). I guess I felt I deserved it, or maybe I just wanted to be naked in front of him, I don't really know. And yes, part of me hoped he would ravish my body (not that I even really understood what that meant at fourteen).

Mr. S kept me there for about half an hour before calling me over. He didn't ravish me, or otherwise take advantage of me as I wished he had at the time. Instead, he had this look of understanding, like he could read my thoughts. He wasn't mad at me, but he told me that for the next two weeks, I would do half an hour of nose-tits-n-toes every day and that I had to ask for it no later than the end of dinner. He then made me fix the drawer before giving me permission to get dressed again. We hugged for a long time after that.

That night, I rubbed myself to the best orgasm of my young life. And every day for the next two weeks, I asked for my time on the wall. I looked forward to being naked in front of him, him in complete control.

Dumping the silverware became like a code between us. Whenever I felt out of control (and that happens a lot as a teenager...), or if I just wanted to feel closer to Mr. S, I would dump the silverware and he would exert the slightly harsh control I sometimes so desperately craved. He never got mad at me for it, and he never held it against me. And he always hugged me afterward.

Jess and I had more or less been isolated from the other kids all these months, living in our own little wonderous world. Then in September, I had to start joining Bunk 7 (now made up of about half my old bunkmates) for the academic classes (Jess tagged along) and both Jess and I had to do the wilderness and Phys-ed classes with Bunk 8, which also had kids from my old bunk.

About twice a week we had to join Bunk 11 for a chore, but only for an hour and a half of it, because we had to make it to class. The girls we worked with were happy for our help—our work counted towards their quota, but our bodies didn't enlarge their quotas. Those extra hands can make all the difference in the world! Besides, I really liked the extra structure this gave our days, I didn't constantly feel like I was supposed to be doing something I was neglecting.

I never was formally promoted past Level 3, but when I was with the Bunks for classes and chores, I was treated like an upper-level girl. I couldn't make anyone wait on the wall, but I wasn't chewed out for every little thing. I could look girls in the eyes, run errands for staff, ask questions, take Jess to the bathroom as needed, and I got other upper-level privileges as well.

Unlike the other girls, points were not assessed to Jess and me. We were not given points for classes or chores or doing extra things, but we didn't have points taken from us either. I liked not having the constant pressure of the points, but not having them also meant I didn't have that instant feedback on if I was doing good or not, and that was hard. On top of that, being the only girl whose points were not called out every period was just really weird. I wished they would have at least told me what points I would have earned, even if they were not tracked. It also didn't help me socially with the other girls.

The bunks' daily chore was now broken up by the classes. I also found out that Brother Mark and several of the other creepier staff, including Sister Jean, had parted ways with the school. The new Bunk 7 parents were kind of OK, but I didn't like the Bunk 8 mother. She was mean, she carried that paddle everywhere.

About a month after I started attending classes with Bunks 7 and 8, Mr. S informed me that he was planning a fancy formal staff dinner. This wasn't the honey-glazed rabbit staff meetings he did every month, this was to be a big formal affair. I was told to pick 3 girls to help prepare and serve the meal, and two more to help clean up after. I chose Nancy, Brittany, and Meghan (friends from my old Bunk 7) to help prep and serve and Tonya and Julie (new friends from Bunk 8) to help clean up. They were mostly not at the right levels, but no one said anything about it!

Nancy, Brittany, and Meghan were excited to get three extra showers, a clean uniform, #6 meals, or maybe family dinner, and three days off pulling the plow.

Wednesday came and we were supervised by Sister Beth. Sister Beth was not part of the church like the other Brothers and Sisters, she was Mr. S's sister and was visiting. She stayed in my room, and I bunked with Jess for the 6 weeks, sharing her bed. She wasn't one of the normal staff. She made it clear that if we misbehaved, it wasn't her job to punish us, she would send us back to bunk (or in my case, Jess's room) if we misbehaved, where bunk parents would no doubt do the punishing!

Sister Beth had us scrub and polish the house till it shined for that party, and more importantly, made us take pride in the work, and in turn, she took pride in us. It was so different than the bunk parents shitting on you no matter how hard you worked. We absolutely loved her! We helped her make food (and boy did she know how to cook!). She even taught us how to serve food at such a formal event.

It wasn't supposed to happen, but Mr. S was working late, and Sister Beth just kept Nancy, Brittany, and Meghan for family dinner and lesson (Sister Beth did a lesson on critical thinking) and even for story. We didn't sit on her lap, but we all sat on the couch together, Jess on her lap and two girls on each side of her, snuggling in as she read to us.

After the story, she snuck us a bottle of red nail polish (an absolutely forbidden item) and sent them to sleep with me and Jess. She literally gave us a sleepover where we got to be giggly girls and do our nails for a few hours! We all slept in a puddle of girls on the floor of Jess's room that night, sharing blankets and pillows and snuggling with each other.

Sister Beth woke us up in the morning. She didn't call us to formation, but Nancy and Meghan jumped into line and the rest of us then did too, more as a force of habit. I don't think Sister Beth quite knew what to do with us in formation like that, she didn't give us any of the normal commands or say any of the normal things, like what our day was.

I remember that when Nancy finally asked Sister Beth if we could have permission to get dressed and be dismissed, she teased us about how if we were naked all day, she wouldn't have to worry about us soiling our uniforms while cleaning.

Just as we were all internally panicking that we wouldn't be allowed clothes for the day, she laughed and told us to get dressed and be down for breakfast in 30 minutes. I remember wondering if that meant we had been dismissed and thinking that 30 minutes to get dressed was such a long time. We all giggled about that and about just how close we came to having to spend the day without clothes!

Mr. S came home after we were all asleep. And because Sister Beth made breakfast (pancakes!) and let us sleep in, he didn't discover the sleepover till we all sat down for family breakfast. We all knew the orders were to have them back in bunk by ten p.m., and we figured we would all be spanked for the sleepover and nails, but we also figured it was well worth it.

When Mr. S questioned it (and our red nails), we were sure our butts were going to be roasted. Sister Beth told him that keeping them was her decision and that she had needed us later than expected and needed us earlier to get ready.

She said the red nails were part of our serving uniform. I think he knew it was all a lie, but they then seemed to have a complete conversation in a few looks. He asked Sister Beth if she was sure and she said no, but she was following a hunch. We were shocked that Mr. S accepted that. From anyone else, he would have needed really solid reasoning, and going against an already made decision was just not something you did with him.

Mr. S said OK, but that she had to contact the bunk parents and let them know what happened. We were floored by that. We didn't even get any punishments for it. Sister Beth kept them for Thursday and Friday nights too.

Thursday went much like Wednesday, with more cooking and less cleaning. We got a chemistry class from Mr. S, after dinner on yeast and fermentation, then Sister Beth had us bake a loaf of bread, showing us the chemistry of what Mr. S had just covered. They were amazing teachers as a team like that!

We even got two stories that night. The first story was from Sister Beth as the bread was baked. She didn't read to us from a book but instead told us a story about a cloth becoming a coat, then a jacket, then a shirt, and eventually a button and a story. Then we got a second one from Mr. S as we ate the bread. He too told us the story instead of reading from a book. His story was about soldiers making sourdough bread. Sister Beth said they were stories their mother told them as children. I liked Sister Beth's story more, but I liked snuggling into Mr. S's chest more.

By Friday Sister Beth seemed to have gotten the hang of the morning line thing. She called us to attention, told us about our day, and even officially dismissed us to make bunk and dress, though 30 minutes still seemed like such a long time for that.

Friday night, the five of us girls (including Jess) got to wear matching dresses, complete with nylon panties. This was a luxury compared to the itchy wool panties of our uniforms!

Dinner went off amazingly! We did exactly as we were taught, one girl removing the old dish and the next girl placing the new dish. It was like a well-choreographed dance complete with costumes, and we loved it!

After serving dessert, we were to go to Jess's room until we were called so the staff could talk. I forgot to get Jess her antibiotic before we went upstairs (she was at the end of a two-week antibiotic for a respiratory infection), and she was fast falling asleep, so I snuck down to get it.

I wasn't intending to spy, but I couldn't help but overhear what was being said. They were talking about what to do with kids like me! Kids who didn't really need an adolescence of the schools' tough love, but who were here until they were 18 or 21 anyways. Or kids who were snapped out of bad behaviors, and that was now doing well, but would certainly fail if just dropped back into typical home life.

Most of the staff felt it would be best to leave us in the tough love program anyway. Sister Beth made an impassioned plea to do something different, pointing to Nancy, Brittany, Meghan, and I, and how far we had come in just a few days.

Other staff was now ganging up on Sister Beth and I couldn't take it anymore. I burst in and screamed hysterically for them to stop it and to leave Sister Beth alone. The room went dead silent.

Maybe we screwed up. Maybe we deserved all of the bad things that happened to us. Yeah, maybe we deserved to be treated how we had been. But if we learn and grow, and if God can forgive us for our sins, when would the time come when we had been punished enough? When do we get to grow past stumps and plows and shoveling shit? What will it take to earn being a human again? Then I ran back to Jess's room, tears streaming from my face.

I expected a major punishment for that. But they never even called us to clean up dessert. The next morning, no one called us to get up. We eventually got dressed and went downstairs to find Mr. S, Sister Beth, Sister Carol, Ericka, Kate, Michelle, Tonya, and Julie were sitting at the dining room table.

Mr. S told us all to sit down. I figured I was in serious trouble for last night. Instead, he said it was time to figure out how to bring kids who were ready, back to being human again. I was sure this was Sister Beth's doing, I mean, who else could it have been?

Our mandate would be helping girls that were ready to become humans again and trying to get the rest ready. We spent the entire day mapping out how we thought this would work. This moment was the birth of the Guardians, though we wouldn't get our name for several more months.

Sister Beth spent a lot of time with Jess and me the next few weeks. It was like having a mom again. Sister Beth thanked me for standing up for her, but she also told me that she was quite capable of standing up for herself and that she knew I would be able to do that too.

Sister Beth had a number of superpowers. She was able to get Mr. S to agree to almost anything just by saying she had a hunch. But she had two others as well, neither one of which was fair to fourteen-year-old me.

A few days after our big meeting at the dining room table, Sister Beth and Jess were both tired, and it wasn't even lunch. After lunch, she said we were all taking a nap. I protested that I wasn't tired and wouldn't sleep; I told her I was too old to take a nap, but she didn't care, she said I was taking a nap with them. She laid down on her side on the couch and made me lie on my side with her and Jess laid on top of us.

She started rubbing my nose. The next thing I knew, she was waking me up, telling me it was 2:30 and time to wake up. I sat up and snuggled into her while she wrapped her arm around my shoulder. I loved her, but I remember feeling that being put to sleep like that just wasn't fair and I didn't understand how she made me fall asleep like that.

I told her that it wasn't fair using her "make you sleep" superpowers on me. She laughed as she hugged me tighter and told me I would develop my own superpowers as I got older.

Her last superpower was being able to reduce me to a pile on the floor. I wasn't ticklish. I stopped being ticklish when I was 9. Many had tried, but no one could tickle me. But somehow, she had the power to tickle me and instantly reduce me to a squirming giggling mass on the floor at will. I both loved and hated this superpower of hers. I loved it because it was Sister Beth, and it was kind of fun. I hated it because she could make me agree to anything she wanted with that superpower. It so wasn't fair.

I can't put into words how much I loved her and how much that time with her meant to me. When you haven't had a mother, and suddenly you do, even if just for a little while, it's the most amazing feeling.

Seeing her go was extremely hard for both Jess and I. I missed her terribly, but I was allowed to write to her, which I did every mail run (when the boat came). I got a letter or postcard from her every mail run (she wrote me more than she did Mr. S!). They didn't even censor mail to or from her like they did all the other mail. It was about the only mail I ever got, and I always looked forward to it.

Sourdough Bread Recipe

Ingredients:
- 7 cups Flour
- 2 tsp Yeast
- 3 cups Warm Water
- 2 tsp Honey
- 1/3 cup oil or melted butter
- 4 tsp Salt
- 1 cup of shelled Sunflower Seeds

Instructions:
1. Pour flour into a large bowl and shape into a volcano
2. Dissolve yeast & honey in 1 cup of warm water, then pour into the center of your flour volcano
3. Let yeast mixture rise for 10 - 15 min
4. Add salt, oil, and 2 more cups of water
5. Add in Sunflower seeds
6. Mix, knead, and shape the dough
7. Let rise for 20-30 min in a warm location
8. Knead once more and place it on a baking sheet
9. Bake in preheated over at 325 F for one hour
10. Enjoy!

This is the story Sister Beth told us:

The Button

There once was an old lady who was given the finest of cloth. She LOVED that cloth. She looked at that cloth and said "Hmmm, I know what I'll do!" And with a stitch here and a snip their and a snip here and a stitch their she turned that cloth into a coat. She loved that coat so much she wore it up, she wore it down, she wore it all around the town. She wore it here, she wore it there, you know she wore it everywhere. She wore it and she wore it until she wore it all out.

This old lady looked at that worn out coat and said "Hmmm, I know what I'll do!" And with a stitch here and a snip their and a snip here and a stitch their she turned that coat into a jacket. She loved that jacket so much she wore it up, she wore it down, she wore it all around the town. She wore it here, she wore it there, you know she wore it everywhere. She wore it and she wore it until she wore it all out.

This old lady looked at that worn out jacket and said "Hmmm, I know what I'll do!" And with a stitch here and a snip their and a snip here and a stitch their she turned that jacket into a vest. She loved that vest so much she wore it up, she wore it down, she wore it all around the town. She wore it here, she wore it there, you know she wore it everywhere. She wore it and she wore it until she wore it all out.

This old lady looked at that worn out vest and said "Hmmm, I know what I'll do!" And with a stitch here and a snip their and a snip here and a stitch their she turned that vest into a shirt. She loved that shirt so much she wore it up, she wore it down, she wore it all around the town. She wore it here, she wore it there, you know she wore it everywhere. She wore it and she wore it until she wore it all out.

This old lady looked at that worn out shirt and was sad at how much had already been lost. But she looked harder and said "Hmmm, I know what I'll do!" And with a stitch here and a snip their and a snip here and a stitch their she turned that shirt into a hat. She loved that hat so much she wore it up, she wore it down, she wore it all around the town. She wore it here, she wore it there, you know she wore it everywhere. She wore it and she wore it until she wore it all out.

This old lady looked at that worn out hat and was now really sad at how much had already been lost, and really concerned about what to do. But she looked harder and thought about and then said "Hmmm, I know what I'll do!" And with a stitch here and a snip their and a snip here and a stitch their she turned that hat into a button. She loved that button so much she wore it up, she wore it down, she wore it all around the town. She wore it here, she wore it there, you know she wore it everywhere. She wore it and she wore it until she wore it all out.

This old lady looked at that worn out button and was now so very sad. Almost all of it was gone. She looked and thought and looked and thought and finally said "Hmmm, I know what I'll do!" And with a stitch here and a snip their and a snip here and a stitch their she turned that button into something bigger and better than the cloth had ever been. She turned it into a story. She gave that story to me, and now I have given it to you!

It is a story my children grew up hearing, and one that will stick with me till the day I die.

Chapter 6:
Learning to Fly

It was the first week of December 1991. Sixteen girls were selected, all lifers, here till they were eighteen or twenty-one, just like me. Most of them were upper-level girls. One of them was Ericka. She was the oldest girl selected and a natural leader. I don't think the Guardians would have worked without her leadership, her tenacity, and her enormous heart.

Our first job was to resurrect the dilapidated bunkhouse 1. This building was attached to Mr. S's house and had not been used in a long time. But it had flush toilets (no more latrines for any of us!) and a group shower in it. We spent two weeks cleaning it up, building bunk beds and a large table, putting on new shingles, and doing other repairs. This would be our living quarters and base of operations.

Tonya and I worked together a lot in rebuilding Bunk 1. We quickly became best friends. We shared a bunk bed and hanging rod. We ate together as often as we could, we shared secrets and quickly became inseparable. Tonya even sometimes got to sleep in my room with me and I brought her to as many family dinners as I could.

When we started fixing up Bunk 1, we would have Jess with us. It was really hard to do what everyone else was doing when I was the only one that Jess would go to. Sometimes Mr. S would take Jess to his office, like when we worked on the roof, but mostly she was my responsibility.

We were building bunk beds when it happened. Jess needed some attention. Tonya sat with me as I read Jess a story, and Jess talked in front of her! Then we sang the Green Grass song, and much to my surprise, Jess sang with Tonya! She even talked to Tonya and then gave her a hug!

A little while later that day, we were building the table and I was working on nailing the top boards down. It was the first time in my life I actually started to get the nails going in straight. Just as I was really starting to get it, Jess started to meltdown. I can't blame her, it's really hard being so young in a room full of teenagers when no one is paying any attention to you for so long, but I was really excited that the nails were going in and I wanted to keep doing it!

Tonya scooped up Jess and made a big deal to her about how it wasn't fair that only I got Jess turns and that she wanted one too. At first, Jess had this very unsure look on her face, and I thought she was going to meltdown, but then Tonya very excitedly asked Jess if she wanted to go with her on an adventure to the maintenance building. Jess thought about it for a moment, looking back and forth between me and Tonya, then said "YES" very loudly. Most of the girls had never heard Jess talk before, everyone looked. Tonya told me that she got me and that this is what best friends are for. Then she and Jess skipped out on an adventure to the maintenance shed.

Tonya was my best friend, but she also became closer to Jess than any other Guardian besides me. Not only was she the first person besides me and Mr. S that Jess would talk to and even sing with, but she got Jess climbing trees and even taught her to do cartwheels. After a while, Jess would talk to and even play with all of the Guardians, but that took time.

The first week of January 1992, we started training for the task ahead. Mr. S had gone to the mainland for a few weeks to deal with some fundraising thing. So, we were working with Brother Sam at the intake center. We were taken through the intake process with the new arrivals from the Staff side. Mr. S had made major changes to the intake process.

One by one, the new arrivals were brought into room A and cuffed to the benches just like I was. It was so hard to watch this, I kept remembering how tough this was on me, how scared I was. Our first task was to explain to all the girls what the next steps of this process were, and some of us were assigned to shepherd the youngest girls through the process.

Most of the older girls acted like wild animals, itching for a fight, while the younger girls were just as scared as I was when I arrived. Two by two, they were taken from room A to the intake shower by two large maintenance men, where they were stripped and cuffed to the wall.

Many of them were covered in puke and God knows what. You could see the fight leave them as they were hosed down with the cold salty water. Brother Sam explained that it's just safer for everyone to sap their energy with cold water like this before delousing them, doing a body cavity search, and putting them in cells. I mean, I could see his point, but I hated that he had a point.

The youngest girls were still hosed down and deloused, but instead of being cuffed to the wall like the older girls, they held the hands of two Guardians, one of whom was their shepherd.

I asked Brother Sam if I was like this when I got here? Brother Sam pointed to two girls and said I was more like them. Scared, but compliant. He also told me that those are often the most dangerous, as they will lull you into a false sense of security, so you can't trust them until you get to know them. He told us about a staff member who had an eye gouged out this way a few years ago.

I asked why the body cavity searches. It was perhaps the most traumatic part of my intake. Brother Sam told me that it was for two reasons. First, it's where they find the most contraband. Indeed, this batch of girls produced a quantity of coke and pot. Second, as more than half of us were juvi diversions, they had to meet contractual standards that required it. I still can't believe that courts would require that, but they do.

Unlike when I came through, they had a woman, the nurse from the infirmary, doing the searches. She was a lot gentler about searching these girls than what I went through. I think the explanations these girls got made a huge difference, but the fact that they were given the opportunity to cooperate instead of just being manhandled into place was a major improvement.

When I went through intake, it was not knowing what was happening and what to expect that was the most difficult and scary thing. I envied these girls a little. I wished that I had had a Guardian to hold my hand and shepherd me through intake like the twelve- and thirteen-year-olds in this group. I would never want to go through intake again, but I envied how much better they were treated than I was. But I guess that's part of making progress.

After the search, they were taken to cells. The cell block was made up of sixteen 10x10 cells. You had a central hallway, with eight cells on each side. The back walls of each cell and the side of the hallway towards the cliff and the shower was walled off, but the side towards the lane were bars. Girls were put two to a cell and prohibited from making physical contact. Brother Sam explained that this was to hasten the detox and "tantrum time", as well as to establish that they were firmly in control.

Shepherds spent time in the cells with their charges every day. As a Shepherd, we were allowed to comfort the younger girls and talk to them about what was to come. Shepherds had to visit their charges at least three times a day while they were in cells. We even gave our charges rubbing stones. They settled down far faster than the older girls, I think we could have started teaching them the commands on day 2, but we always waited until day 4.

All of the other girls in the cells tried begging, bargaining, crying, tantrums, making promises, offering sex, and anything else they could think of to get out. I felt so bad for these girls. It was hard to ignore them and their pleases, though I now understood why we were laughed at. Brother Sam said the most humane thing we could do was to ignore it. I am not sure I agree with that, but I understood. I tried, but at times it was either laugh or cry, and crying wasn't an option, it wouldn't help anything. Not them and not me.

They were fed soup 3 times a day. Chicken broth in the morning, a beef broth with grain soup in the afternoon, and tomato soup in the evening. 950 calories a day. The mostly liquid and fiber diet was to help them detox, as most were either hungover (like I was when I arrived) or on something illegal.

We had a meeting at the end of each intake day where we went over things and then we had one at the end of intake process where we tried to come up with ways to make it better for the girls and make a new game plan for the next intake. We did this meeting after every intake, usually once, sometimes twice a month.

The next two days were spent in the chow hut (kitchen). We knew higher number meals were better meals, but we didn't really know why we would get them. We learned that all of us girls were on a low-calorie, high nutrient diet. We learned that the numbers we were given for meals each week were the calories and were related to us being weighed after our weekly shower. If you were overweight, you got meal 1 (800 calories a day). If you were underweight, you got meal 5 (1600 calories a day). Most kids got meals 2, 3, or 4.

We learned that the salad (something we could eat as much as we wanted) was made up of foods that were calorie neutral, like lettuce, celery, and cucumbers. Fills the belly but doesn't really affect the diet.

I thought about how Jess had gotten Meal #6 a lot when we were in bunk, before family meals. I suspect it was because of her age and the fact that she was losing so much weight. They called it "failure to thrive". I thought a bit about when Jess would only eat what I ate, which mostly meant she was eating off my plate. We in bunk 1 could now have Meal #6 nine times a week at the chow hall, or about half of our meals, though I usually did family meals with Mr. S and Jess.

We went back to intake for day 4. You could see the change in these girls. The tantrums had mostly ended. Whatever was in their systems was now mostly gone. You could talk to them now, where a few days ago that was just about impossible.

Brother Sam told us that the next few days were mostly for the staff to start getting to know the new girls and for the new girls to start learning some basics of how to behave here.

We were assigned to take family histories. We made the girls stand in front of us and answer the questions on the form. Many of them had major issues. One girl I interviewed was here for the attempted murder of her parents. She had stabbed both of them. Others seemed to be here for comparatively trivial things. One girl was here for sassing her parents too much. Another girl, Mary, was here for running away from foster homes. Other staff had other questionnaires that had to be filled out, like health and school histories.

Later in the day, we went back and started teaching the basic responses and commands and making them practice them. Attention, Parade rest, Rest, At Ease, Fall In, Fall Out and Sound Off, Wait on the wall, Watch the wall, Nose-tits-n-toes, Mongra and Assume the position. We also explained to them that Strip was another common command, and it didn't matter where you were or who was watching. Because they had already spent so much time naked, this was almost never a shock to any of them, though we did sometimes have to explain to them that they needed to get over themselves with it.

We went back twice a day, every day for the rest of the week until every girl had those commands and responses memorized. Well, all except one girl, I will get to her in a minute.

Brother Sam had us spend time observing groups. The first group we observed did the heart thing, where they had girls write all their happiest memories on a red heart of paper. Then they talked about these memories and about getting back to them.

When I did this, they stood us each up and had us tell the group about the memories. Then they passed the heart around and had the other girls say the meanest things they could think of about these memories, each tearing off a piece of the heart and grinding it into the ground with their foot. This was definitely better than when I went through it, I was so happy they didn't have to endure the groups of Sister Jean.

In the next group, they talked about a few of the mantras. They didn't just drill them into your head like they did with me, they talked about what they meant. Some of them were still stupid, but a few made sense.

The last group we watched was a confessions group. They still made girls confess truths from their life, but they didn't have the group go around and say mean things about them anymore and they didn't do horrible things to make them confess. I wish my groups had been more like these.

Back at the intake center, we kept working with the new girls on the commands. As the girls passed the basic commands test, we took them to the quartermasters and then to shower. We still didn't let them dress until we gave them permission, but we did that before taking them to the bunk. This was different than when I arrived, but I think it was a lot better. They were scared enough as it was entering the bunk and meeting their group, they didn't need to be dirty and naked for it.

The new girl welcome party beatings were gone. In its place was an explanation that for the first week, they were to silently watch and observe. They got a Level 5 girl assigned to tell them things, and the Level 5 girl now had to answer some questions. Girls still were not allowed to talk to them for the week, but I think it was better.

One of the new batch of girls was Jenna. She was only 8 and one of the most innocent kids I ever saw. Her older sister, Marci, 15, was sentenced here till her 20th birthday for armed robbery. Jenna was here because she wanted to stay with her older sister and some bonehead thought it was a better option for her than foster care. Nancy was her Shepherd through intake, but I held her other hand a lot.

I guess they told the school that she was 11. Since Mr. S took over as head, the school no longer took any kids younger than 11, usually not younger than 13. But Brother Sam told us the agency lied and we were now stuck with Jenna.

Jenna didn't have the commands down, but she copied her sister, and like with Jess, we felt it was good enough. Jenna and Marci were assigned to the same bunk, Bunk 16. We were over capacity, and it was the only bunk with two open beds. But it was probably the roughest bunk in the place, other than Bunk 22. Brother Sam started making plans to transfer them to a different bunk, but as we were over capacity, they would have to go to Bunk 16 for the night.

Four of us had been assigned to take these two to the bunk. When we got to Bunk 16, they told us that the house mother was in the bathroom with half of her group (more likely smoking a cigarette somewhere...). We were a bit uneasy, especially as Nikki, a seventeen-year-old Level 6 girl, a particularly low-life scum, and generally the leader of Bunk 16, seemed to know Marci, and *not* as friends. But we left them in the bunk as Brother Sam had ordered and started back towards the intake center.

When we looked back and saw the circle form through the window, we all knew what was about to go down. Jenna had grown on us and none of us were going to let Jenna be beaten up like that, especially not me and Nancy.

Laura was the smallest of us (one quarter of an inch shorter than me), but she had also been a track star off the Island. We sent her running for reinforcements while Tonya, Nancy, and I charged back into Bunk 16.

We were outnumbered over 3:1, but we didn't care. We just had to hold out till the others got here.

Tonya, 16, was the biggest of the 3 of us. She started yelling at them. Nikki started arguing with her. Tonya made clear that this welcome party was not going to happen, and Jenna was coming with us. Nikki felt that the party was going to happen, Jenna was her special guest and since it was going to happen anyway, she may as well make us her guests too. The fight then erupted. It was basically 3 of us plus Marci versus 10 of them. We were holding our own, but as outnumbered as we were, we were going to lose and lose badly, and we knew it – it was just a matter of time. So, we concentrated on protecting Jenna as best we could.

Tonya was fierce and she was damn scary when she was angry (which I only ever saw a handful of times). She took on the 4 biggest of them, including Nikki. I think if it was just 3 of them, those girls wouldn't have stood a chance against Tonya, but she still more than held her own against the 4 of them. The rest of us struggled with 2 each. Nikki broke away and got a hold of Jenna. I tried to get to her, but I couldn't.

I saw Nikki punch Jenna in the face when out of nowhere came Laura. She jumped on Nikki's back and took her to the ground by her hair. Nikki, who was twice Laura's size, tossed her off, then 12 more members of Bunk 1 burst through the door. It was now 16 of us plus Marci and 10 of them, and as a group, we were older, bigger and we had far more gas in our tanks than they did. Ericka and Christi now had Nikki and as quickly as that, the fight was over as we pinned them all to the walls.

In all my time on the Island, I only once ever wanted to do a circle beating, and this was it. I think we all wanted it at that moment. I think Nikki was lucky that Mr. S had put a stop to them because I don't know if she would have lived through the beating Tonya, Nancy and I wanted to give her.

Brother Sam wasn't nearly as fast as the girls were. He got into the bunk well after we had them all pinned. They knew they were royally screwed when they saw him come in. Brother Sam ordered us to take Nikki to his office and take Jenna and Marci with us to Bunk 1 for the night. Tonya and Christi started to take Nikki to Brother Sam's office and I was taking Jenna and Marci to Bunk 1. Just before she was taken through the bunkhouse door, Nikki screamed at Jenna that her guardian angels wouldn't always be there to protect her, and she was going to make Jenna pay for Marci ever being born. Christi told Nikki that she didn't have a chance in hell of laying a finger on Jenna, that we would be there to stop her.

Nikki may have sparked it, but it was Brother Sam that first started calling us the Guardians when he said, "Guardians, I need 4 volunteers to take the remainder of Bunk 16 and have them empty the latrines by hand (about the most disgusting job in the place, often given as a serious punishment) before allowing them to get dinner". Every single Guardian not already assigned raised their hand for the job.

Jenna and Marci shared my bed in Bunk 1 that night (I slept in my room). We figured they had been through enough. We talked to them that morning and told them a lot about how the Island worked. We told them a lot more about how things worked than new girls usually got. Later that day, just before dinner, they were sent to Bunk 5. Nikki got hotboxed for two days.

The day after Marci and Jenna were sent to Bunk 5, we had our first assignment with Bunk 22. The Bunk 22 compound was the supermax inside of the prison. It was made up of 3 buildings, 2 bunkhouses, and a community building. The compound had a fence around it to keep them in. Every cult-like program needs someplace worse that they can send kids to as both a threat and as the ultimate punishment. On the Island that was Bunk 22.

Bunk 22 assignments were the worst assignments Guardians could pull. I would rather supervise shit chores for a week than so much as walk the Bunk 22 girls to lunch – and lunch in the chow hall was a major reward for them!

These girls were the older girls who just refused to level up. They were between 16 and 22 but I don't think any of them were past Level 3 and they just didn't care. They all had the worst attitudes, and they were perpetually on punishment of one type or another. I think they got a quarter of all the office punishments, and their house parents gave out more lashes than I think the whole rest of the school combined.

Barely a day went by where you didn't see a Bunk 22 girl standing nose-tits-n-toes or nose-tits-n-knees right out in front of their bunk. Unlike the other girls, they just didn't care if they got in more trouble, they mostly saw the Guardians as just another annoyance.

Assaulting a Guardian was not quite as serious as assaulting a regular staff, but it was still serious stuff on the Island. Assaulting a Guardian was an instant office punishment and a serious one at that. Some of the Bunk 22 girls took that as a challenge, so the general rule was that if we were taking one of them out of bunk, we brought at least an entire operations team to do it. It didn't help that they were generally bigger than us. Yeah, those assignments sucked.

One of the Bunk 22 girls, a twenty-year-old bitch name Rory, had stuck her hand down the pants of a maintenance worker during lunch. The guy was on a ladder changing a lightbulb, she just reached down into his pants and assaulted his junk just because. He fell off the ladder and broke his arm. The guy was maybe 23, he hadn't even been on the Island three days. He had never even seen this girl before. He reported the details of the incident in the infirmary. Her nails drew blood.

Brother Sam asked if we could get her, or if he should get maintenance staff. Ericka said we could do it, so he sent us to get her and take her to a solitary cell under the office.

Bunk 22 girls were bad news, but Rory was bad news even for Bunk 22. She was physically bigger than any Guardian and was well known for taking on as many as she could in a fight. Even Tonya (our best fighter) wasn't a match for her. Rory was the one who started the Bunk 22 riot a month or two earlier. All sixteen of us guardians went for this, we didn't know what kind of trouble we would face.

We decided deception was our best chance. Laura and I (the two smallest Guardians) approached her in the middle of Bunk 22. We told her she had won this week's prize drawing, and she won an extra 10-minute shower and a clean uniform (they were on a shit chore, so this was *very* welcome news!). We told her she even got to take that shower in a stall with a shower curtain and hot water (the Bunk 22 shower was only cold water).

Rory was so cocky, strutting around Bunk 22 and holding it over the other girls when we told her that. She quite eagerly grabbed her towel and came with us for her shower. We let her have her 10-minute hot shower in the upper-level girl stall (we did promise it to her). We even gave her time in the shower room to leisurely dry off. We told her that we would have to meet a staff person to get her the new uniform. She followed Laura and I out of the shower and the next thing she knew, a bag had been thrown over her head. She was taken to the ground by all of our biggest girls and handcuffed.

Even so, it took six of us to drag her to solitary, and even then, I got kicked hard in the face.

Rory spent two weeks in solitary for assaulting the staff member. When we went to let her out and bring her back to Bunk 22, she managed to jump on me and pound my face. Brother Sam pulled her off me and gave her another week in solitary confinement for that. I always hated Bunk 22 assignments.

Nikki got out of her two days in the hotbox the same day we put Rory in solitary. She was dropped to Level 1 and given a week on a leash. This was one of those 'creative punishments' I normally wouldn't have wished on my worst enemy, but I delighted in her getting it. Being on a leash meant she had to remain naked, except for her dog collar, handcuffs, and maybe her shoes. At all times someone had that leash (and for two days, it was the Guardians), or that leash was tied to some object.

While on a leash, she wasn't allowed to use furniture of any kind (including a bed or toilet), she had to walk behind whoever had the leash, she was not allowed to speak unless spoken to and given specific permission to speak. She even had to eat with just her mouth from a plate on the floor. Basically, she was a dog.

Nikki on a leash was a test for us that we failed, badly. I think things would have been very different if Mr. S was here for this, but he wasn't, and we had not been Guardians long enough yet to understand. Our mandate was to help make the girls more human again. We were all so mad at her, instead of following our mandate, we made her life as hellish and inhumane as we possibly could.

Her first night with us was the day after we put Rory in solitary. We tied her leash so short to the base of the center pillar that she couldn't even rollover. We made her crawl everywhere. In the morning, we made her crawl out into the front yard where we made her lift her leg and pee on a tree as we all laughed at her. We made her eat the scraps from our breakfast – including the stuff we chewed and spit out.

Not only did we let Jess and Jenna whip her with a riding crop, but we also made Nikki ask them to do it. We even made her hang her boobs off a table so Jenna could whip them more easily, then we punished Nikki for using the table we put her on.

We spent an hour plucking her bush (pubic hair) clean. We plucked out one hair at a time as we made fun of her as meanly as we possibly could. There's a reason people shave down there—if you've never plucked out pubic hair, it's extremely painful and gets worse as you continue. After we slowly plucked her clean, we took her outside and made her tell every girl that passed by that she was a stupid, worthless cunt bitch not even worth having a bush.

We took her over to Marci and made her tell Marci how stupid, fat, and ugly of a drunk and druggy slut she was. We were brutal. After the second day of this torture, we had to return her to her bunk.

Nikki's house mother got in trouble for the welcome party, and she took it out on her bunk. She made her girls, even the 10 who were not at the party (but not Nikki) crawl in shit for several days. She literally made them crawl in and turn the wet latrine waste on the drying pads, making sure they knew it was Nikki that got them into it. Someone told me that Nikki was made to lick each of her bunkmates to orgasm. Given that the House Mother for Bunk 16 left on the next supply ship, I tend to believe it.

After Mr. S got back, we had a long talk about this. We did the right thing by stopping the welcome party, and he was proud of us for charging in like that, he said it was very brave of us to have taken on such long odds as we did. Leashing may be a traditional punishment on the Island and beating up an innocent little kid like Jenna was bad, but if we are to meet his expectations, we would have to live up to our mandate to make them more human, not less.

He was clearly disappointed in us, and that was devastating to all of us, but especially me. I cried a lot that night in my room. I was so relieved when I was told Brother Sam would whip each of us the next day. What was the mantra? "Better a pink bottom than a black soul"? It didn't really cover the shade of purple we got, but we definitely deserved it. It's funny how being punished like that when you have let someone you respect down can relieve a portion of your feeling of guilt, whereas punishments from someone you don't respect just breed anger and resentment.

Sister Lisa made us shave our bushes off for having plucked Nikki's, but it hardly seemed like payment for what we had done—not to Nikki, the whipping was more than enough for that. But it was hardly a down payment to the loss of Mr. S's trust and faith in us. This is where the tradition of Guardians being shaved came from. Being shaved was never spoken of to us again, but we all kept shaved after that. Even today, I pay that small penance.

All of us would have happily taken a week on a leash rather than have Mr. S disappointed in us like he was. I even offered to take a week on a leash if he would forgive me. He hugged me and told me that he expected more of us, that he knew I was capable of more than that and that he expected more than that of me in particular. He said that more than any of the other girls, I was a reflection on him. We were all going to work hard not to let that happen ever again, especially me.

This was when Mr. S started talking a lot about power corrupting, how we needed to ensure we were accountable for our power, and how we had to be ever vigilant against becoming tyrants with our power. That took time to really understand.

Nikki went to Bunk 22 and aged out about 6 months later. She was never the same after being leashed and her bunk broken up. We clearly broke something deep inside her when we did that to her. I don't know whatever happened to her after she left, but I still look back and feel horrible about what we did to her.

In my time as a Guardian, we had a few more leashed girls spend time with us before Mr. S finally abolished the practice the next year. We never did to them the kind of things we did to Nikki. And while we enforced the rules, we spent a lot more time caring for them and talking to them about what got them put on a leash and how not to get to that point again.

That they had to eat off a plate on the floor didn't mean we couldn't use a fork to feed them. It didn't mean that they had to eat half-eaten scraps off our plates, and it didn't mean we couldn't give them a mattress and a blanket. But most importantly, no matter what the rules, we should be striving to treat them more as people, not less. That was a hard-earned lesson, one I wish we could have learned without having broken Nikki as we did. The worst part was that besides Mr. S, no one else seemed to care about us having broken Nikki as we did. But *he cared*, and because he did, so did we.

Many of the bunk parents were already upset with all the changes Mr. S was making. Because of that, many of them wanted the Guardians punished over the Bunk 16 fight. The green team even got the belt from a few bunk parents over it. It was then that the official rules came down about Guardians and punishments. Guardians could be punished only within our own chain of command. Team sergeants' could punish their team members with wall time, pushups, extra assignments, and whatnot. Ericka could punish any Guardian, including the team sergeants the same way (not that it happened very often). But only Mr. S, Brother Sam and Sister Lisa were authorized to inflict more severe punishments on Guardians, though staff could refer incidents to Brother Sam.

At about this time, Mr. S and Brother Sam started talking to us a lot about how we had to show an impeccable image the moment we crossed the staff fence line, and we took that seriously. We never wanted to give anyone any reason to doubt us, and we worked really hard to build and maintain our image. Screwing around was strictly reserved for when we were alone in Bunk 1.

The Bunk 16 mother was replaced with a young couple, Father Fred and Sister Denise (they were married). Father Fred was about 26, but he graduated from a real seminary college and was an actual ordained minister. I really liked him, and Church became a lot better under him.

Ultimately, Mr. S decided that Jenna would share a room with Jess and like Jess, would be a responsibility of the Guardians – now our official name. Marci was still assigned to Bunk 5, across the lane (and fence) from Bunk 1 to be close to her sister. Twice a week we took Marci out of chore to spend special time with Jenna. I liked supervising that and tried to always take that duty, especially as the other Guardians didn't love the assignment - it made most of them a little sad and homesick. I would usually take Jess for it, so we got special time too. I always kept Marci for family lunch when we did that. They loved each other at least as much as Jess and I did. Marci and I became good friends during those special times.

The Island's Honey Glazed Roast Rabbit

Ingredients:
- 2 lb. of Rabbit
- 2/3 cup butter
- 2/3 cup honey
- 4 tablespoons mustard
- 2 teaspoon salt
- 2 teaspoon pepper
- 2 teaspoon curry powder

Instructions:
1. Cube the rabbit meat into one-inch cubes
2. In a large bowl, mix the butter, honey, mustard, salt, pepper and curry powder and blend well to form the glaze.
3. Dip the meat in the glaze and then arrange the meat on a high walled sheet pan or in a shallow baking dish, leaving a little space between each piece of meat.
4. Pour the remaining glaze into the bottom of the sheet pan.
5. Bake at 350°F for hour to an hour and fifteen minutes.
6. While baking, baste the rabbit frequently with the glaze mixture.

Chapter 7:
And the Jedi Moved The Mountain

In February of 1992, Mr. S introduced Jodies to the Guardians. Jodies are marching cadences (you can think of them as call-and-response songs) that are just fun to sing. He had taught Jess and me a lot of them on Sunday mornings, but now we were using them to help with marching. They really made boring drill a lot more fun, especially as many of them made fun of the Marines! There was even one about a Navy Seal beating up Superman! How did that one go? I think it was:

Whooo-a-whooo-a-whooo
Superman is the man of steel
He ain't no match for a navy SEAL
Whooo-a-whooo-a-whooo
Chief and he got in a fight
Knocked his head with kryptonite
Whooo-a-whooo-a-whooo
Superman is no more
Chief crushed his head into the floor
Whooo-a-whooo-a-whooo
Whooo-a-whooo-a-whooo

Guess he ain't so super no more
Whooo-a-whooo-a-whooo
Whooo-a-whooo-a-whooo!

Even though Mr. S taught them to us, and he worked hard to get us all to be good callers, because it was initially done in secret in the field behind his house, and because you know, singing, it always felt so rebellious!

The bunk parents and even Brother Todd, the drill guy, definitely did *not* do Jodies with drill. They would only call lefts and rights. We only did Jodies with the girls when the bunk parents and Brother Todd took a walk during drill (that happened a *lot*) and stopped the moment we saw any sign of them! If we Guardians felt rebellious with them, you can just imagine how the girls felt!

While we were now allowed to use Jodies, under no circumstances were we allowed to call them songs! Songs were 'unauthorized celebrations' whereas Jodies were 'military tradition'. Talk about splitting hairs! But it's amazing how much easier it was to get girls to do drill correctly when you introduce a little bit of fun!

March came, I turned 15 and Jess turned 6. The Guardians were split into 4 teams – red, blue, green, and purple (the colors of fabric we scavenged for our flags). One team would be assigned to Jess and Jenna, as well as assisting with administrative things. One team would be in training and two teams would be operational. The teams would rotate every two weeks unless a situation dictated otherwise.

- Purple team: Tonya (sixteen), Vanessa (me, fifteen), Julie (fifteen), and Meghan (fourteen)
- Green team: Christi (sixteen), Shawn (sixteen), Sarah (fifteen), and Laura (fourteen)
- Red team: Michelle (sixteen), Nancy (fifteen), Brittany (fifteen), and Nora (fourteen)
- Blue team: Ericka (seventeen), Kate (sixteen), Kat (fifteen), and Tori (fourteen)

Tonya, Christi, and Michelle were team sergeants. Ericka was both the team sergeant of the Blue team, and the overall Captain of the Guardians.

The first area of training was learning to saddle and ride a horse, which we did as a whole. This was taught by Sister Martha, who grew up on a ranch. A few of the girls (Kate, Sarah, and Michelle) already knew how to ride, so they helped the rest of us. Once we had the basics, we rode every day we could.

The second training session was on common repairs. Fixing doors, floorboards, replacing bulbs, and most importantly, all the emergency water shut-offs. The Island got most of its water from the ship, which filled the large tank and water leaks could be deadly. We had enough water to last eight weeks if we were careful (the ship came every six weeks), but we had to be careful about wasting water. This is why kids only got showers once a week; if they did it twice a week, we wouldn't have enough water to get past week four. But every two-week training session was focused like this.

During the second week of training, Mr. S, who had the only TV on the Island, got a tape with a movie about an invisible man. Jess, Jenna, and I watched it with him, but I think we were all still too young for it. After we watched it, he watched it again with Brother Hastings, a young Missionary maintenance guy. After Brother Hastings fell asleep, Mr. S filled us all in on his plan. He wanted us to pretend the guy was invisible. Not shunning, but as if he were invisible like in the movie. We were supposed to comment on his moving stuff and things like that. We were even told to reprimand girls that spoke to him for talking to imaginary people, especially as he was "currently missing".

We kept this joke up for a little over two days. All the staff were in on the joke, and we actually got him thinking it was real for a hot minute! We even launched a 'search party' for him, which was hysterically funny, as he went with us to look for himself! Boy was he panicked! While this happened mostly out of the sight of the girls, it confused the hell out of the girls who saw it, making it even more fun!

Lower-level girls were not allowed to talk to the maintenance staff anyways, and the upper-level girls didn't know what was going on, but they still went with it. One Level 6 girl even put her fingers in her ears, closed her eyes, and chanted, "I'm not seeing things, I'm not seeing things," over, and over again until he walked away from her. It was so hard to keep from cracking up when that happened; the dejected look on his face was just priceless!

At the end of two and a half days, he suddenly "reappeared" after Parade. Staff kept asking him where he was, and we Guardians even got to tell him how uncool it was that he played that prank on all of us and we had to spend so much time searching for him. Then, at the staff meeting, he tried to explain, and we all laughed hysterically, and he finally got the joke! It was the biggest and best prank I ever saw played at the school. After that, we were allowed to tell the girls what happened and it became both the month's big excitement and, more importantly, it became another part of the school's lore. Officially known as an 'Island Accomplishment', this was a 'war story' girls were allowed to tell each other without getting into trouble for it.

By this point, it was obvious to everyone on the Island that we had become Mr. S's 5th column. We were his eyes and ears. If staff wouldn't do something he wanted to be done, we would. Often, he came to us first, and only after we were doing it and making it work would staff pick up the ball. We did things to protect the girls, we were a huge part of the change he was trying to make. I honestly don't think he could have made many of the changes he did if he didn't have the Guardians to help force those changes.

But doing those jobs let us spread our wings in ways we otherwise wouldn't have been able to, it let us develop autonomy in ways other girls on the Island were not able to. It really made a difference to the Island, and to us.

Operational teams started as helping staff wherever needed but quickly grew to help the girls directly. My first operations rotation started the third week of April. We were stopped by Brother Paul. He told us that he had a moment of anger, and assigned a new girl, Alex, way too harsh of a punishment (staff don't take back punishments here, even if it takes the girl a year to complete, it's against tradition).

She was assigned to move a rock the size of a small car and given a shovel and a hammer. Alex deserved to toil for about two weeks for her crime (I don't even remember what her crime was), not years. He wanted us to solve it. I took this issue back to the Guardians. We had our first real mission, two weeks to plan and execute the impossible.

The operations team spent the next two days planning. Mr. S never let us tell him exactly what the problem was or how we planned to deal with it, but he made us break the problem down. First, we needed to know the scale of our problem. We learned to calculate volume and mass. The rock was about 465 cubic feet. Granite is about 168lbs a cubic foot, so that's about

80,000lbs. The rock just had to be moved; Brother Paul would accept a few inches of movement. We wanted to make a statement. The rock was at the top of a small hill, but we knew we couldn't dig that in two weeks, and the rules prohibited anyone other than Guardians from assisting her.

That night Mr. S had Ericka join us for family dinner. At family dinner, Mr. S talked about coordinating teams in the military for a secret mission. The job was too big for the special ops team itself, so they used compartmentalization. Teams were given jobs to do where they had no idea how something connected to the whole. In this way, they would use regular soldiers to get a top-secret job done, without ever having to reveal any secrets to them.

Mr. S then told us that two staff, from Bunks 9 and 14 (24 girls a bunk), had food poisoning, and he would need Guardians to supervise their groups' chores for the next week or so. They were on shoveling compost — turning rotting food scraps in with horse and cow dung and sometimes human waste from the latrines—a *very* dirty and disgusting job.

At first, we thought that our operations team had lost half its strength. It took us a few hours to realize that Mr. S had solved our manpower issue for us (what an epiphany moment that was!). We just had to change the chore to digging a trench. It was a lot cleaner than compost, so the girls wouldn't mind, and the compost would be fine if it wasn't turned yet again. We raced out to the rock with string and sticks to mark out the new "drainage trench". The top of the trench would begin 4 or 5 feet from the rock. Close enough that Guardians could finish it in the night.

The next morning, purple team (my team) started early at the horse barn. Tonya and I mounted horses, while Julie and Meghan dealt with the wagon (shovels, water, and lunch). Tonya and I road over to the chow hall and got the two bunks.

Mr. S said that our authority would go way up just by being on horseback. He was right. Here we were, fifteen and sixteen, and even the nineteen- and twenty-year-olds didn't argue with us. We took them to start digging the new trench. It took them 11 days to dig the trench we needed. We sang a lot of Jodies. Father Fred came out to do extra-long religion class with all of us each day, but we didn't stop for other classes. Father Fred and those classes are why I started to pray at night.

While we were dealing with the trench, the Green team still had to solve the issue of starting the rock rolling. They spent several days with Mr. Walker, the head maintenance man, learning about levers and pulleys. It took them all week to put a system together. They calculated that if we used a 10-foot lever, every pulley on the Island, the horses, and all the Guardians, we might get the rock rolling to standing.

Someone told Sarah that old I-beams could be found on the other side of the Island in the abandoned military buildings. I really wanted to see them, so I traded duty with another girl and rode out with Sarah and Laura to investigate. We found a big old 15-foot-long I beam on a truck right by a sandy beach. After a quick dip (my first time ever being in the ocean), we used the horses to drag it back to the woods by the rock. This would be the big lever they needed.

It was now all hands-on-deck for the Guardians. We got the beam in place, installed the pulleys and rope, hooked up all the horses, and pulled with everything we had. The rock didn't budge.

We would need a lot more force. The red team put the horses away for the night, while the rest of us tried to come up with a solution. We checked the duty roster. Bunks 9 and 14 would rotate to plow duty the next day (both in the plow fields), and Bunk 11 (Brother Paul's bunk) was on Stumps.

We asked the house parents of the three bunks if we could borrow the bunks for a day or so, that they would be doing the same thing, but different. Brother Paul was quick to give us whatever we needed. The other two grudgingly agreed but insisted the girls be locked to the yokes except for lunch.

Each yoke fit a maximum of twenty-four girls: four across and six long. The yoke stations each had a padded bend in it for the girl's shoulders. The arms would then wrap around the bar, and a leather strap held the yoke in place. Each station also had a set of shackles that could be used to lock their hands to the yoke. The use of the shackles was usually up to the preferences of the plow operator (bunk parent), but there were other reasons for using them, such as an uncooperative girl or very often, new staff. I guess we fit the new staff reason.

After the bunks had breakfast and a turn in the bathroom, we attached the three yokes in sequence, giving us spaces for seventy-two girls (we had seventy-five girls to yoke up). We yoked them up as a single team, not by bunk but by size (biggest in back, smallest in front). This was a bit weird for the girls, but it would give us the most power possible. Alex and the two smallest girls we made quick rope harnesses for and had them at the very front. We then attached the yoke train to the wagon (lunch, water, and tools) and had them pull us out to the field just out of view of the rock. Pulling the wagon like this was far easier than pulling the plow! With this many girls, it was barely harder than just marching.

Alex was sent to work with the green team. Once the horses and the yoked girls were hooked up to the proper ropes, the rock was quickly pulled to standing and it wasn't even ten a.m. This was much faster than we anticipated.

After the other teams secured the ropes, we hooked the yoke train back to the wagon. I led on horseback, while the rest of purple team road in the wagon. We took the girls out to the beach we had found, almost an hour's walk from where we were.

Then we gave them a choice. We could have them pull old trucks around – about as much work as plowing

– or, if they met our conditions, we would let them have a beach day.

The conditions were simple: 1. They *never* tell *anyone* that we did this. 2. Any fighting by *anyone* gets everyone put back on the yoke and they will pull trucks till breakfast. 3. Anyone not immediately following the instruction of a Guardian would get her and 5 of her friends punished and yoked early. They all eagerly agreed.

Row by row, we unlocked the girls, making them leave their shoes and clothes on their yoke spot. Then we gave them their bagged #3 lunch and let them play in the sand and water till it was time to head back. Playing on the beach, laughing and happy, they could have been kids from a summer camp or even kids on holiday. For an afternoon, none of them were troubled kids. The closest we had to a disagreement was judging the sandcastle contest.

We had them rinse off in the stream to get the salt and sand out, hiding our trip to the beach. The bunk parents must have known something was up, as this is likely the happiest and cleanest any girl had ever returned from plow duty! Between swimming in the ocean and rinsing off in the stream, most girls were far cleaner than after a shower!

Then we had them get dressed and re-yoked for the journey back. They didn't even complain when we took them the long way around so they didn't see the rock (not that they were allowed to talk while yoked, that was strictly forbidden and would typically earn girls a spanking or other major punishment).

We had all these kids for two days, so the next day, May 4th, we yoked them up again and took them back to the beach. This time we did make them work moving an old truck and some other junk off the beach for a few hours before giving them bagged lunch and free time on the beach. We did have a few kids not follow directions and had to punish a few times, but we stopped short of re-yoking any of them. What was it Sister Martha said about horses? You can let up on the reins, but you always have to let them know who's in charge. Guess that's true for packs of girls as well.

On the way back, we met up with everyone at the bottom of the hill, a good way away from the trench but in view of the rock. Brother Paul was there. The ropes and I beam were gone. The rock was standing up and looked precarious, but it had moved more than enough to satisfy Brother Paul.

Alex screamed, "Brother Paul!" and we all looked to the top of the hill. She swung the sledgehammer into the rock. On the third hit, it started tumbling, landing in the trench, and sliding down it, just as we planned. The rock came to a stop about 100 feet from where it started. Everyone cheered!

It was years later, when *Star Wars: Revenge of the Sith* came out and they did the big 'May the 4th be with you' media day, that I finally understood why Brother Paul referred to us as the Jedi.

Alex became a legend that day—the girl who moved the mountain. Over eighty-five kids witnessed it, most never knowing the parts they played. Brother Paul knew. Brother Sam knew. Mr. Walker knew and we were sure that Mr. S knew, but everyone kept the secret. The Guardians obviously denied any involvement, which became our tradition in such matters.

Not everything we did was so spectacular. Most of it was rather mundane – leading drill, being subs, taking kids from place to place, acting as additional muscle when needed, fixing things that needed fixing, talking to girls about things (we did that a *lot*), demonstrating things as needed (like milkcrate steps or PT stuff or fancy marching formations), working our special magic if a girls punishment was too severe and otherwise helping to make things at the school just work. But even a few of those mundane things had a big impact, especially just talking with the girls like they were people.

Mr. S's Jodies

Here we go again
Here we go again!
Same old day again!
Marching down the avenue
Few more days and we'll be through
I won't have to look at you!
You won't have to look at me
So, I'll be glad and so will you!

Turn up the volume
Turn up the volume.
Just like a rad-i-o.
A high-fi ste-r-eo.
Turn it up in front.
Turn it up In the middle.
Turn it up In the rear.

Early in the Morning
Early one morning in the pouring rain,
Master Chief said it was time for pain,
grab your ruck and follow me!
It's time to do some PT.
We jogged nine miles and we ran three,
The Chief was yelling follow me!
Then we walked two miles and ran eight!
Navy PT sure is great!

Hey, Hey Marines

Left, left, left, right, left
He-ey Marines
Bullet-sponge marine corps
Cannon fodder marine corps
Crayon eating Marine corps
Left, left, left, right, left
He-ey Marines
March in the sun until your pink
I really wish you didn't stink
At least you know how to drink
So come and have a drink with me
Left, left, left, right, left
He-ey Marines
We know you can't learn math
One day you'll learn to take a bath
Good thing you can't smell yourself
That's why you're at the bar all by yourself
Left, left, left, right, left
He-ey Marines
Hear you can't get their on your own
You smell so bad can't get on the bus
Rather have you in the fight
Guess you'll have to ride with us
Left, left, left, right, left
He-ey Marines
Navy's here to save the day!

Sailors Alphabet *(Call / Response)*

If sailors need to know the Alphabet
   This is what your gunna get
A / the anchor that holds a bold ship
B / the bowsprit that often does dip
C / the capstan on which we do wind
D / the davits on which the jolly boat hangs
E / the ensign the red, white & blue
F / the fo'c'sle holds the ship's crew
G / the gangway on which the mate takes his stand
H / the hawser that seldom does strand
I / the irons where the stunsu'l boom sits
J / the jib-boom that often does dip
K / the keelsons of which you've told
L / the lanyards that always will hold
M / the main mast, so stout and so strong
N / the north point that never points wrong
O / the orders of which we must beware
P / the pumps that cause sailors to swear
Q / the quadrant, the sun for to take
R / the rigging that always does shake
S / the starboard side of our bold ship
T / the topmasts that often do split
U / the ugliest old Captain of all
V / the vapors that come with the squall
W / the windlass on which we do wind

X, Y, and Z / Sorry Cap, we can't put rhyme to that!

Up from a Sub

Up from a sub 50ft below
Up swims a woman with a tag of gold
Backstroke, sidestroke
heading for shore
She hits the beach and
she's ready for war
240 Bravo, Kabar by her side
These are the tools she lives by
How to kill, search team, hostage snatch
Out of the sub and back to the hatch
Hand-to-hand combat behind the lines
Seal Team 5 is just killing time

They Say...

They say that in the Navy the coffee's mighty fine
it looks like muddy water, it tastes like turpentine.
They say that in the Navy the toilets are mighty fine,
you flush them down at 7, they come back up again at 9.
They say that in the Navy the pay is mighty fine,
they give you 100 dollars and take back 99

They say that in the Navy, the meat is mighty fine
Last night we had ten puppies, this morning only nine
They say that in the Navy, the shoes are mighty fine
You ask for size eleven, they give you size nine
They say that in the Navy, the hours are just right
Start early in the morning and work on through the night
They say that in the Navy, the biscuits are mighty fine
One rolled off the table and killed a friend of mine
They say that in the Navy, the pancakes are mighty fine
You can try to chew them, but you're only wasting time
They say that in the Navy, the beds are mighty fine
But how the heck would I know, I've never slept in mine

We are the daughters of UDT
(Underwater Demolition Team)

Heey, Army!
Backpacking Army!
Pick up your packs and run with me!
We are the girls of UDT!
Heey, Marine Corps!
Bulletsponge Marine Corps!
Pick up your steps and run with me!
We are the girls of UDT!
Heey, Airforce!
Low flying Airforce!
Get on your planes and follow me!
We are the girls of UDT!
Heey, Coast Guard!
Puddle-pirate Coast guard!
Get on your boats and follow me!
We are the girls of UDT!
Heey, Navy!
World finest Navy!
Get on your ships and follow me!
We are the girls of UDT!

I Don't Want To Be No Green Beret

I don't wanna be no green beret
They only PT once a day
I don't wanna be no airborne ranger
I wanna live a life of danger
I don't wanna be marine recon

I wanna stay til' the job is done
I wanna be a seal team member
I wanna swim the deep blue sea
I wanna live a life of danger
Pick up your swim fins and run with me

Let 'Em Blow

Let 'Em Blow Let 'Em Blow
Let those trade winds blow
From the East and From the West
A SEAL Team member is the Best
Hooyah
Ah ha
Hooyah
Ah ha
From the East, From the West
A SEAL Team member is the Best
Hooyah
Ah ha
Hooyah
Ah ha
Let 'em glow, let 'em glow
Let those nuke, the nukeheads glow
From the East and From the West
A SEAL Team member is the Best
Hooyah
Ah ha
Hooyah
Ah ha

Chapter 8:
New Responsibilities

One of the things about being a Guardian was that we had to deal with the after-effects of the rain. We dreaded the rain. We always had so much more to worry about when we were on operations duty after a storm, or really, anything more than a light sprinkle. We had to think a lot about how we were going to get our girls to be clean. Was there enough sand in the sand stations? Was there a dry place where we could let the girls dry the mud off? Was this going to cause another infection? Were we going to have to deal with yet another foot fungus outbreak? All in all, the rain sucked for the Guardians.

Intake was an admin job for the Guardians. It was a job I mostly hated. On the one hand, I had been traumatized so much my first time through, on the other hand, you couldn't help but see some of the necessity of it. What I really hated was that intake was necessary. I hated the fact that so many girls, myself included, had to go through detox in the first place. I hated the fact that those body cavity searches turned up drugs and other contraband. I hated the fact that so many of us girls were violent and so out of control when we arrived. I hated the fact that sitting in cells may have been the safest way to gain control of them, us, even me. Most of all, I hated myself for having once been like that.

It would be so much easier if I could just say the intake process didn't serve any purpose and was just an evil, vile torture. Unfortunately, I can't deny that it did serve its purpose of both detox and gaining control. Being a shepherd at least made the job bearable, we could treat the younger girls more like humans.

Shepherds were a major improvement for the younger kids. We did try it several times with the older girls. While it worked for some, on the whole, it didn't work out well. Detox was generally far worse in the older girls and the manipulation tactics were far harder to ignore when you had to interact with them several times a day. The tantrum time was a lot longer. We also had several cases where Guardians and staff got hurt when we tried to give older girls shepherds. I think giving them adult shepherds would have been more helpful, but the Brothers and Sisters were not on board with that.

One of the high-impact things we did was to make a marriage happen. The latest batch of Missionaries (they rotated in about every 6 months) included Sister Gretta and Brother Daniel. These two young missionaries were crushing on each other something awful, with this weird mix of trying to hide it and being too scared to do anything about it.

Mr. S was so very amused by this and did things to encourage the relationship. When that didn't work, he had Laura deliver flowers to Sister Gretta with a card that said it was from Brother Daniel asking her on a date. At the same time, he had Nancy deliver a pie to Brother Daniel and the card said it was from Sister Gretta and asked him on the same date. They both arrived at the spot to find the blanket and picnic basket Mr. S and I had made for it. Mr. S was very excited to see his plan work, and partway through the date, he had Tonya and I deliver a bottle of wine to them, with a note from Mr. S telling them to kiss each other already. It worked, and they ended up getting married later in the year.

About this time came another big change that Mr. S made was with the level system. Up until now, it had really been a fiefdom. Who leveled up and who leveled down was really just at the whim of the bunk parents. But now the promotions from level to level had specific criteria. The Level two promotion now had a test, and it was the Guardian's responsibility to administer that test and to do remediation if a new girl didn't pass within a week. While this rankled a few bunk parents, by and large, they didn't care, because it was easier to have girls on Level 2 than it was on Level 1. The changes to the higher levels promotion system were a lot more controversial, especially having Guardians observing the peer councils and serving as the appeals board for it.

We also started having weekly level meetings. On Mondays, between first and second breakfast, Erica would lead a meeting of all the Level 9 and 10 girls from all the pods, as well as all operational Guardians. We would work to teach them things and cover the things they would need to teach to the girls the next levels down. The idea was that Guardians would work with the Level 9s on becoming Level 10s. Level 10s would work with the Level 8s to get them to Level 9. Level 9s would work with Level 7s. And so on down the line.

The Level 7 and 8 meetings were always run by the operations team sergeants on Tuesdays, with the Ops teams and a few of the Level 9 and 10 girls. We would go over with them what the Level 9/10 girls would be working with them on, what we wanted them working on with the Level 5/6 kids, and what we wanted everyone to work on with the lower-level girls. In these meetings, we always drilled the mantra "Be the leader others want to follow, not the tyrant they fear to cross". That was Mr. S's mantra and of all the mantras on the Island, it was the one that made the most sense to me.

On Wednesday, we did the lower-level meetings as part of breakfast with each pod. Those meetings were run by rank-and-file Guardians. I remember being so terrified the first time I ran one of these meetings. Standing in front of an entire pod for the first time was just terrifying!

Mr. S decided that the not taking back punishments tradition needed to end. As part of that, we Guardians became the school's JAG office. The Guardians generally supported the upper-level girls in their authority, as well as the bunk parents and their authority. But our mandate was to help the girls become more human and to do that you have to be able to appeal bad decisions. This was a big change, as we now had a real system in place for kids to challenge a host of punishments and decisions (like being dropped levels). We wouldn't usually get involved if a kid was being stood on the wall or spanked (though there were exceptions to this...), but we would get involved with appeals of excessive punishments or in cases where upper-level kids went power crazy.

If we got a complaint from a girl, one Guardian would represent the accuser, and another the accused, just like JAG does in the Navy. Usually, we would end up telling both sides they were being ridiculous, but we would say it a lot better than that, and we always had to take great care to preserve the chain of command. That usually meant that we would side with the upper-level girl or staff member, while at the same time reining them in and letting them be seen as reducing their own punishment to be fairer. Sometimes girls would try to game this system. If we saw that we came down on them hard for it, so most girls learned not to try that more than once. Trying to game the Guardians that way earned girls an office punishment.

If we couldn't come to a resolution that way, the next step was to involve the team sergeant and the bunk parent. Almost everything got resolved there, even when girls were appealing things the bunk parents did. If that didn't work it would go to the head bunk parent for the pod and Ericka, then Brother Sam, and finally to Mr. S. I can only think of three occasions where it went past the head bunk parent and only one time where it got to Mr. S. Brother Sam and Mr. S always sided with Ericka.

The girls that were upper level when we started had the most problem with it, especially since we could have the most power-hungry girls reduced in level, but even they quickly got used to it. Some girls resented this, but the girls that came up under this system were a lot happier with it than they were with what came before.

Most of the bunk parents hated this system at first, as it was no longer just their own fiefdom, they could be held somewhat accountable. But everyone got used to it within a few months and it just became normal. You still had the times when other means were necessary and we had to do our special kind of magic, but not nearly as often as if we didn't have the appeals system.

But it wasn't always smooth sailing. Sometimes girls did what they had to do to survive, and it was often us Guardians that took the hit for it. I once had a girl from Bunk 12, I think her name was Ginny, she walked up to me, said she was really sorry for this, and then hauled off and punched me in the face! She did it so she would be taken in for an office punishment instead of facing a clique of girls in her bunk, but boy did that hurt!

When I brought her in, Mr. S talked with her and got the story out of her. He asked her if 3 days would do it and when she said yes, he sentenced her to 3 nights in solitary and during the days moving a big stack of bricks solo. She even got to keep her normal meals! He made me supervise that chore and he wouldn't let me hold a grudge over it, saying she did the only thing she could to survive. He only dropped her one level and then put her in a new pod and bunk. I still think she should have told me about what was going on instead of sucker-punching me as she did, we would have protected her. But Mr. S said it had gone too far for that and this really was her only option. Learning to let go of things like that was really difficult, but it was now expected of us, so we learned to do it.

The Church's view on gay was extreme. Any kind of gay sexual activity was about the worst sin on the Island. Girls doing it would be given some of the most severe punishments dished out on the Island. Any girl that knew about it and didn't report it didn't get off much better.

Girl-on-girl sexual assault (or even girls just playing sexually with each other) was a huge sin and something we had to watch closely for. It's part of why showers were so closely monitored. Girls found doing that would be given only one chance to change their ways. They would usually be severely spanked by the bunk parents, then sent in for an office punishment, dropped at least a level, and sent to a new bunk, usually of older girls. If it happened again, then they would be sent to Bunk 22, and no one wanted that. It kept it from being a huge issue in most of the school, though I wouldn't ever want to take a shower in the Bunk 22 group shower, that's for sure!

But then I also know of it being used as a punishment, like with Nikki. The humiliation of being forced to commit a sexual act in front of a group, especially when you are taught that doing so is a mortal sin against God, was about the most dehumanizing thing I ever witnessed on the Island.

The tween bunks were a little different. They got punished for it, but it was usually more exploration and not gay or abuse so to speak. Typically, in a tween bunk, a very sore butt was enough of a deterrent for it to just not happen again, it didn't even rise to the level of an office punishment, as it did with older girls.

About this time, Bunk 22 assignments started to change. We were now allowed to take Bunk 22 girls that earned it for walks outside of the fence line. They had to be cuffed, shackled, and on a leash, but for 15 minutes or half an hour, an ops team could take two at a time outside of the fence line for a walk. They were so very different away from the group. I often felt really bad for these girls. We would sometimes sneak them little snacks when we did this, or occasionally, a half-done rubbing stone (pickings in the Bunk 22 compound were slim to say the least). This really changed how we were treated by most of the Bunk 22 girls, as we were often the only safe people they could talk to, though Bunk 22 assignments still sucked.

Molly was a recent arrival. She was generally this sweet fifteen-year-old girl in Bunk 3, I think she was Level 4 or 5, I know she advanced quickly. She was allowed to talk with the maintenance staff at any rate. Anyways, she always did what she was told, worked hard, and was generally the kind of girl you just liked working with. But Molly had another side to her, it's what got her sent to the Island. Molly had some kind of a psychiatric condition. Molly would randomly, and without warning, flip out and become seriously violent. Not only that, but when this would happen, she would suddenly have this superman-like strength that made it even more dangerous.

The first time I saw her flip out was during a lunch period. Purple team was on Office duty. We were having lunch and planning out a project for Bunk 16 when it happened. Molly had been helping one of the maintenance staff, Brother Joe, fix a bench, then we heard him calling her name and asking if she was alright. The alarmed tone of his voice made us all look.

Molly's face looked strange, and she was drooling. Molly made this deep throaty sound, and the maintenance guy called her name, panic in his voice. He reached out and shook her shoulder. Brother Joe was about 180lbs, Molly was maybe 110lbs soaking wet, but

Molly was suddenly in a rage! She picked him up and threw him on his head, this primal scream coming from her.

Tonya was the first to react, with Julie, Meghan, and I hot on her heels. Tonya tried to take her down, but Molly knocked Tonya to the ground as easily as if she were a toddler. Julie and I tried tackling her but we both got tossed. I landed on a table, the wind knocked right out of me.

Someone hit the alarm. The bunks who were in for lunch were now being herded out by bunk parents. The two Ops teams, Green Team, and Blue Team, came running in as I was getting up off the table. Ericka, Kate, Kat, Christi, Shawn, Sarah, and Tonya were the biggest Guardians, and together they couldn't restrain Molly. More than two full Ops teams couldn't hold her down.

Mr. S. and Brother Sam came in. Mr. S. waived us all off and started talking to her about soccer (she played it off the Island). He sounded so calm, like he was just talking to a friend. At first, she grunted at him, but he just kept talking to her about Manchester United as he kept his distance, then her grunts slowly became arguing with him over soccer players. Eventually, Mr. S sat on the floor, and then as she argued with him, she sat down with him and the flip-out was just over. She was then asleep, like, mid-sentence, she was just asleep.

Mr. S said the flip-out wasn't her fault, and that we can't hold it against her. Mr. S called her sleeping a "post Ictal state" and that we had to wait that out, making sure she was undisturbed. He had Tonya and I wait with her until she woke up and then had us take her to the infirmary. She didn't even get in any trouble for hurting the staff and Guardians, interrupting lunch, or even the smashed tables, that we had to fix.

The next day, Molly asked about what happened, as if she wasn't there for it. When I told her about it, she cried a lot about having hurt everyone like that. As a Guardian, you quickly learn the difference between real and fake tears. Hers were as real as they get, she was really upset about what she did. This confused the hell out of me. After that, our 'Molly orders' were to form a perimeter around her until it passed, then take her to the infirmary. While most of the maintenance staff and even bunk parents tried to avoid Molly, Brother Joe was quick to work with her and kept requesting her.

We did try talking to her about soccer when she had a flip out, but that only ever worked for Mr. S, the rest of us never managed to develop that particular Jedi mind trick.

Mr. S had a real knack for doing things that really got at the center of you, even if they were weird, they worked. Like the whole purposely getting in trouble with him thing that I did when I was fourteen (and fifteen and sixteen. . .). It's weird that he let that happen, but I think it was the best way he could have dealt with it. Whenever I did that, he would do morning lines for a few days and call me to attention just because and otherwise take control and it just felt so safe. But

Mr. S seemed to know everyone. He did things like that to every girl he worked with. He had more of those Jedi mind tricks than anyone I have ever known.

It wasn't long after the first Molly incident that Brother Sam woke us up in the middle of the night. Two girls from Bunk 9 were missing. We were tasked with finding them and bringing them back. We broke up into teams of 2 and went searching for them. Julie and I found them out near the farm.

They were just looking at the stars and talking with each other, one of them was even telling the other the story about the constellation Gemini, the twins Castor and Pollux. How the twin's mother had two more kids with Tyndareus. Mr. S had told me a different version of the same story. Julie wanted to take them in immediately, but I wouldn't let her. In that moment, I felt it was important to let them finish the story, after all, what difference would another 5 minutes make to us? But I knew those extra minutes were really important for them to have, so I insisted on giving it to them.

We listened as the first girl told the second girl how Castor and Polydeuces grew up together and were very close. How the brothers clashed with a set of twins, fighting over two women. How one of those twins, Lynceus, killed Castor by stabbing him with a sword. She talked about how a devastated Polydeuces asked Zeus to share his immortality with his murdered brother and how the god Zeus placed them both in the sky, where they remain inseparable to this day as the constellation Gemini. We listened as the two talked about how they would do the same for each other. Then they were quiet.

After a few quiet minutes, we went over and got them and took them to the office. They were ready, I think if we didn't find them, they would have gone back to bunk on their own. This wasn't the only time we had to do that. I always felt bad about that. It's not like it was possible to run away, we were on an island. They still always got punished for it.

The third week of May, two weeks after Alex moved the mountain, we were all pulled into a meeting with Mr. S, Brother Sam, and Mrs. Thompson (the office secretary). A lot of regulations were about to change, and we were given the tedious task of mapping it out. We were given a pile of paperwork and the last map (over 10 years old!) as a guide to do it. And we started sorting through it.

The number of places one thing references another was mind-boggling. This contract referred to this law which referred to this policy, which referred to this other definition. The school took kids from over 40 jurisdictions, each with its own rules and regulations, standards, and definitions.

Ericka and Kate took the lead on this project, with the rest of us doing whatever we could to help them. It made our brains hurt. Our walls were covered in big sheets of paper with writing everywhere. Ericka used string to map from place to place.

We ended up with 20 handwritten pages of a report. The crux of it was that some places were easing up on searches, while other places were requiring more of it. As I understood it, body cavity searches used to be required for everyone. Now they were prohibited for those 11 and younger unless the school had a reasonable suspicion to conduct one or if they came from one of 4 jurisdictions that still required them. Strip searches were required by most of them whenever moving from one facility to another.

When you drilled down into the definitions, that meant any time a girl goes from one building to another or goes to anywhere outside, they should be strip-searched. May as well just keep us all naked at that point. Other contracts required searches to be done with "regular frequency" and still others required they be done randomly.

Many of the policies required girls' possessions and living spaces be searched (or tossed) regularly, and limited what they should have (in bunk, you basically had nothing that was yours). Operations teams carried a backpack that included a knife, needle and thread, matches, a basic tool kit, and other items that these contracts prohibited us from having.

We mapped the rest of the policies to the Guardians. It occurred to us that we had not been strip-searched, undergone a BCS, or even had a staff member inspect our bunk since our first or second week as Guardians. We were treated more like staff, we definitely were not under direct observation at all times. Under these contracts, we should not exist.

We mapped the policies to the other bunks. We came to the conclusion that to actually follow everything outlined in all of these contracts, you would have to put us each alone and naked in a rubber room and never let us out.

At some point, Ericka found a way to simplify it. She grouped the contracts by what they required, then she re-sorted who was in what bunk. By doing that, it was possible to meet most of the contract requirements by having each bunk go by different policies. This worked for every group except for the Guardians.

The first week of June we formally presented our findings to Mr. S. He assured us that the contracts would not end the Guardians, but he would likely need to do something so that we were at least somewhat in compliance. But he took the rest under advisement.

He did start moving all tweens (11 – thirteen-year-olds) into specific bunks. Bunk 16, now Father Fred's bunk, became the first dedicated tween bunk. He insisted on giving his girls playtime, and we often assisted with that. New students were placed in bunks partly based on the contract groups we identified.

Fearing that something worse would be imposed on us, we eventually bit the bullet and presented a plan to bring the Guardians mostly into compliance. The backpacks would be stored in the kitchen of Mr. S's house instead of in the bunk area and signed in and out at breakfast and dinner. We also would log our plans the day before.

We figured that if we had to be strip-searched, it was better to do it as a group and just get it done than to do it individually. Besides, the Devil you know and all that. We proposed resuming the morning line routine for the Guardians (sans the whip). Eventually, that's what happened, though it definitely wasn't every day, more like once or twice a week, sometimes less. Sometimes it would be weeks between searches. I still liked it when Mr. S would do them, even if it wasn't the game version we did in the house. I don't think he liked doing the morning lines, though I really liked it when he did them, I still got the tingles from it.

Chapter 9:
Gulliver on the Island of the Amazons

July of 1992 brought the Island two special guests, Sister Marie, and Tony. Sister Marie was Mr. S's oldest sister. Tony was a fifteen-year-old boy, Mr. S's nephew. At this point, I was mostly sleeping in Bunk 1 anyways, so giving up my room for them was easy. Jess and Jenna had a more difficult time with it, but we made a big deal about them staying with us big girls, and it was OK.

Before they arrived, the Guardians had a big meeting with Mr. S about it. Mr. S expected problems having one teen boy on an island of hundreds of teen girls. We were to be his friends, guides, babysitters, and security. Mr. S was clear that there was to be no hanky-panky between any of us and him, and we were not to permit any girl to even try.

Tony would be hanging out with us, and he would be our primary responsibility (as well as Jess and Jenna) while he was there. He would attend wilderness, math, and church with us and he would do a music class for Jess and Jenna twice a week. Other classes, training, operations, and other administrative things came after that, and it was fine if they didn't get done. We were to keep the girls in line around him and we could use any means necessary to do so (we could liberally give out wall time or ask bunk parents to punish).

The Friday before they arrived, we had an extra parade. Mr. S announced that they would be here and set out the law about him. It wasn't often that any kid here would go against Mr. S, even the Bunk 22 girls, but this was different, this was about a teenage boy! One girl yelled out that she wanted him to have her baby, and was then cheered by, like, everyone.

Mr. S was *not* happy. His voice boomed "Atten *'hut*!" over the PA so loud, sharp, and angry that everyone snapped to attention. He told the school that the Guardians would be with him at all times, and if any girl gets the least out of line around him, we would come down on them *hard*, and if they wanted a day in the hotbox that the Guardians would put them in there so fast their heads would spin!

Now, you have to understand that we had levels of punishment. It started with yelling, and it ended with hotboxing and public whipping. Mongra, Nose-tits-n-toes, and circle beatings were powers Mr. S had taken away from upper-level girls. Guardians were generally allowed to give out up to watching the wall on our own authority, we could do short-term removal of privileges in certain and very specific circumstances, and we could refer girls for an office punishment for specific offenses (fighting and rebelling mostly). Technically, we didn't have the authority to strip them for the beach days, though they didn't seem to know that, or they accepted it as part of the trade, or they just accepted the utility of it.

Bunk parents and teachers could spank or give major punishment tasks. Head bunk parents (you had one for every pod of 5 bunks) could paddle. The rest was only given out by Brother Sam or sometimes Sister Lisa. Mr. S's statement shocked everyone, and I mean EVERYONE, especially us Guardians! But it also made clear how serious this situation was to be taken. After parade, Mr. S and Brother Sam had a talk with us. Mr. S explained that he said what he did in a moment of anger (that was rare for him), but since it was done publicly, now we were stuck with it. They explained we were not to let this authority go to our heads and that we were to use the lowest level of authority possible to get the results we had to get. In most cases, that means not exceeding our previous authority unless absolutely necessary.

They knew some kids would test this and we would have to come down on them swift and hard, but where possible, leave that to the bunk parents and teachers. We were told not to give out any major punishment tasks unless we were prepared to follow through and supervise them (generally not something we could do). He said it might come to spanking, and if we had to, we could (team sergeants only), but if possible don't, and anything more than a spanking should be done through

Brother Sam. We understood: Do what you have to do, but no more.

On the day they arrived, they were welcomed with a parade formation and introduced to everyone. After the parade was dismissed, we had to stay at attention while the other groups filed out. Then we were individually introduced. One by one we stepped forward, said our name, then stepped back into formation. When we were dismissed, we took Tony on a tour of the place.

Tony was autistic and today he would be described as having 'high' or 'substantial' support needs. He was semi-verbal, something none of us had any experience with. We were totally blindsided by this and had no coaching or experience on how to deal with him. From a distance, he looked *hot*, especially with that guitar of his. Spend more than 5 minutes with him, though, and most of us had lost any sexual interest, especially us Guardians, who couldn't wait to get five minutes *away* from him! He smelled bad (even for girls who only got one shower a week), and he couldn't socialize with any of us effectively, which was probably a mix of just how different "socializing" on the Island was and his own social delays.. None of us really wanted to be around him, but we had to, it was our job.

We started the tour with Mr. S's house and Bunk 1. Then we went around showing him the other bunks (they were empty, as everyone was now at chore or a class). We stopped into the English, Science, and Math classes. Then we went to the wilderness class with Mr. Jennings. Mr. Jennings did a lesson on some of the edible plants of the Island. Basically, we walked in the woods and tasted various plants. Many tasted better than what we ate at the chow hall. We now knew why we almost never saw Mr. Jennings at chow. . .

After wilderness class, we showed him the stable (the horses terrified him), the farm fields, the plow field (where you pull the plow when it's not needed for farming), the rock Alex moved (though we didn't tell him about helping her), then we went to show him the chow hall.

As we walked to the chow hall, we hit our first issue. We passed the shower hut, not even thinking about it – I mean, why would we? Then it happened. The line of girls waiting for the shower saw Tony and screamed. Two girls were flaunting themselves at him. Tony froze like he was a deer in the headlights looking at those two girls. A bunk walking to chow started screaming. It was suddenly chaos! Ericka and I hurried Tony along, while the rest of the Guardians called those girls to attention and chewed them all out for acting like that.

I guess I should explain something. The Island is about 80 degrees year-round. We only have girls here. The only males here are the adults, the authority figures, and we were used to them seeing us. You don't really think about it. Nudity was just so common for so many things on the Island, it just wasn't that big a deal when it was expected of a group. If you are going to an academic class from a messy work task, you change outside. Sometimes you just leave the work uniform outside and do class in your underwear or even just nude, especially on really hot and humid days or from really messy chores— especially shit chores.

If you are waiting for your turn in the shower, you are already undressed, your uniforms, sheet, blanket, towel, and washcloth already in the bin to be washed (you pick up a new bundle on the other side of the shower). You sleep in the nude. Strip searches are a normal, everyday thing. Lining up naked for morning lines was normal. Nudity was something that just *was*. It (mostly) wasn't sexual, it was just an everyday part of life that you just got used to. Nudity was only embarrassing if you are singled out for it, such as when a single girl would be given nose-tits-n-toes, or if it included a spanking or being made fun of for it.

But having Tony here was *different*. He was a teenage boy—the *only* teenage boy most of us had seen in years. With him, it *was* sexual. Given the lack of choices, he was the Island's heartthrob. *Every* girl (who didn't actually know him) was dreaming of or at least thinking of him as they rubbed themselves in bed at night. So having him see was just *very different* than having a teacher or bunk parent, even a hot new teacher, walk past. With Tony, sexual feelings came into play in a way that was, well, just different. Tony's mother didn't want him to see any naked girls. He, however, was still going through puberty, and wanted to see as many naked girls as he could.

On his second day, we went to math class. We did a lesson in quadratic equations. Apparently, this was part of what Tony needed to learn. We girls had never seen them before. It wasn't something typically taught on the Island, so it took us a while, but we all started to get it, and by the end of class, we had it better than Tony.

On the way home from math class, we ran into our next issue. A girl in one of the bunks was taken out for nose-tits-n-toes at the front door of her bunk. Tony got quite an eyeful of well-developed nineteen-year-old flesh. As we hurried him down the lane, he tried to get a better look. His mother saw this and blamed us for letting him see "the evils of her naked flesh".

The next morning, we had Wilderness again. We took Tony early, before the shower lines started. We sent out scouts to make sure the way was clear, had a sentry at the shower door, alerted the bunks we were coming, and started to run him up the lane as fast as we could get him to go. Then we had a girl start to shake the mud out of her shirt out the front door of her bunk. We pushed Tony to the wall of a bunk, blocking his view of her, and sent someone to put her back inside. When we turned back to Tony, he was at the wall where we shoved him, looking right through the window of the bunk. Another eyeful we didn't intend for him to get.

He, of course, told his mother about it and she chewed us out for like half an hour over it.

We tried putting a bag over his head to walk through. That just caused him to fall and scrape his knee – and yep, you guessed it. He landed on some girls waiting for the shower. If a girl had gotten that kind of a scraped knee, it would hardly be worth mentioning. Tony? He went on grunting about it for two whole days! To top it off, we got chewed out by his mother for days over that one too.

From a practical standpoint, we all wished his mother would just get over him seeing naked girls. We knew that our headaches would have been over in a week - when we would get new missionaries, especially the young males, they would gawk and stare for a week but by the end of the week they got used to it and they pretty much stopped gawking and staring. Naked girls were just normal. With Tony, it was always a big deal, and that made it so much worse.

It felt like we were always running him away from naked girls while he was trying to run towards them. And then we had the exhibitionists. You never knew where they would come from, but we were most wary of thirteen- and fourteen-year-olds and the 18-21 set, as it always seemed to be one of these two groups. By the end of week 3, we gave up. Two older girls accidentally-on-purpose found a way to walk into him while we were distracted shooing away tweens. Yes, the older girls were basically naked.

We had had it, or more specifically, Ericka had had it. We started to run Tony, but Ericka stopped us. She had had enough. If they wanted to be seen like this badly enough to sneak away from their group and he wanted to see them like this, then fine. Instead of chewing the girls out, Ericka made them finish stripping and then stood them at attention. She gave them a choice, they could be hotboxed, or they could have what they apparently wanted. They chose the latter.

The two girls were ordered to put their hands on their heads, stand with their feet wide apart and not move. She then gave Tony permission to look, touch and feel, but only with his hands. We let that go on for, oh about 7 seconds until Tony obviously lost his load. It was the first time I noticed what a funny face boys make when they do that. With his tent now folded, he lost all interest in the girls. The girls seemed very unsatisfied with it. Ericka then ordered Christi and Shawn to spank the two girls until they were truly sorry before returning them to their bunk—where I am sure they got the belt for running off. The rest of us took Tony to wherever we were off to.

At the end of week 3, we had Brother Sam publicly hotbox a girl for crap with Tony. It was only for a few hours, but the rest of the girls got the point. Between that and Ericka working with Brother Sam to change a bunch of bunks' shower and class schedules, we were more or less able to control it the rest of the visit.

During his visit, we took Tony to see and try each of the typical chore tasks (except for the ones related to shit, like latrines or compost). It's very different to pull a plow for an hour with the blade at 2 and put a smiley face in the dirt, then it is to plow for 8 hours with the blade at 6, 8, or (God forbid) 10.

We laughed and had fun with how much Tony struggled with something that was so easy for us girls. We never would have laughed or joked or talked had it been chore (talking while yoked would get you a beating!). Likewise, chopping wood for an hour can be fun, not so much when it's a 9-hour shift with quotas. I think Tony left the Island with a very skewed view of our life here.

I think the last naked girls he got to see was an eyeful of Guardians. Unless we were having a line inspection, Guardians were usually called to attention in the mornings by Ericka, who would tell us what was up for the day, then give us some words of encouragement for the day, and then give the order to make bed and dress.

Mr. S did a single line inspection of us while Tony was on the Island. He kept apologizing for how much he didn't do with us. We understood, but I really missed my time with him, especially family meals and storytime. So, I was very happy to see him when he woke us and called us to fall in – I was so excited knowing that he had not forgotten us, not forgotten me!

I was beaming when he smiled at me as we lined up and stood at attention.

Then Sister Marie called him. She called him by his first name, Theodore, in her super annoying voice, drawing out his name ridiculously "Theeeeeodooooore," she called. He rolled his eyes, tilted his head back, shaking his head back and forth, raising his arms to the sky and said, "Arghhh!" obviously annoyed. We all smirked and giggled at that. I know I covered my mouth to stifle a full-on laugh.

Mr. S was always the picture of calm and cool, it was really funny to see him so annoyed at his sister like that. He called us back to attention in that sharp, but this time slightly playful don't-even-think-of-disobeying-me voice of his. I remember him saying to us "Do you see what I have to deal with?!" We all stifled more giggles at that. Then in the same voice, sans the playfulness, he ordered us to wait while he went back to talk with Sister Marie for a minute.

It was hard to stifle the smile, and we all giggled more than a little bit as he walked out, and we heard that call of "Theeeeeodooooore" again. Mr. S yelled back for us to be still and silent, and we knew we were now pushing our luck a little too far. A fourth call to attention would even earn us Guardians a sore bottom!

After a few minutes, Tony came in. We had been ordered to wait at attention and we had already pushed our luck with the giggles, so there was really nothing we could do but wait silently at attention, especially as

Ericka had called for us to hold fast. It didn't matter that Tony was being a tot being a total voyeur and even touching us, while we had to stay at attention.

Tony got to see all of us that morning and it was absolutely humiliating, especially as he had a hand in his pocket the whole time and we all knew he was getting off on us. His unintelligible grunts didn't make it any better. Tony only left when he heard Mr. S starting back to do the line inspection. He ducked out the bunk door. What a little fucking chicken shit he was, he couldn't even be man enough to face Mr. S after pulling that crap.

Mr. S came back and rushed the inspection, obviously annoyed at his sister. But he told us how well we were doing and how proud of us he was. After he dismissed us to dress and make bed, he called me over for a much-needed hug. You have no idea how much I missed his hugs those weeks. I didn't even care about Tony's crap anymore when I got that hug.

Ericka spoke to Mr. S about Tony, he was really mad about it, and we didn't have another line inspection until after Tony left, when we got them just about every day for a while. It was nice to hear his words of encouragement all those mornings. For a few weeks after Tony left, I slept in my room almost every night, just to be close to him and get those morning hugs. I went with him to the Bunk for the morning inspections, even though I didn't have to do that when I slept in my room.

Unlike the other bunks, we would have meat regularly (mostly chicken, rabbit, and fish). Beef of any kind was a really big deal, but even we never saw steak. To thank us for all that time with Tony, we got a huge steak dinner, complete with the biggest T-bone steaks I had ever seen, mashed potatoes and gravy, corn on the cob, Mr. S's stuffing, macaroni salad, deviled eggs, chocolate ice cream, and all the fixings. I think we ate a weeks' worth of calories in that one night!

Then we got to watch a movie in Mr. S's bedroom (the only TV on the Island) with popcorn! We all eventually fell asleep on his bed or the floor of his room. The 6 weeks with Tony were difficult, but the after-party was epic! We found Mr. S sleeping on the couch the next morning. We didn't wake him, and he slept in till almost eleven a.m., by which time we had everything cleaned up.

Mr. S's Angel Eggs ("Deviled Eggs")

Ingredients:

- 6 large hard-boiled eggs
- ¼ cup mayonnaise
- 1 teaspoon yellow mustard
- 2 tablespoons sweet relish
- Dash of Tabasco sauce
- Salt and pepper to taste
- Paprika, or chives for garnish

Directions:

1. Hard boil a dozen large eggs. Let cool and peal.

2. Slice the hard-boiled eggs in half longways and place the yolks in a medium-size bowl. Feel free to add the whites to your serving dish.

3. Mash the yolks using a fork until it crumbles nicely. Add in mayonnaise, mustard, relish, hot sauce, salt, and pepper and mix well until combined and as smooth as possible. As an adult, I use my Food processor to blend this, then fold in the relish by hand.

4. Use a spoon to divide the yolk filling between the egg white halves.

5. Chill in the frige for an hour.

6. Garnish with paprika, or chives and serve.

Chapter 10:
School Begins Anew

September of 1992 brought a *lot* of changes. Some unexpected legal thing meant that Kate, who was court-ordered here till age 21, got to go home. We had a goodbye party on her last night, complete with cake and ice cream and Polaroid pictures. Sister Lisa didn't even cuff her for the flight out.

We had to choose another Guardian. This was no small task. The only two criteria Mr. S gave us were age (had to keep the spread we started with), and lifer status. It was left to us to figure out what made a good Guardian.

We made a list of every girl we thought would be a good candidate. Mr. S looked at the list and said that we needed to come up with criteria, not names. He asked us to think about what made each girl Guardian material?

We spent a long time talking about what made us good Guardians (lucky was my answer). Ultimately, we hit on the following criteria:

First, girls needed to be repentant of what brought them here. Not fake, but real.

This led us to an unexpected conclusion. All of us were here less than 9 months before we became upper levels or Guardians. Almost all of our candidates had been here 9 months or less before becoming an upper-level girl. Those here more than that were too angry, too damaged, or too jaded to be Guardians. They were no longer repentant of what brought them to the Island. That became our second criterion.

Our third criterion was being a team player, being able to both follow orders and being able to lead other girls. If you couldn't be a team player, this was the wrong job.

Our fourth criterion was intelligence. This job took a *lot* of thinking! You had a lot of problems to solve, you had a lot of planning you had to do, it just takes a lot of brain power to be a Guardian!

Our fifth criterion was that candidates needed to be able to do all of the chore tasks, PT exercises, and all of the marching drills. A significant part of our job involved chores, PT and drill. If you were not proficient at all of those things, you couldn't do the job.

Our sixth criterion was that candidates had to be caring people and treat people humanely. This was a tough criterion. The Island was a brutal place, finding girls who were still caring, and treated people humanely was just not so easy!

Last, we figured that we should let each bunk group nominate candidates for selection based on those criteria. After all, Guardians have a lot of power, in some ways not as much as staff, but in other ways, we had more power than staff did. We felt that the girls should have a say in who was given this power.

All in all, we got 22 nominations. We whittled that down to 5 (the names that matched our original list), any one of which would have made a good Guardian. For the final selection, we did the only fair thing we could think of – we had Brother Sam pick a name out of a bowl. Marci was our new Guardian. It was extra special as she would get to live with her sister again.

Another big change was that the bunks and the level system were all reconfigured. For a few weeks, we had to have a hot response Guardian team in each pod to help with this major transition. As difficult as that was, it meant that you no longer had limits on the number of girls who could reach the higher levels. That helped with the previously really nasty politicks that the upper-level girls had to play to stay at the upper levels.

Kids who reached a certain level were now grouped together in a bunk within the pod. Those kids in the upper levels only had chores 3 times a week instead of the 6 the lower levels had, and only for 3 hours a day, not 8 or 10. They were also assigned more useful chores. If they pulled the plow, it was for farming, not the plow field. Upper-level girls were no longer assigned stumps, unless they were helping a lower-level bunk.

We, along with the upper levels, had a lot more classes, making it much more like a real school. To go with these new classes, we got a bunch of new teachers, all ex-military. I don't know what rank they had in the military, but from some of the things they said, they all worked under Mr. S's command. We called them all sergeants, though we occasionally heard them refer to each other as other ranks (Sergeant Davis was sometimes called Major, and Sergeant Richards was sometimes called LTC, whatever that means).

I remember the first time I met Sergeant Mitchel was on a Bunk 22 assignment. A twenty-year-old Bunk 22 girl randomly started to beat up an eleven-year-old from Bunk 6 as my ops team walked 8 girls from Bunk 22 to the shitters (the Bunk 22 shitters were down). I ran to intervene, but that bitch was twice my size. Sergeant Mitchel got to them before I did. He challenged that girl to try fighting someone who would fight back. Boy did she back down *fast*, and he never even laid a finger on her. I can tell you that there was no way in hell I would have challenged him! She didn't even resist when I took her in for an office punishment.

The sergeants only worked with the higher levels (7-10) and they expected a *lot* from us, like way more than anyone other than Mr. S. Levels 7 and 8 used real books (something only Guardians had had before), and Levels 9 and 10 even got to take books from class to bunk to study (again, something only Guardians had had before). I think if we had enough copies of the various Naval Training Manuals, Technical Manuals, and Field Manuals, they would have even let the Level

7 and 8 girls take them to bunk. But then again, no one was allowed to take the *Human Behavior* Naval manual out of class, as we only had one copy of that one - though I did eventually get Mr. S to bring it home for a few days so I could get a turn to read it. I still remember the cartoon pictures in that book!

While the official rule was that Guardians could only be punished within our own chain of command, we didn't resist when the sergeants gave us pushups. If they gave them to us, we earned them, and we knew it.

A major construction project also started. They were building a water pipe to the mainland and a new academic building. They were even going to have real phone lines (as opposed to the one sat phone we had at the school for emergencies). It was said that kids may even get phone calls home at some point, though that didn't happen while I was there.

As Guardians, we had even more to do. We had one more class each day than everyone else, and in place of chores, we had duty (training, admin, or operations). As part of ops, we were now also tasked with teaching a class to the tweens on treating people like humans. This was a lot harder than you might think. We worked with both Father Fred and Sergeant Davis on this.

And while we didn't make any more miracles as big as Alex moving the mountain, if we felt a punishment task was too unfair, we would make our special kind of magic happen under cover of night.

We once dealt with a twelve-year-old having to do 25 stumps by herself as a punishment for rolling her eyes. She didn't appeal her punishment to us, but we heard about it. We took 3 bunks of girls, yoked them up, and used that massive amount of force to pull 75 stumps (3 rows) out of the ground in under 3 hours. You should have seen the look on that asshole Brother Thomas's face when he saw that little girl pulling the last of those stumps out of the ground after only 2 days. We, of course, denied all knowledge.

Not everything went so smoothly. We had the great shit storm. Purple team was supervising Bunks 15 and 17 emptying the latrines. We knew that we had a big storm coming in. Protocol was that you don't risk spilling the shit carts in a storm, and for good reason. But I was sure we would have enough time to get the carts done before it hit if we worked the girls extra hard. Big mistake. We got the carts out and about halfway to the shit pads, right on the little hill near chow hall, when it happened.

We should have followed protocol and left that chore until after the storm, or at the very least, we should have chalked the wheels or moved the carts another 50 feet, so they were over on the other side of the little hill and not left directly uphill of Chow Hall. But I thought I knew better. We panicked when we saw the lightning hit the tree. I gave the order to run, and we just left the carts, running the girls back to bunks.

All 4 of the carts we were moving got hit by a tree that fell. The carts rolled downhill, right through the front doors of Chow Hall. What a mess that was! The carts knocked the doors off the hinges and spilled over 1,200 gallons of shit everywhere, and I mean everywhere! Shit literally covered everything in chow hall! Every bunk had to work overtime for the next 4 days cleaning that up, and the worst part was that we used so much water cleaning it up that we almost completely depleted the tank.

Thankfully, the water pipe was filling the tank and while we had to ration, we had water to drink. But after 4 days of cleaning up all that, we only got 2-minute showers. We depleted so much water that we even had to get the boat to fill the tank, which we had not had to have done since the water pipe went in. Boy, did I get my butt whipped good for that one! Believe me, we never made that mistake again! But that too, became part of our lore, forever known among the girls as "the great shit storm". In front of Mr. S or most of the staff, it was known as "the great poop storm".

The sergeants did military training stuff together two days a week, and they often included the older Guardians (sixteen and up only). Rumor had it that they were Delta Force or Marine Recon or Navy Seals or some such, but they would never actually answer those kinds of questions, only give these vague statements about military traditions. The older Guardians got to learn to swim, scuba dive, shoot guns, and do other insanely crazy things with the sergeants. I was so very jealous of them, especially when Mr. S would join them, and we would miss family time.

The sergeants did a lot of the Guardians' training. We used these books called Field Manuals for a lot of it. In one of those, we learned about rigging and hoisting with Sergeant D and we found out just how crazy we were when we moved that rock with Alex. I guess we were lucky that we didn't kill anyone. Turns out that Mr. S didn't actually know what we were doing with that project until after it was already done. I guess he wouldn't have let us do it like we did if he had known. Oops!

The sergeants had two modes, covers (hats) on, or covers off. When the covers were on, it was formal military. When the covers were off, they were informal. If it wasn't class or drill and they didn't have covers on, you didn't get in trouble for missing sirs or salutes or things like that. With the covers off, some of them, like Sergeant Davis, were even huggers, and we *all* hugged him at the end of every class.

You could talk to them, and they all actually cared about us in a way the other teachers and the bunk parents just didn't. They made it more like family than anything outside of Mr. S's house had been.

Sergeant Mitchel's classes were *very* different. He would pose ethical questions to us, and we had to attack those questions from all sides. You were never wrong in his classes, so long as you were open to new ideas.

Very often my brain hurt leaving his classes. I guess that's normal when you expand your mind.

But the thing that made his classes so different was that we met in a grassy field, and he didn't just allow us to, but he encouraged us to be puddles of cuddling girls in the grass as we debated the topic at hand. So very different than never touching each other. Somehow in his class, we were the most innocent kids.

In one class, someone said that to him, and he made us discuss what being innocent meant. We didn't reach any firm conclusions, but we agreed it was a state of mind, and one we all liked being in, we liked who we were when we were innocent. We also couldn't understand how we could be so innocent here, given the things we all had done in our lives. What was it that made us so innocent in this one class? I don't think I will ever know. But we were, and that was a special thing. He was another one we hugged at the end of every class.

Speaking of innocents, I don't know where this came from, but somehow it was decided that Jenna needed some help growing up and coming into her own. She needed an adventure. The Guardians were tasked with giving her one. We planned a quest for her, a trek for her across the Island, through all sorts of dangers to find the Chalice of Honor.

We got the sergeants to teach her the little things she would need to complete the tasks ahead of her and we worked overtime for a whole month setting up the challenges she would have to face. Sergeant Mitchel provided us with the chalice, a gold cup with fancy metals glued to it.

It was a big deal when Mr. S sent her on the quest. This was done at Parade, in front of the whole school. He said she was the only one that could retrieve it. She was shocked, but when you are picked out for something like this, you rise to the occasion, and Jenna was no exception.

It took Jenna 3 days to complete the quest. We Guardians were up 24 hours a day with that, always far enough away that she didn't know we were there, and close enough that we could step in if she got hurt. The water bottle drops were the hardest. We made her believe she had a magic water bottle that refilled itself! She completed the quest without any help, and the growth she showed was remarkable.

She was no longer Marci's helpless little sister, she was now Jenna, the girl who braved the Island to bring back the Chalice of Honor, and she could do anything! We had a big ceremony for Jenna's return with the entire school. We had a gathering in the chow hall where she got to proclaim Chocolate ice cream for everyone (monthly ice cream was only ever vanilla). The Chalice of Honor, along with Jenna's photo and a writeup of her quest got a place in the new glass cabinet in the chow hall, right next to the picture/writeup of Alex and her rock and that of Adrian and her stumps.

These were now part of our history and tradition, and we told those stories to every new girl. They were about the only "war stories" girls were allowed to tell. While "war stories" were officially prohibited, Mr. S believed that "Island Accomplishments" were important, so they were allowed to be shared if they helped to inspire girls to succeed. And I will say, telling those 30 or so stories made a huge difference. It let girls believe that they, too, could accomplish the impossible and helped restore a glimmer of hope in girls' hearts. That really makes a difference.

Later, after I was off the Island, I found out that the metals glued to that cup were the metals and honors Mr. S and the sergeants had earned in the military. I wish I knew which ones they were, and I think they all deserved another medal for doing that for Jenna.

The Guardians were way overstretched, especially Ericka. After Jenna's quest, Mr. S decided that the Guardians' numbers would grow to 21. 5 teams and one overall captain.

In early December, we had to choose 5 more Guardians, this time one sixteen-year-old and four fourteen-year-olds. We followed the same processes as before, except now we would consider kids in the higher levels that had been here longer than 9 months.

Ericka (eighteen) was our beloved leader and would be the overall captain. The rest of the teams were:

Purple team: Tonya (seventeen), Vanessa (me, fifteen), Julie (fifteen) and Maxine (fourteen).

Green team: Christi (sixteen), Jennifer (sixteen), Sarah (fifteen) and Sasha (fourteen).

Red team: Michelle (seventeen) Nancy (sixteen), Brittany (fifteen), Paula (fourteen).

Blue team: Kat (sixteen), Meghan (fifteen), Tori (fourteen), Susan (fourteen).

Orange Team: Shawn (seventeen), Marci (sixteen), Laura (fifteen), Betty (fourteen).

As part of ops, we had to do Bunk 22 rotations. Every Tuesday and Thursday, the Ops team spent 3 hours in Bunk 22. Usually, we would cover for the bunk 22 staff meeting on Tuesdays, but on Thursdays, we started to be able to give girls that earned it certain privileges. The big one was the 15-minute walks outside the fence.

This girl from Bunk 4, Emma, got sent to 22. She should have appealed the sentence to the Guardians, but she didn't. We didn't find out about it until she was already in Bunk 22, and then it was too late. But Emma really didn't belong in Bunk 22. I went to Ericka about it and tried to get her to intervene. As much as she wanted to, the rules of appeal left us no options for getting her out. But she didn't belong there, and I just couldn't let it go.

Tonya and I hatched a plan. Purple team was getting her out. If we could get her to go with the program and level up while she was in Bunk 22, we could use that to show that she didn't belong there and maybe we could get her out that way. We spent a couple of weeks working with Emma to get her back up to Level 4. That meant a lot of extra time in Bunk 22 and as much as we hated time in Bunk 22, we were determined to get her out.

For a girl to go from Level 1 to Level 4 in a few weeks is a major accomplishment anywhere on the Island. For a girl to do it in Bunk 22, well it just doesn't happen. But with our help, Emma managed that impossible task and that gave us the opportunity to get her out. So, we took our case to Brother Sam. It took an awful lot of convincing, but ultimately, he agreed, with conditions.

If Emma got sent back to Bunk 22, our ops team would have had to take a whipping for it. We really (and quite literally) put our asses on the line for her. Emma was on probation for 6 months. Even when our team wasn't on ops, we had to check in with her every day and twice a week had to do a "fence check-in" where we stood her at the Bunk 22 fence and talked about what things could get her sent back and how not to do that. But Emma never went back to Bunk 22, she worked hard and became an upper-level girl.

This was another 'Island Accomplishment', and more importantly, it was a path we could use to get other girls out of Bunk 22. This island accomplishment was when Mr. S put a binder in each bunk with typed versions of these stories for girls to read. Lore is really important in a place like the Island, it really makes a difference.

Christmas brought another major change. Christmas services were a very serious and somber matter, but also the only real celebration on the Island. For this event, Guardians were placed strategically around the chow hall, especially around the lower-level kids to help keep them in line. My team got stuck with Bunk 22. God, I hated Bunk 22 assignments!

In the middle of Father Fred's sermon, he stepped off stage to get something, and, in that moment, we were visited by Santa (Sergeant Davis in a red Santa suit with a ridiculous fake white beard). "Santa" and his "helpers" (Mr. S and the sergeants in equally ridiculous elf suits) hammed it up as they passed out small boxes of chocolate to every girl in the hall. We all cheered for Santa and his elves. Then, just like that, they disappeared. Father Fred came out and played the whole thing up, though he did make everyone eat their chocolates before leaving the chow hall.

This was the first time I ever saw the whole school, and I mean the whole school laughing. For the first time, we all played a game together, and the rewards of the game (and the chocolates) outweighed the alternatives. Even the Bunk 22 girls enjoyed Santa's visit. It was just a lot of fun.

The next major change came with my sixteenth birthday. I was now old enough to join the sergeants and the other older Guardians in the Saturday and Sunday training. In my first training session, we got to blow things up!

Under the *very* watchful eyes of the sergeants and Mr. S, we learned to set charges of C-4, run detonation cables, put in detonation caps, and blow the charges.

In the afternoon of the second day, we blew up two of the old and crumbling buildings on the other side of the Island. We all knew the reason we did that was that the buildings had partially collapsed and had become too dangerous to leave, but we pretended that we were on a super-secret spy mission to blow up Dr. Evil's secret base anyways.

We started on the two Zodiacs, rounding the Island. We landed the boats and moved in on the buildings, the older girls practicing moving with the paintball rifles and cover formations that I had not yet learned. One of the sergeants shot at us with a paintball gun as we made our way to the first building with Sergeant Davis. The other girls got to shoot back, while I carried the bag with the explosives! We did just as we had practiced, setting the C4, detonators, and wires.

Then, after it was set and we were all outside and under the cover of a big rock, we blew the first building and watched, cheering as it collapsed in on itself.

Afterward, the sergeants went over how to do better next time. I guess if you are a top-secret super-spy, you don't jump up and down cheering after you blow up a building... Teenage girls, right? But for us, this was *very* serious stuff! Even if Sergeant Davis had trouble keeping a straight face when he told us that and even if Mr. S and the other sergeants were doubled over in silent laughter behind him; to us, this was serious stuff!

Then we were tasked with trying to stop them from blowing the next building. If we hit them once with a paintball, they were out. They had to hit us 3 times before we were out. A blast area was set that we had to stay out of.

It was a slaughter! They had most of us covered in paint in like 6 seconds flat and I don't think they were even trying! Tonya had gotten a good hide, and she kept trading fire with them. It was against the rules, but we kept sneaking her our ammo so she could keep shooting at them. She even managed to take out Mr. S and Sergeant Mackey!

Then, as they were trading fire, the charges blew, and the building collapsed in on itself. We were stunned, we didn't even see them set the charges! Then all of a sudden two of them were behind us and then we were surrounded! We all got covered in paintballs, including Tonya (they shot her three times right in the butt as their opening salvo! Boy did she scream in surprise!). We, of course, all shot back until we ran out of ammo, even though we were hit like 100 times each, at least we got them some too!

When every paintball had been fired, only Sergeant Mitchel was left unscathed, he didn't have a drop of paint on him. We girls just had to share our paint with him. We said it was time for his hug and we all chased him down and hugged him, making sure he got as much paint on him as we had on us! Sergeant Richards, who was so very, *very* amused by all this, said he had never seen any group use that tactic on a sergeant before and this would have to be added to the book!

We girls may have gotten slaughtered, and those paintballs may have left big bruises all over us, but we had so much fun those two days that we didn't care! Mr. S said we did better defending than some of the military units they did this drill with. I guess most never got a single one of them of them and we got two!

Most trainings were not quite as exciting, but I enjoyed them. I learned to swim, and I got really good at shooting. I loved my Barrette M82. Everyone else preferred the MK4s we had (a navy version of the M16), but I fell in love with my M82 sniper rifle. I was even good at hitting targets as far as 1,760 yards (one mile) with that sniper rifle. Not nearly as good as Sergeant Mackey (he never missed a shot), but I could hold my own shooting that distance with most of the sergeants, even when shooting the floating target. The trick to the floating target is you shoot at the bottom of the swell.

We learned all about the differences between 'Boats' and 'Ships'. We learned about Ships having a Commander, whereas a boat just has whoever happens to be on it. We learned that a 'boat' can fit on a 'ship', but a 'ship' cannot fit on a 'boat'.

We learned that all submarines are boats, even if they are 500 feet long. We learned about hull shapes. We learned about V-shaped hulls being for deep water, thus belonging to a ship, and we learned how a flat-bottom hull was for shallow water and thus for boats. We learned all about various hull designs - displacement hulls, planing hulls, round-bilge hulls, and others. We learned about hard-chined hulls, soft-chined hulls, semi-displacement and semi-planing hulls.

And we learned all about the exceptions to each rule, like how the PT Boats of WWII could carry a lifeboat on its foredeck, was made for deep water, and had a permanent crew with a commanding officer. Yet, a PT Boat is a boat, not a ship. The same goes for Vietnam "swift boats". We learned that all Coast Guard vessels are Cutter boats, no matter what the puddle pirates say. And we learned several other exceptions.

We learned all about maps and charts and how to make them. We learned first aid and so much more those weekends!

When we went on trainings, we had special backpacks and vests and other gear we had to have. We wore belts with both a kabar knife and a 9mm Hushpuppy gun (though they only gave us ammunition when we were practicing shooting). I don't know why they were called hushpuppies, they were Smith and Wesson 9mm semi-automatics, but you could add a suppressor to them. They were a lot more fun to use when they gave us suppressors and we got to pretend that we were on assassination missions! And sometimes we even got radios. The backpack radio could even pick up a radio station that played music!

One of my favorite Jodies was 'Up from a Sub'. The idea of a women with a tag of gold swimming up from a sub to do a secret mission was just so enticing! I had an idea that a 240 Bravo was a gun, but I really didn't understand what it was. I was so excited the day we learned that '240 Bravo' was really the M240 machine gun, and now we got to fire it, along with the Browning M2 machine gun! We had fired guns on automatic a few times but firing a real machine gun for the first time was both exciting and terrifying all at the same time! We absolutely destroyed that stone wall with those two guns! Ericka loved the M240, whereas Shawn loved the Browning. I would shoot those guns when I had to, but I would much rather shoot my beloved M82.

My Beloved M82

Life went on that way. I still did some lessons with Mr. S, and I tried to be at as many story times as I could. I was now too big to sit on his lap for stories, so I sat next to him with either Jess or Jenna on my lap, his arm around my shoulder.

School became more challenging. Training became more intense. We got to be *really* strong working out with the sergeants! Guardians got to wear skirts. Those of us training with the sergeants got highly coveted black uniforms, like they had.

We got a projector, and once a month we all went to the chow hall to see a movie. The new cooking class in the chow hut was popular.

Sergeant Mackey got a CD player, and we got to listen to pop music. I don't know how he got to do this with the no celebration rule, but he did. I remember the first song I heard on that CD player was one of Madonna's songs. That opening music was just so magical and wonderous. It was like being transported to another world! The feeling of hearing music for the first time in forever was just so indescribably awesome!

Mackey did a weekly music and dance gathering. Once, when it was like 110 degrees out and humid as hell, we all just did the dance gathering naked. No one told us to, but it was just too hot. Mackey was very uncomfortable with this and we had so much fun tormenting him! He actually ran away and hid behind the other sergeants as we danced after him! He could stare down a whole friggin army with nothing but a Bic pen, but he couldn't face a bunch of naked teenage girls dancing to Madonna! Boy did we (and the other sergeants) torment him for that! Well worth the pushups we all got! We LOVED Mackey. About a week later,

Mackey turned that Madonna song into a marching Jodie, I think just to torment us!

We had the big water crisis, where the pipe failed and drained the tank. We had to do a bucket brigade from the stream to have drinking water and couldn't shower or do laundry for a month and everyone had to stay in bunk the whole time (even Guardians) because we barely had enough water to drink. Staff were not even permitted to use the flush toilets! Staff, and especially male staff, having to use the open latrine stalls was a sight to see!

You would think that was torture, but everyone stayed low-key, and the sergeants went bunk to bunk for thinking classes every day, even to the lower levels. But we didn't have any chores and we got to chat and just be girls more in that month than I think the whole rest of my time on the Island.

The new water line was repaired, and while it didn't work as they wanted, it worked well enough that girls got showers and laundry twice a week and higher levels got a third shower every other week.

We had a big parent weekend, where 24 moms of Level 9 and 10 girls came (out of over 650 girls currently on the Island). That weekend was so much work for the Guardians, as we had to shadow the moms the whole time. Those parents also got a *very* skewed view of life on the Island, they didn't see any chores or any of the life of the lower levels *at all*!

It felt like a real school. Life generally got a lot better for everyone. This was the happiest year since my parents died, and boy did it go by *fast*!

December was here before I knew it, and Mr. S wanted me to apply for college. Tonya, Christi, Shawn, and I worked every day on those applications. I applied to UT Austin (where Mr. S went) as my first-choice school, I even selected psychology as my major, as that was Mr. S's major. Mr. S wrote one of my letters of recommendation and Brother Sam wrote the other.

Christmas was even better than the previous year. Not only did Santa come with chocolates, but we all got journals with attached pens (I still used my Leather one).

Only staff were allowed to have watches on the Island, even Guardians were not allowed to have them. Mr. S gave me his Rolex Submariner watch as a gift. He said it was a family heirloom. It was the best gift I was ever given, and I wore that watch every day.

Life was good, the best it had ever been for me.

Guardian Nominations
Guardian Nominations
now being accepted!

Nominations are to be done by the girls of each bunk. Nomination deliberations by your bunk are confidential and will be supervised by a Guardian. Each bunk may nominate up to 2 girls for consideration in the Guardian selection process.

Girls do not have to be on any specific level to be considered for the Guardians, but they do have to meet the following criteria:

1. Nominees must be a lifer, ages _____

2. Nominees must be repentant for what brought them to the Island.

3. Nominees must be on the Island less than 9 months or have reached level 5 in less than 9 months

4. Nominees must be team players, able to follow orders and lead girls.

5. Nominees must be intelligent. Being a Guardian takes a lot of brain power.

6. Nominees must be proficient in all of the chore tasks, PT exercises, and all of the marching drills.
7. Nominees must be caring people who treat everyone humanely and who you want as a Guardian.

Bunk #_____ Guardian: _____
Nomination 1 _____
Nomination 2 _____

This nomination form must be signed by all girls in the bunk to be valid!

Chapter 11:
Fall of the Guardians

On February 22, 1994, Mr. S had a heart attack. I didn't even get to see him before he was taken by helicopter to the hospital on the mainland. He died four days later.

After Mr. S died, the whole school was in mourning. I know we had a funeral for him, as I visited his grave regularly. I think I spoke at the funeral, though maybe I just cried, it's all such a blur.

There were a lot of military people on the Island for it. It was only at his funeral that I learned his rank was Commander, and he only retired from the Navy 2 months before becoming our Headmaster.

We tried to carry on as best we could. Brother Sam, Sister Lisa and the sergeants kept as much the same as they could, and we Guardians stepped up to fill in whatever gaps we could. The house felt so empty without him. I turned seventeen and Jess turned eight. It wasn't a happy birthday for either of us. Even the news that I was accepted to UTA for the Fall didn't cheer me up.

In May we heard that we would be getting a new headmaster. Her name was Miss Rawlings. We were told she had previously been the head of another troubled teen school in Mexico and was a great choice to honor Mr. S and his legacy. She was supposed to be a whiz at fundraising and was going to raise the rest of the money to finish the new academic building. The new school building was to be named after Mr. S.

Miss Rawlings arrived the second week of May and immediately clashed with the sergeants. These were the guys getting the most out of all of us girls, making us be the best people we could be. They were the ones making us family.

They would get mad at you if you screwed up, but beatings or really anything more than pushups or making a kid watch the wall for half an hour was practically unheard of at the upper levels anymore (though not in bunk, kids were still punished harshly for various things by bunk parents...).

It mostly just wasn't necessary given our relationships with the sergeants. According to Miss Rawlings, if discipline slips were not being stacked up, they were not doing their jobs. They flatly rejected that idea, as did us Guardians and a lot of the other staff.

It was about this time that Sergeant Richards had a talk with me. He told me what was coming and that they wanted to wait for me, but because this is when the ship could come, I would not be able to come with them, at least not yet. If I wanted to join the Navy, in 4 months and 12 days I could use the sat phone and call them, and they would get me out and into the Navy, same as the other girls. He made sure I knew that it won't happen the same day, but he assured me that it would happen.

He also assured me that if I needed to leave before then, he was leaving me the resources to get both me and Jess out. He made me promise that I would stay a Guardian until I left, no matter what that meant, even though it wouldn't really be the Guardians anymore. He said it was about my survival, and that I would honor Mr. S the best by surviving the rest of my time here and then living a life with the lessons he taught me. How could I say no?

Then he showed a hidden cache of stuff. It included huge crates of MREs, school uniforms, civilian clothes, Mexican and American money, a deflated Zodiac boat in a crate, a sat phone, my M82 rifle, a handgun, and two cans of ammo as well as passports with both Jess and my pictures, but different first names and Mr. S's last name.

By the end of June, the sergeants quit. Everyone dreams of leaving with flair. The sergeants landed a friggin Navy ship on the dock, complete with huge guns, police-type people, and some kind of Navy lawyer. They took with them any of the upper-level older girls (seventeen and a half or older) that were eligible to join the US military. They had papers to take 56 of the girls to Basic training, including every Guardian older than me except Marci, who wouldn't leave her sister. How I wished I could go, but I was 4 months too young.

A lot of other staff, including almost every trusted staff member, left at the same time or on the next supply boat. They called it 'The Great Resignation' and it was the largest change of staff in my time on the Island, and not for the better. At the same time, most of the girls on Levels 6, 7, 8 and 9 that didn't go and were not close to going home purposefully got themselves dropped to Level 5 to screw up the system even more. And it worked! The school was in chaos.

Julie, Maxine, Sasha, Paula, Tori, Susan, Betty, Marci, and I were all that was left of the Guardians. Marci and I were now the oldest of the Guardians and I was now the de facto Captain. To make matters worse, Brother Roid and some of the other creepy staff were back.

Marci and I went to Miss Rawlings to start the Guardian selection process. Our plan was to fill the ranks with fifteen- and sixteen-year-olds. She told us that it was covered. Two weeks later, on July 4th, 10 new girls, many from Bunk 22, moved into Bunk 1. They called themselves Guardians, but really, they were Miss Rawlings's new Jr goon squad.

Miss Rawlings laid out her new plan for the Guardians. Gone was training or office support or caring for Jess and Jenna (who were moved to Bunk 16 with Father Fred) or even our usual operations. We now had a single job; we were now to patrol and watch for infractions and punish harshly for them.

She then had two girls, Kayla and Julie, both upper-level girls that had gotten themselves dropped to Level 5, brought into our bunk. She was clear that these girls had done *nothing* to deserve a punishment, but that was irrelevant, this was not a punishment, it was "training". She made them strip. I noticed they both had the same fairly small, firm, perky tits Brother Mark liked my first year. It wasn't lost on me that I had the same kind of perky tits. I learned that this was Miss Rawlings preferred type of girl.

Then she explained a new procedure we were to use when questioning girls or giving out punishments or just to exercise our power. She called it "the Nurples". Miss Rawlings told Julie to keep her hands at her sides, then she pinched Julie's nipples, twisting and lifting them as she dug her thumbnails into them.

Julie screamed, her face contorting in pain. Miss Rawlings was obviously enjoying it. Her voice was excited as she told us to roll the nipple as she rolled Julie's nipples. This caused fresh screams and tears. She told us it was effective to move girls as she dragged Julie in a circle around her by her left nipple. She told us it was effective to get compliance in almost any situation as she used her nipple to drag her face to the floor.

I was horrified. This was so far from what Mr. S had wanted, I felt sick. The look on Kayla's face was one of sheer terror, knowing she was next, and I could do nothing to stop it.

This was the moment I knew the Guardians had fallen and it was on my watch. This once vaulted institution created to help girls become human, to protect and help them was now nothing more than another goon squad.

Miss Rawlings told us that a girl's tit was tougher than it looks and was effective in correcting behavior. Then she pulled Julie to standing and smacked Julie's left tit so hard she left her handprint on the tit, and a fresh wave of tears from Julie. She told us that using a switch on girls' tits was now fair game for even the most minor infractions. And with that, she used a crop on the inside of her tit as her other hand continued to hold on to that nipple, Julie crying the whole time. I counted 37 lashed she gave with that crop, but I don't think Miss Rawlings was counting.

Then she told us we were to practice this with these two girls, and we would only be done when they both ran out of tears, the four tits were a good shade of purple on all sides, and we all got this down pat. She told us to look in their eyes as we did it, to make them look us in the eye and for us to have fun with it. This sick, twisted bitch expected us to take the same pleasure in torturing these girls' tits as she did. I wanted to throw up. With that, she left. I now had to organize us taking turns doing what we were just told to do.

Resisting wasn't an option. The real Guardians did the bare minimum, but we all knew that if we resisted, we were next. The fake Guardians enjoyed themselves.

Those two girls' tits were purple, bloody, and raw when we were finished with them. Sometimes, when I close my eyes, I still see the flesh of the girls' tits covered in angry welts. I open my eyes and want to throw up. They couldn't even cry anymore when they were tossed naked out of Bunk 1 like trash.

Nurples were a new and terrifying normal on the Island. They were inflicted by us and by the staff, especially the new "teachers" (torturers she brought in from her previous school) on all of the other girls. Miss Rawlings told us that for serious issues, we could "nurple the pussy as well".

"Pussy". She didn't even have the decency to call it a clitoris. Mr. S may not have been comfortable talking about those parts, but he never would have let me get away with using such a vulgar term for it, let alone doing something like that. I never nurpled a girl down there, the thought of it made me sick, though I heard a few of the fake Guardians bragging about having done it to girls.

A few days later, we had a staff meeting. The brutality of the school was now worse than ever. The circle beatings were back with a vengeance. Caging was back and now automatic for any circle beating. We could hold heads under latrine waste water if we wanted to. Staff and even Guardians were told to liberally beat girls for *any* infraction. Leather belts were now a part of Guardian uniforms, and not to hold our pants up. Office punishments, which had steadily declined under Mr. S, were now expected to go up 1000%. All "for the good of the girls" of course. The real Guardians knew what BS this was, but we had no choice.

Miss Rawlings covered what the legal definition of sexual abuse here was. A male teacher inserting a penis into a girl's vagina was sexual abuse. Teachers would be fired for that. If a baby was produced, they could be arrested. Because of the Island's weird legal status, the jurisdiction had no other laws on sexual abuse that applied to us.

That night, she ordered us to bring a girl to her room. I was tasked with removing the girl in the morning. I remember Miss Rawlings making me hand her my underwear, then telling me that the girl upstairs had a real talent with her tongue and that I should make use of it before taking her out. It wasn't a suggestion, it was an order.

I went upstairs to her room. Standing outside the door, I remembered how this bedroom used to be the safest place in the world for me. When I first came to the Island, the big storms really scared me. We had to sit in the center of the bunk during the worst ones. It was the only time the bunk parents let us all hold and comfort each other without getting into trouble for it.

When I moved into Mr. S's house, we were right on the cliff, my bedroom window facing the ocean. At thirteen, the storms were far scarier when you were alone in your room and saw them out of the window at night like that. The bunks didn't have a view of the ocean.

My first big storm in the house (I was thirteen, Jess was 4), Jess and I were so scared by the storm that in the middle of the night we ended up running to Mr. S's room and begging for him to save us. Jess and I hugged him with everything we had.

He tried to console us and send us back to bed, but just as we had calmed down and were agreeing to go back to our rooms, lightning violently struck the ocean right outside his window, the room a flash of bright light, the boom so loud I thought the world was ending and the electricity went out. I prayed to God not to let us die that night, crying the whole time.

The storm lasted all night and into the next day. But that night he let us sleep in his bed with him. I think he did it more out of exhaustion than anything else that first time, but it was safe, even in the scariest of storms. Jess and I slept with him whenever the storms were too scary until I was fourteenish, and the storms didn't scare me so much. It was, for me, the safest place in the whole wide world.

I opened the door and saw the girl. Her name was Mary, she was fifteen and a lifer from Bunk 14. I did her intake back in January of the previous year. She was here for running away from foster homes.

Mary was thin and pretty, with long flowing blond hair. She had the perky breasts Miss Rawlings liked. It was so gross—she was naked, tied spread-eagle to the bed on her back, her body covered with welts and her face covered in what had to be Miss Rawlings' bodily fluids. This room that was once so safe for me, was now her torture chamber. I wanted to be sick.

Mary begged me not to make her eat me. I was shocked. I had heard a few of the older girls talk about being eaten out, but only ever had a vague understanding that it was the person's tongue in my vagina, which seemed gross to me. I was 17, I had never really understood what it meant.

Then came Miss Rawlings's voice, telling me that I only had 10 minutes, unless I wanted to be next on her bed. I grizzled at her calling Mr. S's bed "her bed", but there was nothing I could do about that.

Hearing her voice, Mary and I were both resigned to what we had to do. I had never had any kind of sex before, other than rubbing myself and giving a few blow jobs when I was 12. I told Mary that I was really sorry.

Biology is a funny thing. You can be disgusted, angry, and afraid and your body can still betray you in unimaginable ways. I still don't understand how, at 17, I could have orgasmed like that while forced into doing something that was so revolting to my whole being, to a fifteen-year-old no less! It left me with very complicated feelings I still struggle with today.

I tried to never be the one to take girls out of her room, but sometimes I didn't have a choice. Miss Rawlings delighted in making me compare how well the different girls did. It was so hard to put on the required face and smile through that. More than once I legitimately threw up after leaving her house.

The girls changed, but the order was the same every night. And she was not the only one. Miss Rawlings had a saying: "tongues, tits, and asses". The new staff and the fake Guardians made liberal use of those parts of girls' bodies. The words and their implications alone made me sick.

Then came the 'visitors'. They were 'rich donors'. They came by boat. They would stay a few nights and leave. Girls were brought to them each night, and then get taken back when they were finished.

The girls who went were given time off chores, Meal #6 for a few days, and little necklace charms, I guess as payment for what was done to them. A few girls got pregnant, but because it wasn't a male staff member, and no one seemed to know anything about these boats, it all got swept under the rug. They got pills and time in the infirmary.

A few of us talked about resisting, but even the words were incredibly dangerous. We were just a handful of teenagers with no real power, no idea how to effectively resist, no one to help us, and no place to go. Even if we got the guns, it wouldn't be enough to stop it. Miss Rawlings controlled every resource. She had the junior goon squad, a staff of one hundred and she could call in guys with guns too.

Father Fred now had both Jess and Jenna in his bunk. Somehow, his bunk stayed protected through all of this. Miss Rawlings never gave orders involving his bunk (she sometimes took girls from the other tween bunks for herself and the visitors) and the fake Guardians avoided it, while the real Guardians were welcome. It was the only oasis of sanity left in this hell hole.

Miss Rawlings and I had a fight over my going to college. The school and the judge would have to sign off on my leaving early. She was clear she wasn't letting me do that. I argued with her over it, pointing out it was Mr. S's wish that I go as respectably as I possibly could have.

She yelled at me that if I thought I could survive without them, that I was to take Jess and see how well I did in the woods for a week. If I survived, maybe I would have learned my lesson and could rejoin the Guardians. If not, or if we were caught, oh well, the hotbox would be waiting for us. She then gave me 10 minutes before she would be sending the (fake) Guardians to hunt me and Jess down.

I ran, grabbed Jess, and headed to the horse barn, where I knocked over one of the new torturers and took the horse she had saddled. The new staff member didn't know the Island and the fake guardians didn't know how to ride so they had no chance of keeping up. We made it to the equipment hide and settled in for the night. I kept the guns loaded and close. I set a perimeter at 50 yards, complete with claymores on trip lines, and told myself that my rules of engagement were that I could shoot if they came inside that line.

Miss Rawlings and the fake Guardians came looking for us the next day. They didn't know about the guns or the equipment hide. They had clubs and Miss Rawlings had a riding crop.

I don't know whether I would have actually shot or not if they had crossed that line, but at one point, I had Miss Rawlings's head in the crosshairs of my scope. She was basically unarmed, standing still and about 100 yards out. It would have been an easy shot. Part of me wishes I took that shot, but I didn't. Killing a human for the first time, even one as evil as Miss Rawlings, just isn't so easy.

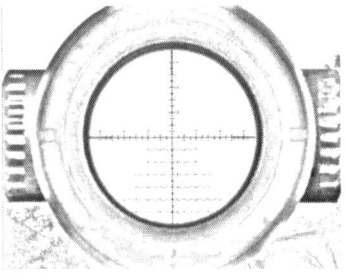

Besides, I didn't think Mr. S would have approved of me breaking my own rules of engagement. They eventually gave up and left, taking the horse back with them. Jess and I hardly left our hiding place. The boat was too heavy to move without the horse and I didn't think of taking it out of the box and moving it in pieces.

Two weeks later, Jess and I went to Mr. S's grave, then we went to Father Fred, one of the last of the trusted adults on the whole Island. I wouldn't tell him where the equipment hide was, but I told him everything else, including that I had the rifle and ammo and about having Miss Rawlings in my crosshairs. I agreed to let him hold the handgun I had with me, and he took us back to his bunk. He hid the gun under the floorboards in his room.

I don't know what happened with Miss Rawlings and Father Fred, but I was returned to Bunk 1 two days later. The fake guardians kept their distance. They didn't even make snide remarks.

I was a member of the Guardians in name, I ate the better food every meal (more often than we were allowed, but I didn't care), I showered every day (again, more often than allowed, but I didn't care about that either), I wore my skirt and black uniform, but I didn't organize anything anymore, I didn't patrol, I wasn't given any orders, I didn't deliver girls, I didn't go to any kind of groups or classes (not that the classes were real anymore…), I just helped Father Fred with his bunk and occasionally helped Brother Sam. Even Miss Rawlings avoided me.

Brother Sam took a vacation shortly before I got back from the woods. It was the first one he had ever taken in my time at the school. He said it was "family business". I guess he wasn't even gone for a week.

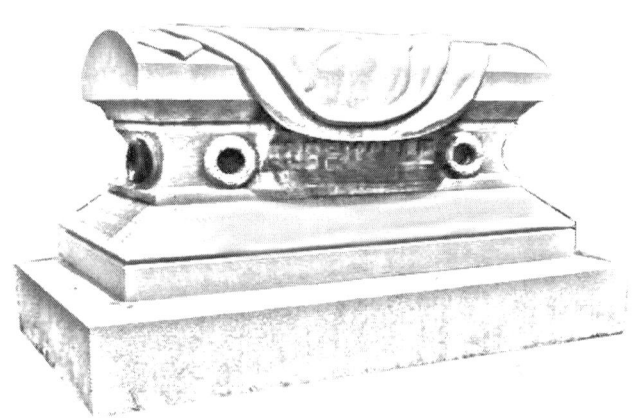

This picture isn't the actual memorial, but it's really, really close, like they are the same model that came from the same factory close – stone carved blanket and all. This one is only missing the insignia and symbols of the church, as well as the engraving of Mr. S's real name.

Vanessa

Chapter 12:
An Angel Takes Flight

On September 1st, Brother Sam came into my bunk early. He woke me up, then he put a set of cuffs on me and made Marci pack my stuff into a bag. He said I was being transferred. He then walked my naked seventeen-year-old ass to his office, standing me nose-tits-n-toes in the outer office.

I figured I was going to get it good. Publicly whipped, hotboxed, raped, I didn't know, but I didn't really care either. Once we got into his office, he closed the door, unhooked me, and told me to get dressed quickly, giving me a new skirt uniform to put on. He handed me my bag, putting an envelope of papers into it.

Then he very loosely put the cuffs on in front of me and took me out the back door and to the airfield, telling me he was getting me to college and not to talk under any circumstances until we landed and were out of the airport. We boarded the plane with the girls going home and he sat next to me.

Eventually, the overhead speaker announced that we would be landing in 30 minutes. A few minutes later, the pilot came back and told me that a mistake was made, and that I had to be returned to the Island. I wanted to cry. He also told Sam that his vacation was canceled, and he would be returning as well. I knew this wasn't good for either of us, but I stayed silent. Brother Sam was oddly quiet.

We landed at the same airfield this started at. I was taken and put in line with the girls that would be going to the Island for the first time. Sam stood nearby, two big goons behind him. I was numb, my heart cold. I was planning out how I was going to get my M82 and what I was going to do with it. 500 rounds was a lot of shots to plan, and I was determined that I was going to make every one of them count. I was planning out how I would take out the water tank, the water line, the boiler, the plane, the fake Guardians, the staff, and most of all, Miss Rawlings. I was resigned to doing what I knew I had to do to end that place once and for all, no matter what the cost.

Then there was a commotion outside. Sergeant Richards came in with a bunch of guys. They flashed some kind of badges at the one security officer. I could see that they were military by how they walked. I recognized how they swept in as one of the things we had been taught about urban warfare, how to take control of a large space. But they were in civilian clothes, and I didn't see many weapons.

One of them, a really big guy I later learned was Seaman Jones, he had a big sign for UTA students. They came over and Sergeant Richards snatched my paperwork from the goon behind me, and without even opening the envelope, said that since they have the paperwork, I was heading to college.

The goon started to protest and Seaman Jones, who was quite a bit bigger than any of the goons, loudly said "LTC?". Richards nodded his head and Seaman Jones stepped around me and backed the two goons up hard as Richards took the cuffs off me.

My cuffs now gone, Seaman Jones beside me and Richards behind me, I looked the goon right in the eye as I took my bag from him. All of my earthly possessions were in this small tote bag. I staired defiantly into his eyes as I put my watch on right in front of the goon. I was free and I wanted him and everyone else to know it!

Then Sam and I left with Sergeant Richards and his men. It was tense, with more goons than Richards had men, but the goons must have known they were way outclassed because they didn't put up any kind of a fight. I guess kidnapping helpless teenage girls was all the fight these chickenshits had in them, facing real men and women who could fight back was too much for them.

It was only in the car that Brother Sam told me that he had been a college friend of Mr. S (why Mr. S took the job), and that he stayed when the sergeants left because he promised Mr. S that he would make sure I got to college and Jess got out. Sam said that Jess and I were the closest Mr. S had ever had to having children, daughters of his own. I cried when I heard that, wishing Mr. S had told me that himself.

I learned that Sam went to court for me on his last trip, and he wasn't ever going back to the Island. He called Richards to meet the plane a few days before we left.

Sam assured me that Jess would get out shortly – she was private pay, and the family wasn't paying any more after his talk with them. Sam said that they would send her home on the next plane because they only did this for the money.

Richards assured me that if it didn't happen, he would personally go get her, and he would have no problem finding volunteers to go with him, including Sam and everyone that came to get me, though he said I couldn't be one of them for legal reasons, that they might try to claim custody of me if I went. He also said I didn't need to see what would happen if he went back, my M82 might get a workout.

We spent a few nights at hotels on the way to Austin. I had never been in a hotel before. Richards and his men stayed with us the whole time. Said they were making sure nothing happened before getting me to school. I guess they were afraid that Miss Rawlings would send goons for me again.

We stopped at a Walmart and the one woman on Richards team, Sara, took me in to buy school clothes. I remember being so overwhelmed at all the choices. I picked 3 outfits (that's what I had on the Island, skirt uniform, work uniform, and black uniform). She told me I was crazy and made me pick out like 20 different outfits and then she made me get all these things for my dorm room, like blankets and lamps and a laptop computer (I had never even used a computer!) and a dorm fridge and a trash can and notebooks and pens and markers and other "college stuff".

She was a lot of fun to shop with and she got two of the cutest guys on Richards's team to push around the carts for us as we shopped and tried things on. They said nice things when I tried things on, I loved how that made me feel so special, like a superstar magazine model.

Sara made a joke about hoping I had money to pay for all this, then laughed, saying it was a good thing she had the gold card. It occurred to me that I had no idea what this stuff cost, I didn't really know how money worked, or what a gold card even was. Just one of the many, many "normal" things I missed out on that I would have to learn.

We filled the bed of a pickup truck with all the stuff we bought. Till now, my possessions all fit in a little tote bag. I had never had so many things that were mine. It was overwhelming.

Then they took me to my college orientation. 25 big guys taking me in made me feel like a million bucks. They cleared the way for me like I was a princess! They hung around while Sara and I went on orientation. They had my dorm room set up when we got back and then they helped me pick my classes. Picking classes was a new experience for me, something I had never once done in my life. I don't think I could have done it without their help.

After orientation and meeting some floormates and selecting classes and doing some other paperwork, they hooked me up with the NROTC people. I guess it's unusual for a new NROTC recruit to be dropped off by so many military people and it was clear that Richards counted for a lot with them, as they all called him Sir, even the CO (who called him "Lieutenant Commander"). He told them I was Commander S's daughter. I almost cried at that. Then he told them that I had been through a lot, the same hell as being a POW and that he expected them to do right by me.

I didn't have to retake any class I took with any of the sergeants, only retake the final exams, which was fairly easy. Richards gave them a hand-scribbled list of the classes I had taken, saying I got As in every class, even the ones I really struggled with. They referred to them as transfer credits, which was funny as they basically rejected everyone else's fancy paperwork transfer credits from all these impressive-sounding high schools and JROTC programs.

The NROTC people were impressed with my training, especially my marksmanship. I qualified as a sharpshooter my first time, and I qualified expert on my first try with an M107 (newer version of the M82). I even got to show them a few 1,760-yard bullseyes and a few 1,000-yard swell shots. The urban warfare and the demolition stuff I had learned impressed our NROTC CO. Even our NROTC instructors had not done Urban Warfare training, like I had, and I even got to run our NROTC class through some of those drills.

NROTC was a big part of my college life. While most of my peers couldn't relate to any of my experiences growing up—let's face it, being grounded doesn't really compare to being publicly whipped. Being questioned about some transgression doesn't compare to a body cavity search or to the Nurples. Taking out the trash doesn't compare to emptying out the latrines onto the shit pads. Having to do an extra chore as a punishment doesn't compare to having to turn wet latrine compost by hand for 8 hours. Soccer just doesn't compare to stumps. Raking the yard and being yoked are just not comparable. At least the NROTC people understood being chewed out, military training, and drill.

They treated me very well in the NROTC and I advanced quickly, though not without struggle. I had a *lot* to learn about normal life and that wasn't easy. I went with the NROTC for most vacations. A few times, and to the absolute envy of my NROTC peers, I got to go with Lt-Commander Richards instead of going to NROTC drill. That was always amazing!

I once got to help him with a training where I got to dress up really young looking (I looked twelve in that yellow sundress!) and played the undercover spy. I got to 'assassinate' the whole team he was training. They didn't expect the innocent little girl to be the super spy sniper!

I got them all twice before they figured out it was me! I was supposed to let them win on the third try. They even took me prisoner right at the start and brought me to their base tent to keep an eye on me. But I saw the training grenade just sitting there and I had an idea. I got them again by being a suicide bomber. seventeen-year-old me in my yellow sundress and pigtails, looking all of twelve years old getting to take out sixteen Marines like that was epic!

Richards' really chewed them out for letting a teenage girl take out their entire team three times, even after they had identified me as the spy. He said 3 minutes was the fastest loss he had ever seen.

I had to let them win on the 4th try because Richards said so. They duct-taped me to a chair this time, but they never figured out I put another training grenade in my bra. Richards had me show it to them after they were all cocky about having won. I then followed Richards out, whining something about "But Uncle Matt, you can't be mad at me, I did what you wanted, I didn't kill any of them this time…" Boy did we have a good laugh over that back at his office!

The next day, Richards had me tell them that I wasn't allowed to play with them today, as I had been too rough on them yesterday. Instead, I had to play a boring hostage. Boy did that fry those Marine guys! When they "rescued" me, I kept telling them what they got wrong and asking if I should do it for them…They were Jar Heads, how could I not pick on them? But they did take me out to a really nice dinner. . .

I visited both my Aunt Marsha and Sister Beth (now Aunt Beth) a few times in college. Reconnecting with my Aunt Marsha was hard, but she was the only biological family I had left, the only connection left to my parents, the only one that could tell me more about them. While part of me resented her for sending me to the Island, I eventually came to terms with it and we had a good relationship until she passed.

Visiting Aunt Beth was like going home again. Her house even smelled like home and she had a lot of photos of Dad. She often told me stories of Dad when he was younger. She still has her superpowers, though she now uses them mostly on my daughters. Mostly.

Throughout school, Uncle Matt helped me with my school paperwork and made sure I had whatever I needed for school. But he also took a lot of time helping me to learn how to function in the normal world and helping me to see how my time on the Island skewed my sense of what was right and what was wrong.

In one of my first college physics classes, we were presented with a question on moving a heavy object. The question was, given a friction coefficient of 0.3, how much force would be needed to move a 500lbs object. The teachers' goal was to have us calculate the forces needed to pull the object given friction. Everyone else assumed an imaginary winch or some such pulling the imaginary load and came up with the correct answer of 650lbs.

My estimate was based on how many girls I thought would need to be on the yoke. My estimate was seven girls to just get it to move a little, ten girls if you're going under an hour on a flat ground, but real world, at least fifteen because it's never actually flat, and if you're going on any of the less maintained roads or more than an hour, best to use a full yoke of twenty-four girls. But really, we should be using a cart to move that much weight, otherwise you damage the road.

That was a *very* awkward class, everyone laughed at me. Uncle Matt spent 2 hours on the phone with a very upset me that night helping me to understand why I was laughed at over that. Who knew that yoked girls were not a common unit of force? And that was just one of many, many nights I called him in tears.

Uncle Matt is also the one that got me seeing a therapist, though I never was really able to talk to her about my time on the Island. She tried, but she really didn't understand. Even among therapists, it's hard for them to see a "therapeutic" school being what it was.

In a psychology class, I even had a fight with the teacher about such schools. She said I was proof they worked. I told her she was stupid and didn't have a fucking clue and walked out, never going back to her classes. Uncle Matt called the Dean, and I got a new section. I can tell you that I wouldn't have gotten through school, or life really, without him and all that support.

In college, I majored in Psychology and got my Masters in English. My career has been in computer programming. I have a husband I met at NROTC (also a computer programmer). I did two years after college as a Lieutenant in the Naval Reserves working on computer-related projects and only left because of an accident with my knee (third-floor walk-up office and a busted knee…).

When I was pregnant with my first daughter, one of my biggest fears was that she was going to be abused because of my time on the Island. I took a lot of steps to try to protect both my daughters from that. I think it would have been a lot worse without my husband, Aunt Beth, and Uncle Matt.

We now have two daughters. And yes, my daughters grew up learning to stand at attention; they know how to use their "sirs". They know the nine basic responses. They got their share of watching a wall, they did the occasional nose-n-toes, and even got spanked a few times growing up.

They have heard some stories from my time on the Island, mostly about Jess and the man they know as their grandfather, my dad, Mr. S, and not most of the bad stuff. They have never heard any of the stories of the shit chores or groups or beatings or Miss Rawlings.

They know Sister Beth as Aunt Beth and Commander Richards as Uncle Matt. But they never got in trouble with the courts and we never once thought of sending them away, though I did grudgingly let them do sleep away camp when they fought for it (they got my husband, Matt, and Sara to gang up on me over that one...). That month they were away was as terrifying for me as my first month on the Island.

My girls got good grades, did all the normal school things, and most importantly, they were always loved and cared for. I did my best to make sure they learned to treat everyone as people, and that they learned as much of what my dad taught me as I could possibly teach them. Thankfully, I have a husband and family that were able to teach them the things I could not.

My oldest is now attending UTA, majoring in psychology and doing NROTC. I plan on giving her her grandfather's watch when she graduates. My youngest wants to betray family tradition and join the Army when she turns eighteen and goes to nursing school. We will see on that one.

I still have my skirt uniform and I still sometimes put on that old skirt uniform (yes, it still fits!). It reminds me of Dad. I still have Dad's Bible and my journal, though it was filled in college.

Mine may be a story of hope, but it's an unusual one. I know that I was one of the very few lucky ones. Over the years I have met many people who survived the troubled teen industry. None of them had a Jess or a Mr. S or the sergeants or Sister Beth or Father Fred.

Most went in with minor issues and left broken people with drug addictions and mental issues or worse. You have no idea how badly these places remove you from being part of the wider community, how much that screws you up, and how ill-prepared we leave those places for survival in the real world.

For God's sake, at seventeen I didn't know how money worked. I didn't know how to go to a restaurant. I didn't know how to select my own food at the college food court (a #3 at McDonald's isn't the same as a #3 in chow hall). My sense of modesty was way out of touch with everyone else at the college – Freshman year, I was the girl that would walk down the hall naked for my shower. I didn't really know how to fill out a form. I had virtually zero test-taking skills. I didn't know how to choose a class. I didn't really know how to write an essay. I didn't understand the rules of the road. I barely understood the concept of owning something. I didn't know how to make friends that wasn't trauma bonding.

My views on kids and obedience were extreme. I thought it was normal to just yoke up a group of girls. I knew nothing about modern culture. I knew nothing about dating And I could only function in social situations with an authority figure. I needed a boyfriend who would give me rules and permission all the time. For a long time, I needed him to give me permission to get dressed when we slept in the same room—I think I was 30 before it clicked that I didn't really need permission all the time. To this day, if a voice of authority says "Nose-tits-n-toes," I instantly head to the nearest wall and can't make myself come out unless I am told to.

While I can't imagine my life without Jess, Dad, Aunt Beth, Father Fred, and the sergeants, if it weren't for the sheer luck of being sat next to Jess on that plane, I know I would have turned out just as broken as those other kids were, maybe as broken as Nikki was. Drug addiction, self-worth issues, and all the rest.

Almost everyone on the Island thought they were helping us teens get back on track. Most of them, including Brother Mark, were missionary volunteers, true believers in the cause. They really believed that if they were tough enough on us, it would magically fix us. Good intentions just don't equal actual help.

That kind of tough love doesn't help. At least the sergeants had real teaching experience in the military that they could leverage, and they rejected the idea that teens should perpetually be in trouble.

No one deserves to carry the scars and baggage I do from my time on the Island, especially from the first and last 6 months of my time on that godforsaken place, and many, many kids went years like that.

I may have made it, but I know I was one of the very few lucky ones. No person deserves to be in a program like I was in, especially without Jess, Dad,

Aunt Beth, Father Fred, and the sergeants. But people like that are rare.

Chapter 13:
Letters from Home

In the process of working on this book, thanks to Father Fred having kept the full name and date of birth of every girl he worked with in his diary, my co-author managed to track down most of the people I wrote about. He let some of them read an early draft of this book and then worked with them to write me these letters.

Except for changing names and other identifying details, I present these letters as I received them. Many offer views on these same events that are different from what I remember and offer details that I didn't know, but I think their views are just as valid as mine.

When we found Jess, I took out a plea for her to contact me if she ever found this book, but I otherwise did not edit the preceding story in any way to include any of the information they brought to my attention in these letters.

Hey big sister,

I know it's been a minute. Almost 30 years now since we left that Island and we last saw each other. I still can't believe I went there because I bit two classmates in preschool.

I went home about a month after you left. I was so upset that I didn't get to say goodbye to you. That was the hardest part. As long as I had you, I knew everything would be OK.

I was really upset that they never let us say goodbye. You were my whole world and I didn't even know your last name. I left the Island about a month after you did, with the next batch of girls that went home. I didn't get to say goodbye either.

The Island suffered unspeakable horrors after you left. I was lucky to get out when I did. Jenna stayed on the Island almost an entire year after I left. I still talk to her once in a while, she works as an Uber driver in Texas. Marci never made it off the Island.

I wasn't home for two months before I went to boarding school in France. It wasn't a troubled teen program, it was a real boarding school and I got to do an awful lot of normal things. They didn't even make us do any chores!

As much as I love stories, it turns out I was faking reading. I memorized every book we had, I didn't actually know how to read. The new school figured out I needed glasses. But I learned how to be normal and by the time I went to England for high school, I did really well. I even went to college in New York City.

I never married; I don't have any children. I worked for a little while in the tech sector, but my parents left me enough of a legacy that I don't really have to work. I spend most of my time in my garden with my two dogs. I still can't believe that we only live a few miles apart, and you have no idea how much I look forward to seeing you in a few hours.

Not a day has gone by that I haven't thought of you. I think of you every time I touch my rubbing stone. I carried that stone with me everywhere I went right through college to make sure I could never forget you. It still sits on my bedside table. And it's still black from that fire magic trick you and Dad did to it.

I hired a PI to try to find you about 10 years ago, but without a last name, it was just impossible. It was quite a surprise when your co-author called me today. I still don't understand how he found me. But that doesn't matter, what matters is that he did and now I found you. I am counting the seconds till our video call tonight. I can't wait to hear your voice again. Let's never lose touch again, OK?

I guess this means you are going to have to change that ending to your book now?

Maybe we can do Apple Pie for breakfast?

Love always,

Jessica (aka Jess)

Dear V.

You were thirteen the first time I heard about you. My brother wrote to me about how protective you were of a little girl that should never have been on that island, how protective you were of her when everybody else was only out for their own interests. He saw bravery in you standing in that first parade, where everybody else showed nothing but terror of him. He never forgot you telling him to take care of Jess when he took her that first parade. Then you were interested during drill and during science when nobody else seemed to care very much. That made a huge difference to my brother.

You had his heart from the moment you refused to be a rat, willing to take a beating even after the very severe beating you had already taken. That's heart. He saw a love between you and Jess that melted his heart and melting his heart was next to impossible. When he ever saw you saving food for your sister, just like we used to do for each other when we grew up so poor, he knew there was something special about you.

By the time I came to that island to convince him to leave, there was no way he was going to give up the two children that he had claimed as his own. Seeing how much my brother loved you, you were already family the first time I laid eyes on you. Time after time, the two of you showed him the kind of love, the kind of unconditional and never-ending love that every parent dreams of, and for that I am eternally thankful.

We've talked over the years about just how much he saved your life, we've discussed the many things he did to try to give you a better life. He did those things because he loved you and he was so determined that you two do better in this world than he did. He was so determined that the two of you would grow up to have loving families, to have the things he never had. I think you've succeeded in that in ways that would make him forever proud. I know how proud of you I am.

I think it's important to make sure you understand that you and your sister saved his life just as many times if not many more times than he saved yours. The bond you two formed with him was one of the most powerful of his life. In truth I was sometimes jealous, you had the kind of relationship with him that only he and I had ever had before.

His favorite time of the day was reading stories to the two of you. Every time he missed one, I heard about the lost opportunity. He really regretted every night he missed story with you. Did I ever tell you how scared he was that one day you would outgrow story time with him? In almost every letter he wrote me, he talked about how hard it would be to give up that with you. Those times really meant everything to him.

Your interest in learning was incredible to him. You were a sponge that sucked up every piece of information he could give you and he did everything he could to make sure he could keep feeding you more. For every hour you had lesson with him, he stayed up at least another hour planning the next one. You were that important to him.

The one thing I regret about those early days is that I couldn't convince my brother to talk to you about how he felt. From our conversations over the years, I know just how scared you were of losing him and having to go back to living in that bunk. His constant fear was that you would choose to go back and live in bunk, he was always worried that he would screw up and you would stop loving him. He dreaded the idea that you and Jess would stop telling him your stories. I still have quite a few of those stories, he often wrote them down in his letters to me. Your imagination was a better world for him then the real world ever was.

You have no idea the pressure other staff put him under to throw you back into one of the bunks. But he absolutely wouldn't have it. As long as you were willing to live with him, he was keeping you both. Sending you two to do classes with two of the bunks and chore with a third was the furthest he was willing to go to compromise. Even then, he insisted they treat you like they would an upper-level girl, if for no other reason then so you knew you could take care of your sister, but also because he felt you had truly earned it.

When I met you that first time, on that one trip I made to the Island, I understood just how special you were and why my brother loved you so much. In a place as brutal as the Island was, you charged headfirst in and stood up to a whole roomful a very scary adults to try to defend me, someone you barely knew at the time. In doing so you showed the kind of love and bravery that I wish I had at that age. The time I spent with you those weeks were as important to me as they were to my brother. After all, I had the opportunity to get to know my nieces! Oh and the nose trick? I learned that from my mother, and you had the same tickle spots as my brother did.

I know you believe that the creation of the Guardians was my doing, but it wasn't. My brother did that because he wanted you to have something special, he wanted you to have an opportunity to grow and spread your wings, one he knew he couldn't give you just in his home. The only thing I did was convince him to offer that opportunity to more than just you. I think it was the right thing to do. It's fitting that your group was eventually called the Guardians, because he saw you and Jess as his guardian angels just as much as you saw him as yours.

We've talked over the years about just how reluctant the church was for change, how the church refused to spend money to make the Island a better place. My brother spent a lot of his own money to try to improve things. He really wanted every girl on that island to have the kind of wondrous life you and your sister did all those days playing in his backyard.

You have no idea how pleased he was to see you form relationships with his friends, the gentleman you call the sergeants, especially Matt. They were part of his military family and getting to have them come and be part of his adopted family meant the world to him. You and your sister are the only two to ever get him to cross the family and military lines like that. I don't know whether you know this or not, but he was trying to make the Island double as a retirement community for military officers. He thought the girls on the Island could save as many of his friends, as his friends could save girls on the Island. I think if he had lived a few more years, you would have seen it happen.

We've talked about how depressed my brother was, and how you and your sister are the ones that pulled him out of his depression time after time after time. I will never forget the very expensive phone call he made after you sat with him telling him you loved him and please don't die over and over again when he was sick. He cried for almost an hour. I don't think he had cried over anything since he was fourteen. I don't know that I've ever thanked you for that, but I will forever be grateful for what you two did for my brother.

When you ever started doing military maneuvers with him and his friends, he was the proudest any parent could have ever been. He spent a month planning that first outing you did with him.

When you became a better shot than he was, he wasn't jealous, he wasn't upset, he was the proudest parent in the whole wide world. He boasted to his friends for weeks when you made that first swell shot. He wanted to put you up for a medal the first time you hit it at 1000 yards! He told me that it was the first time he understood why some parents acted like they did at graduation. I promise you had he lived to see your college graduation he would have been one of those parents.

We've talked about that incident with the rifle and the headmaster of whom I will not speak her name. For years you've regretted not taking that shot, comparing yourself to what my brother would have done. It's true my brother would have taken that shot, but he wasn't seventeen, he wasn't in the situation you were. He was a Navy man with a whole career of experience behind him. One thing I can tell you with absolute certainty is that he wouldn't have wanted you to take that shot. My brother knew what it was like to take a life, and at seventeen he would not have wanted you to carry that weight. I remember my brother after his first time, you didn't need to carry that at seventeen.

Theodore absolutely adored watching you grow into the amazing young woman you became. If he had any lasting regrets, which would be very much unlike him, it would be that he didn't see you grow to become the adult, the parent and the amazing woman that you are. He would be proud of you. I know I am.

Hopefully I'll be well enough to see you and the family at Thanksgiving, at my age there aren't too many holidays left, but I hope to spend as many of them with you as I can. I hear your little sister may finally be joining us this year.

Love

Aunt Beth

P. S. My brother never understood why you loved those morning lines so much. I never told him the little secret you shared with me about them.

Dearest V

I read the draft of your book, and I can't blame you for holding me accountable. God knows I played my part. I wasn't 26 when I went to the Island, I was 22. My wife was 21. For both of us, this was our first job out of college. It seemed like such an amazing opportunity at the time.

I don't know if you remember Courtney Rogers from Bunk 22, but she and I shared the same birthday. Same day same month same year. We really weren't much older than the girls themselves, and we were in fact younger than some of the girls (some were as old as 24!).

To say that I was idealistic and in over my head would be a dramatic understatement, especially after Mr. S's death. I did the best I could, given my experience and abilities of the time. I really did believe that my leaving would only make things worse for all the girls, so I stayed longer than I should have.

It was almost 18 months to the day that I left the Island after you did. It was after those girls died, when it became clear that I could no longer even protect the girls in my own cabin, with a child of my own on the way, that I knew I could be of no more good in that place. As much as I hated what went on, I loved the kids I cared for. To this day, each and every one of them holds a special place in my heart. Including you and Jess and Jenna.

When I left the Island, I also left the church. It didn't take me long to find a new church, one that has been much more aligned with how I think children should be treated.

It's not an excuse, but hopefully it provides you a little bit of an explanation. Please know that if I had it to do over again, knowing what I know now, I would do it very differently and I will forever be sorry for what you girls went through.

I do not expect you or any other girl that lived on that island to forgive me. While I may have done my best at the time, the wisdom and experience of age has let me see just how badly I failed all of you. I should have done more, I should have stopped many of the things that went on and for all of that and more, I am so very sorry.

That is a burden I will bear for the rest of my life. So many of those things were done in the name of God, in the name of the church and I represented the church on the Island.

I hope the list of names helps you find the others. If there is ever anything I can do for you, for Jess, for Jenna, or for any other girl that lived on the Island I'm here for you.

Your servant in God,
Father Fred

Hey my little Chickee,

You make me out to be such a hero! I promise you I wasn't the hero you think I was. I scammed my way up to being Level 7 by telling them exactly what they wanted to hear and letting them see exactly what they wanted to see and blowing Brother Tim a lot. I didn't actually believe any of the bullshit they spouted, I just did what I had to.

I remember you being sent to Bunk 7 with Jess. That was a weird situation, even for the Island. I was in Bunk 11, I remember hearing your Bunk parents arguing about you and Jess a lot. Your house mother kept giving you tons of points so you didn't drop too low, while your bunk father kept taking them from you. I think everyone in the pod heard those fights! Older teens loved your bunk father, he was predictable and even fun. But he didn't like little kids, even fourteen-year-old' were babies as far as he was concerned. You and Jess were definitely a challenge for him!

I was actually there when your bunk mother had the maintenance guy urinate in Tamaras cheerios. Tamara was a Level 8 girl who was about to be promoted to Level 9. She had already passed all the tests and got voted in by council, she was going to receive her promotion that afternoon. She got dropped to Level 3. That was one of the biggest level drops any of us had ever seen, over 3 years of work vanished in that instant. She wasn't even court ordered; she would have gone home in 6 months if not for that incident. It definitely sent a message about Jess's food!

I don't know why you hero worshiped me, of all people, like you did, but I definitely took advantage of that card and played it quite a lot.

My house mother, Sister Paula, caught me blowing her husband. She put me on a starvation diet. I could eat raw once a day. She told me "learn to swallow because you will need those calories". Brother Tim said I did a better job when I was hungry and did nothing to help. I really hated him for that.

They didn't drop me any levels or take my domestic chore away because she said the starvation would do it for her. She even put me on trash in addition to flowers just so I would have to see the food scraps and know I couldn't eat them. Evil bitch.

I had been on that starvation diet for five days when I met you. I was doing flowers and I was wondering just how long it took to die from starvation. I smelled those crackers from 100 feet away. You two were so eager to share those crackers and I was willing to do almost anything to eat them. I remember some of them had cheese and some of them had peanut butter on them. That first week I conned you into sharing snacks with me every day.

Do you have any idea how much trouble I got in for that tin? Brother James whipped my ass just for giving you that tin out of the trash to make sandcastles with! Then I had to move a big pile of bricks. It took me five freaking days to move all those bricks. I had a whole 12 bricks to go when Mr. S came over to talk to me. I only got to keep my rank and keep my domestic chores because you two liked talking to me so much and I guess told him all about it.

Mr. S knew I was a con man, and he gave me a choice. I could be thrown down into the depths of hell in Bunk 22, or I could pull off the biggest con of my life and become the person who I had tricked you into thinking I was. Really wasn't much of a choice was it?

Mr. S then gave me extra hours every week just to spend talking with you two. At first I really hated having to become the person I conned you into believing I was, but after a while, I don't know, it just sort of became natural. I look back and I still wonder if that was his plan, or if he was just doing it for his little girl?

At first Mr. S restored one of my meals a day (dinner), but he let my house mother keep me eating raw one meal a day too. He said he would restore my other meals if I did well. He eventually restored all three of my meals, but he definitely made me work for that. But that was the Island.

All those family lunches you guys let me do with you really helped. I remember you went through that big kick on those MRE meals you so loved. You would eat half of one, Jess would eat a quarter of one and then I would eat mine and everything you two didn't eat. I never developed the love for MREs that you did, but I must say they were a lot better than eating raw or starving! I had to lie to my bunk parents about those – its why we could never do the picnics under the tree you wanted to do! That island was such a brutal place.

I remember you getting sick. I wasn't on trash duty, I was on my way to do the Tuesday check in chore that Mr. S assigned me. I thought I was going to be in serious trouble for you going down like you did! Brother Sam wasn't going to put me as the one staying with you guys, he only did it because you held on to me so tightly. I thought the staff were going to blow a gasket with how badly I kept that house while I was with you! But you were Mr. S's little girl, and that you were so determined to clean that house is the only reason I didn't get publicly whipped over that.

The part in your story about Nikki leaves out a very important detail. If you remember, I was the reason we broke Nikki. She and I were enemies before the Guardians ever existed, and I took that opportunity for revenge.

When Mr. S sent you into the house to take care of Jess when he got back, the rest of us got chewed out something else. The only reason all of us were not bounced out of the Guardians was because you went and tried to take responsibility like you did. You wouldn't let him blame any of the rest of us, you insisted that you take the blame and the consequences. We all got whipped, I distinctly remember you insisting on going first! But you were his little girl.

Think about it, on any given day you could choose to eat, sleep and shower with us or you could choose to go back to your own room, family meals and a home shower. You had uniforms in bunk and you had uniforms in your room. You could take things to laundry any time, where the rest of us could only take laundry once a week. But then you were also quick to share them and quick to sneak our dirty stuff in with your extra loads (I must say, we all really appreciated the clean underwear...).

You could skip duty if you wanted to (not that you ever did except for that one time to take care of Jess), none of the rest of us could do that. The rest of us were very jealous of you. But we were also thankful that we could hitch ourselves to your wagon. We really did do some incredible stuff, we really made a difference.

Then there was the whole falling on your sword thing. I can't even count the number of times you threw yourself on your sword for the rest of us. So while we all knew what the score was, we all knew the Guardians was just to give you your own little club, that you kept jumping into harm's way for the rest of us did a lot to make up for that. We all loved you, even if you were the Island princess.

It was a weird situation, but I guess it was less weird than the bunk situations we had before? I guess life is all relative isn't it? It was so much better than living in the normal bunks! That and you got really good at braiding all of our hair! I think you did the tightest braids of any of us.

Brother Sam and Mr. S didn't side with me on all those appeals, they sided with you. Did you ever wonder why we made sure you always represented the girl? Everyone on the Island knew that whoever you represented in the appeal was the one that was going to win. You were absolutely the Princess of the Island. The funny part is you never seemed to know that.

When we left... When we left the Island on that ship, we all immediately got seasick. None of us had ever been on the ocean before! Great start for a bunch of Navy recruits, isn't it? We were all still suffering from it when we started basic. That was fun. Most of us were in the same basic training together.

I enlisted and made my career as an NCO. I have a wife and we raised two kids from her previous marriage. I will retire next Summer and plan to move home to Oregon with my wife. I didn't have the level of help and support you got, none of us did. But we had each other, and you didn't have that. I still talk to some of the other girls.

We were all on that island for reasons, we were all lifers for reasons. They're all gonna be very excited to read your book. It's not often girls like us are made out to be the heroes.

Maybe we can get lunch? I'll bring the MREs.

~Ericka~

P. S. I still don't know why you went to Bunk 7. Bunk 7 was the Factory, it was a 15-24-year-old bunk, you should have gone to Bunk 5 with the little kids or at least Bunk 8. It made you both seem even younger than you were.

Hey short stuff!

I read your book and I love it! It's us, but it's not us. You changed just enough that I don't think anyone but a Guardian would ever be able to tell it was us. It amazes me how well you told our story, but still hid exactly who we are and what our program was, but I also understand why. I never would have thought to do that.

You wrote a whole book about us, you told some of our best stories. And yet you never once mentioned why any of us were sent to that Island. Not all of us deserved to be on the Island, but you know I earned my spot in that place, and I thank you for not making me famous for it. It took a long time to put all of that behind me.

Boy, did you ever soft-peddle the violence and inhumanity we all went through, especially the shit they did to us before Mr. S came. Do you remember the first time we met? It was that time Brother Mark caged you and Jess after he forced her to drink all that water and then she wet the bed. Sister Mary and Sister Kendra (my bunk mother) had such a conniption fit when they found out Brother Mark caged you two over that.

Sister Kendra assigned me to watch over you two while they got the key from Brother Mark, but they found Brother Mark while I was still with them. It was the first and only time I ever saw staff members come to blows like that over a student. Were they ever *pissed that he caged you and Jess for wetting the bed! The staff fights over Jess were epic, especially as staff never fought over students on our side of the fence line, except over Jess.*

The things you didn't mention stand out to me far more than any of the stories you did tell. Not even a single mention of the "special groups" and the even more special "counseling sessions" we were put through, you know exactly the ones I mean. No mention of Brother Jonathan lashing girls to that post at the anthill. No mention of the rats. No discussion on the foot fungus and what that did to us all. No mention of the constant yeast infections and begging the Wilderness guy to make that itchy powder to kill the yeast infections because they didn't believe in Monistat. I'm still not sure that stuff was sanitary, but at least it worked.

But of everything you didn't mention, the one that stands out to me more than any other is the ages of the missionary Brothers and Sisters. Most maintenance staff were eighteen to twenty. Most bunk parents were early twenties or even late teens. I know Brother Mark was only nineteen when he became a bunk parent and like twenty-two when you were in his group. How fucked up is it that they routinely put kids barely older than the girls they were supervising (or sometimes younger) in positions of such power over us? Even the head bunk parents were usually only in their late twenties. And yet, despite not having any form of contraception, I can't think of any girl that got preggos because of it. I think only the farm manager, the head maintenance guy, the boiler guy, head office staff, and a handful of others were over thirty-five.

Do you remember how we first became friends when you started doing classes with us? I was trying to level up and since it was always a good idea to make as many upper-level friends as possible, I really wanted to become your friend. I figured you had to be some crazy super-high level if they didn't even give you points! Boy was I wrong! I was in such shock when you were not at that peer council, and I barely lost the vote! Then, a few days later, we cleaned up after that party, and then Mr. S recruited me for the Guardians.

You never talked about how Mr. S recruited every Guardian for specific reasons. With me, he was specifically looking for a real fighter. It should have been Kayla from Bunk 4, she was a higher level and a bit better of a fighter than me, but I guess us being friends tipped the scales in my favor. He said I had a personal stake in it that no one else did, and that was you.

Jess was such a difficult child when she was 4. I worked so hard to get her to like me. You know she only liked me because I was your best friend. When we went on that adventure to the maintenance shed, we got what we needed and she b-lined it back to you as fast as her feet would carry her. When we were on ops, whatever group had her to work with had a really hard time! For the longest time, she either wouldn't talk to them, or just screamed your name! Every other team had so much trouble taking care of her that first year, though Jenna made it a lot better, at least she could translate!

At some point, you and I have to talk about the Nikki fight. Part of my job was to protect you. I really didn't want to walk into that fight, I knew full well that we had no chance of winning it with only three of us! But you two went in with such a head of steam, there was no stopping you. I broke my nose in that fight! But I also regret what we did to her afterward, especially the things you left out of the story, you know, channeling the inner Sister Jean thing we did.

Becoming your friend may have been a strategic move, but honestly, you were the best friend I ever had as a kid. You were the only one on the Island I could share my secrets with that I knew couldn't be made to turn on me. I could trust you when I couldn't really trust anyone else. I think that's what kept me from going insane. And then we had those MRE peanut butter and sugar packets and even those deserts that you kept sneaking to me at the end of class. Those are good memories.

I think that's the thing, most of my best memories from the Island involved you. The goofy radio calls we made. The silly songs we sang in Bunk 1. The hand games. Drawing in the mud. The water fights when we had to drain the standing water. Swimming at the beach. Suntanning! All of my best teenage memories, all of the ones I really cherish involved you.

I almost didn't leave with the others. I came so close to staying with you. Ultimately, I think my leaving was the right thing, especially seeing what happened after I left. But I always regretted leaving you behind. I am glad you made it like you did. I may not have reached your level, but I have managed to raise my kids to be the best people they could be. And to treat everyone like they are humans.

I really appreciate you and Jess paying for me and my kids to come to the reunion. I'm doing alright as a single mom, but we couldn't have swung this trip on our own. It's going to be the first out-of-state vacation my kids and I have ever taken. I guess Father Fred has a family that we will stay with for it. They even have pool for the kids to swim in. It's so unreal that this is going to happen. I can't wait for you to meet my kids; my eldest's middle name is Vanessa. She goes by "V" too.

See you in two weeks.
>   Forever your best friend
>   (even if you still look 12!),

Tonya

What happened to the others?

While we were not able to track down everyone from the Island, we did locate most of the Guardians and others that played a major part in this book. Here is what we know as of 2022:

Guardians and Girls:

Adrian, the girl who pulled 75 stumps in two days, stayed on the Island until it closed. She works as an IV nurse at a hospital in California and struggles with relationships. She is still a member of the church.

Alex, the girl who moved the mountain, stayed on the Island until it closed, what happened to her after that is unknown.

Betty works as a manager at a retail establishment along with her husband. They have a son in college. *(Guardian, Orange Team)*

Brittany is married and is now a stay-at-home mom with 2 kids. *(Guardian, Red Team)*

Christi did 1 tour with the Navy, she now works in Iowa as a waitress. *(Guardian, Green Team Sargent)*

Debbie, from Bunk 7, timed out while I was living with Dad and isolated. What happened to her after that is unknown.

Emma, the girl we rescued from Bunk 22, went to college for art, she works in the art field making stained glass. She is still a member of the church.

Ericka made a career as an NCO in the Navy. She is about to retire with her wife of 15 years and is working on her own book. (*Guardians Captain*)

Ginny, the girl who punched me in the face and got away with it, graduated as a Level 10 a year after I left. She now works in medical billing and is a member of the church.

Gretta, from Bunk 7, left with the other upper level older girls to join the Navy. She did one tour and went on to work in electronics.

Jenna, who shared a room with Jess in Mr. S's house, now works as an Uber driver.

Jennifer did 1 tour with the Navy. She is now working in retail and has struggled with drug addiction. *(Guardian, Green Team)*

Jess and I have reconnected. We live only a few miles apart and spend as much time together as we can. How often do you find your long-lost little sister?

Julie stayed on the Island until it closed. She committed suicide 2 years after getting home. *(Guardian, Purple Team)*

Kat is struggling with drug addiction. She is homeless on the streets of LA. Jess and I hope to get her into rehab soon. *(Guardian, Blue Team)*

Kate, the Guardian that got to go home early, did one tour in the Navy. She works for a defense contractor, has 2 teenagers, 1 of whom went through 9 months in a Wilderness TTI program..

Laura graduated from college and now, teaches Phys Ed and coaches a girls' track team. She is still a member of the church. *(Guardian, Orange Team)*

Marci, Jenna's older sister, along with several other girls, died on the Island. Her cause of death is unknown. *(Guardian, Orange Team)*

Mary, the Bunk 14 girl who was Miss Rawlings's first sexual victim on the Island, stayed on the Island until it closed. She now works in retail.

Maxine stayed on the Island until it closed. She has spent her life in and out of psychiatric institutions and currently lives on the streets of New York City. *(Guardian, Purple Team)*

Meghan works in the adult entertainment field. *(Guardian, Blue Team)*

Michelle did 2 tours in the Navy and got her degree. She now works in mechanical engineering. *(Guardian, Blue Team Sergeant)*

Molly, aka Superman, was eventually diagnosed with a seizure disorder at the hospital on the mainland and was sent to a long-term hospital placement. She is now seizure free and works managing rental properties.

Nancy did 1 tour with the Navy; she currently works for a pest control company in Oklahoma. She is still a member of the church. *(Guardian, Red Team)*

Nikki, the girl we Guardians broke, is currently serving 25 to life in prison. She and Ericka now talk regularly.

Paula is currently serving life in prison. *(Guardian, Red Team)*

Rory "Bad News from Bunk 22" is currently serving 15 years in prison. She has 3 daughters in foster care. We made sure they got a good Christmas this year, and we will continue to support them.

Sarah received a Dishonorable discharge for violating Don't Ask/Don't Tell. She is recovering from drug addiction and with Jess' help, is now in a stable living and working situation. *(Guardian, Green Team)*

Sasha was Honorably discharged from the Navy. She died of a drug overdose. *(Guardian, Green Team)*

Susan is married with 2 children. She works in IT in Seattle. *(Guardian, Blue Team)*

Shawn served as an NCO in the Navy. She died of complications from meningitis just shy of completing her 20 years. *(Guardian, Orange Team Sergeant)*

Tonya received an Honorable discharge from the Navy. She is a single mother with three kids. She supports her family with an OnlyFans site. While we are not interested in the content, both Jess and I are top-tier subscribers – after all, that's what best friends are for. *(Guardian, Purple Team Sergeant)*

Tori received an Honorable discharge from the Navy. She struggled with drug addiction and committed suicide at age 26. *(Guardian, Blue Team)*

Staff:

Brother Sam worked for a construction company until he died of natural causes.

Brother Mark was 23 when he completed his four-year missionary assignment and left the Island. He worked in 1 other TTI program where he met his wife. They now own a ranch in Texas where they live with their 3 children. He is no longer part of the Church and does not work in the TTI. Recently, he has advocated against the TTI.

Sister Mary left the Island as part of the Great Resignation. She now owns a small restaurant in Delaware with her sister. She has a daughter that spent time in a TTI program and is still a member of the Church. Mary still employs a few of the girls from the Island who worked in Chow Hut with her.

Sister Jean is still a counselor with the Church. She still works with teenage girls.

Father Fred and Sister Denise are still happily married and live on the West Coast, where they raised 3 children and still run a small congregation of a different Christian church. They even hosted our reunion and administer the fund we set up to help support those of us that went to the Island. Most of the authors royalties from the sale of this book goes to that fund.

Sister Lisa left the Island shortly after the sergeants did as part of the *great resignation*. She now works for a law firm and is still a member of the church.

Brother Joe, the maintenance guy who took Molly under his wing, left the Island as part of the Great Resignation. He lives in California with his wife, two daughters and his little sister, who has Downs Syndrome and epilepsy. He and Molly are still in contact with each other, and he is still a member of the church.

Sergeant "Uncle Matt" Richards has retired for a second time and lives a mile from me. He enjoys fishing and spending time with his two grand-nieces.

Sergeant Davis recently retired from a private defense contracting firm. He still takes in foster teens and plans to do so until the day he dies.

Sergeant Mitchel works for a defense contractor and does volunteer work with teenagers through the Boy Scouts of America's Exploring program.

Sergeant Mackey reconnected with his own daughter after leaving the Island. He now lives with her and his two grandchildren and a soon-to-be first great-grandchild.

Sergeant Duplessie retired to upstate New York, where he tinkers with old cars and tractors.

Sergeant James taught at a college in Asia until he passed away from natural causes. He is survived by his third wife and a son from his first marriage.

Miss Rawlings is married and has 3 children and 2 grandchildren. She has semi-retired, but still works for the Church part-time in its educational mission. Her specialty is fundraising.

This is not the end of our story; we now have a new beginning. Because of the work on this book, in 2022, Jess and I were able to bring Adrian, Betty, Brittany, Christi, Emma, Erica, Ginny, Jenna, Jennifer, Kat, Kate, Laura, Mary, Meghan, Michelle, Molly, Nancy, Sarah, Susan, Tonya, Aunt Beth, Sergeant "Uncle Matt" Richards, Sergeant Davis, Sergeant Mitchel, Sergeant Mackey, and Sergeant Duplessie and some of the others, as well as many of their families together for a reunion hosted at Father Fred's church. We even got Paula on video for some of it.

Reuniting the remaining Guardians, as well as some of the others to share memories, rekindle old friendships, and mourn those we have lost, was an experience unlike any other.

We are now all supporting each other however we can. Our group text is crazy. Those of us who are doing well are now helping those still struggling. Father Fred even arranged a therapist that does group therapy for all of us via Zoom. She went to a troubled teen program herself and she is the first therapist I've ever met who actually understands.

We all went through hell together and in a special way, that makes us family. And family really is everything.

Come hell or high water, we will stick together for the rest of our lives. After all, we've already been through hell together, high water should be a breeze!

Chapter 14: Afterthoughts

The following questions were submitted to me by various readers and reviewers, most of whom survived their own time in various Troubled Teen programs.

Q. Why don't you name the program?

The short answer is that we don't want to get sued by the church group that used to run it. Also, it is a cult and its members have committed significant acts of violence against its detractors in the past. It's just not worth the risk to those involved.

Q. Was this island off Mexico?

Maybe, maybe not. We took great care to change every name, date, title, and anything else we thought could possibly give away my true identity, the identity of any individual the book talks about, or the identity of the church that once ran this program. And no, UT Austin wasn't even the school I went to. What matters is my story, which is here.

Q. The pictures in the book are haunting. Where did the pictures come from?

Sam's hobby was photography. He brought an album of photos back when we left, and I inherited it.

Q. Looking back now, what do you think your life would look like if you didn't go? Would you like who you are if you didn't go? Would you go back and do it over again?

I certainly hope I wouldn't go back and do it over again. But I have a lifetime of experience behind me now that I didn't then.

As to what my life might look like if I didn't go? That's a really tough question. There's just no good way to answer this question. I can tell you I didn't like who I was when I was drinking and drunk all the time. I didn't like how lost I was and how out of control I was. I can tell you that I absolutely needed help. I needed to be off the booze, and I needed someone to get control of me. If I didn't get help, I likely would have ended up in a really bad place. But I think rehab would have been a better solution. I think with an in-patient rehab, I could have gotten what I needed without the abuse.

On the other hand, I don't know what path my life would have taken had I stayed home with my aunt. Maybe it would have been better, maybe not. But then I would never have met my adopted family: my little sister Jess, my Dad, my Aunt Beth, or my Uncle Matt. I never would have done the things I did with the Guardians. I wouldn't have done NROTC, met my husband, or had my daughters. I can't change the past; my experiences are what they are. I can choose to embrace my history, or I can reject it. What good is rejecting it?

Q. Power corrupts, any way around that?

I believe the old saying is power corrupts and absolute power corrupts absolutely. I think there's a lot of truth to that.

The only counter you have to absolute power is accountability. On the Island, staff was accountable to no one until Dad (Mr. S) was there. My understanding is that many of these troubled teen programs today have almost the same lack of accountability.

Q. What were your feelings on teaching the commands at intake?

There wasn't a lot to feel about it. The commands were integrated into everything we did, the new girls had to know them, it wasn't like it was a choice. It's not like there was a moral choice to be made. The commands were the accepted norm. After my first month or so on the Island, I just accepted them; I never really thought about them as anything but normal until I was in college.

Q. How did you feel about the strip command?

When I first got to the Island, it felt dehumanizing. But when you're given that command every day, and for so many different reasons, you come to accept it as just normal. When I went through intake the second time, I remember thinking that these girls should just get over it. I remember a conversation I had with one girl where I told her that the sooner she accepts in her own head that it's OK for everyone to see her naked, the easier it will be for her. It was just the expected norm.

Q. You talked about girls being returned to intake to start the process over again. Was this ever a positive?

Not very often, although I can think of a few times girls used it to reinvent themselves. Most of the time, it just made girls bitter. The thing is, as a kid with problems, you sometimes really need to be able to reinvent yourself. I got to do that twice on the Island, first when I moved in with Dad, then again as a Guardian. That's one thing I wish the Island did better, giving people more chances to reinvent themselves.

Q. How do you feel about groups now?

I really don't know how to feel about them. Most of the groups I went through were straight-up abuse. They were run by people who had no idea what they were doing, or worse, they were run by people who were out for their own entertainment. Even the groups that came after Dad made major changes didn't seem to really help anybody.

Everything's relative and they were a lot better after Dad's changes than what came before, but I don't know that they actually helped anything. I've heard about many groups in other troubled teen programs that are just as psychologically abusive as what I went through. But then I've also heard about some that made major differences in kids. So, at the end of the day, I don't know what to think.

Q. How did they keep you from revolting against them?

When I was in bunk, they kept us all suspicious of each other. The lower-level girls knew the upper-level girls tattled on them. The upper-level girls were trained to be suspicious of the lower-level girls. And we all knew everyone could be made to turn on you at any time.

By and large, until Dad changed the level system, the upper-level girls had to play their own, really nasty politics to stay at the upper level. It kept us from being able to form the trusting relationships you would have needed to form a real rebellion. While some of that changed under Dad's rule, outside of the Guardians, you never really got to that level of trust with each other. I think that was by design.

Q. You said that girls were required to report other girls, but you also talked about not being a rat. Can you expand on that?

That was always so very complicated. Basically, tattling on a girl that was on a level above you was being a rat. Tattling on something the whole group did was being a rat. But you had to report on lower-level girls, so that wasn't being a rat.

Q. Can you talk about "upping the pressure"?

You learned very fast to do what you were told. They had so many ways of punishing you, they had so many ways of breaking you that your only choice was to do as you're told. Where a lot of places will go from asking to telling to ordering, here it went from telling you to ordering you to torturing you. And the levels of torture they could inflict was just off the charts.

Q. Can you talk about muting and shunning?

Muting and shunning, fun times! When I was in Bunk 7, I would get muted by Brother Mark a lot. Brother Mark liked to mute girls. Muting is one of those things that I think every parent thinks they can relate to, but not really. As a parent, sometimes you just need those 10 minutes of silence from your children. This wasn't that.

When I was in Bunk 7, my house mother wouldn't let me stay muted for very long because if I was muted, I couldn't take care of Jess, and then other people would have to. She really didn't want to, so I never stayed muted for more than an hour or so.

Other girls in bunk were muted a lot more than I was, sometimes for days or even weeks at a time. I remember Brother Mark muted one girl for an entire month. That was brutal. As Guardians we had to make sure muting was limited to no more than a few days and shunning no more than two weeks.

When you're muted, you're not allowed to make a sound, and you're not allowed to have any other communication with anybody. You're not allowed to make facial gestures, you're not allowed to make hand gestures, you're not allowed to communicate in any way.

It doesn't take very long for that to start to eat at you. The longer you're muted for, the more insidious punishment this is. Shunning is worse than muting. When you're muted you can't communicate with anybody, but the higher-level girls can still talk to you. When you're shunned, you're not allowed to communicate and everybody else pretends you don't exist, unless they're punishing you. Just like with muting the longer this goes on the more psychologically damaging it is. At the end of two weeks of being shunned, you're willing to do or say damn near anything just for some basic social interaction.

Q. That 80,000-pound rock story sounds insane. Did no adult try and stop you?

My first co-author, who has an engineering background, had heart attacks every time we talked about this story. In our sessions, he would ask questions but never really voiced any kind of opinion, it's what made our process work. But this bothered him so much that we actually had to have a special session where he outlined to me every possible way it could have gone wrong and asked if we did this or if we did that.

He did the math on all the forces, including what would have happened if the rock fell over with the girls attached. He even showed me things like braking systems we could have used and like a million ways it could have been done safer.

I learned more from that session than I did in the rigging and hoisting class I got with the Guardians. But we were teenagers just figuring it out. The only adult that really knew anything was the maintenance guy, and he really didn't know much more than us. All I can say is, we got lucky with that one!

We also got lucky with the beach! They didn't use the beach because of rip tides. But I didn't learn that until we were training swimming and diving with the sergeants and learned about it from them.

Q. Are you still in contact with Tony and his mother?

I've never spoken to either of them again after they left the Island. I know Beth doesn't speak to them either because of what happened on the Island and the fight over Dad's grave. Part of me thinks that it would have been good for Jess and me to have spent time with them and Dad. We never formed that bond that we did with Beth. But no, we have never had contact again.

Q. How did the other girls on the Island feel about the Guardians?

Some of the girls had very mixed feelings, that's for sure! We had privileges and powers that they didn't have and mostly couldn't earn. So, there was obviously some jealousy over that.

But they also understood that our mandate was to help them. They understood that the only avenue of appeal was through us. They knew that if they were put on a starvation diet, we would put a stop to it. They knew that, for a lot of things, we were the only ones that could or would defend them. If they were muted or shunned, which could last anywhere from a few hours to a few weeks, they could still talk to us, and we would talk to them. If they were having a problem, if they were being bullied, it was our job to listen and help.

But we were also substitutes, it was often our job to oversee chores, it was often our job to bring girls in for office punishments, and other stuff like that. It made for some very complicated relationships.

Q. What habits did you collect from the Island Do you still ration water?

I collected an awful lot of habits on that island. Some good some bad. I still square my shoulders and suck in my gut before I walk through any door. I still make my bed exactly the same way. I still do the same thing with my socks and shoes. I still look at a plate of food in terms of what I can hide in my shirt and save for later. I still snap to attention when it's called. I still find myself saying some of those mantras. I still look for permission a lot. I still always keep MREs at hand (don't look in the trunk of my car). I still sleep in the nude. I still make rubbing stones. And yes, I still ration water. Many of those habits you learn when you are young stay with you for the rest of your life.

Q. What is your relationship with food? How did the meal level system impact your relationship with food?

I think I'm in better shape than most with this. While I lived with Dad, I had enough to eat. My meals were not constantly being watched And I had free access to the kitchen. So while even today I have an irrational need to keep a stash of food, I don't have many of the food problems everybody else from the TTI does. For example, I don't dissect my food to make it last longer, like a lot of girls on the Island did.

When I left the Island, I did take some cooking classes. Those definitely helped me learn to prepare meals for just myself.

Q. What are your thoughts on basic needs as privileges? How does that affect you today?

That's a very complicated question. Our basic needs are air, food, shelter, and water. Everything else is cultural. For example, I know families that happily live in nudist camps. They don't have the same views on privacy most others do. If you've ever known competitive swimmers, they don't think twice about a group shower. There are cultures today where kids must work hard to earn a meal.

It's all cultural, and it's all relative. We live in a culture where, generally speaking, you don't have to earn every little thing we think of as making you human. But I don't think sticking teenagers in a culture where you have to earn every little thing is actually helpful to anybody. It doesn't prepare you to live as a citizen in the United States of America.

Q. As a survivor of a Troubled Teen program myself, I am familiar with the concept of punishment as protection. Can you talk about that?

I didn't understand it at the time, but looking back, it's obvious how much it happened. In Bunk 7, I think Mark kept me on Level 2/3 for long so that I had to stay in his eyesight, and I think that was in part to protect me. Likewise, I think him whipping me in the mornings when I was babysitting was done in part to keep the rest of Bunk 7 from killing me. Dad having me publicly whipped was absolutely punishing me to protect me. Had he not done that, I don't think I could have even gone back to the classes, let alone as a Guardian.

As a Guardian, it was a tactic we used. Many times, we took a kid out of routine to do a punishment chore instead of letting them get eaten alive in bunk. Ginny is a perfect example of that.

Q. You said in the book you got 7 spankings, but you only talk about two of them. What were the others?

Mostly when I screwed up big as a Guardian. Nikki and the Great Shit Storm, obviously. I got one when we didn't take proper care of the horses and one got out - absolutely my fault. I got one for getting into a fistfight with Julie (we both got tanned for that one) and I got one because I was being a "red bitch" to Dad. Not for the red part, but because I wouldn't stop going at him about the tablecloth, even after like 100 warnings and even some wall time. Stupid, right? I got one for lying to Dad to protect Blue team, and I got one for telling Dad to go fuck himself. If I didn't use the word "fuck", it would have only been 6; he had a thing about appropriate language and I knew it at the time, but I was fifteen, I tested the limits and paid the price for it.

Q. That part about you planning out the destruction of the Island was intense. Can you talk about that?

I was heading off the deep end, that's for sure. At that point in time, I was an angry teenager and figured I was going back to die. And if I was going back to die anyways, I was going to take as much of the program with me as I could.

My irrational plan was to get the handgun from Bunk 16, then fight my way to the equipment hide, hopefully, with Marci, Jess, Jenna, and any of the other real Guardians I could find in tow. From there, I knew exactly where I was going to set up my first position to take out the boiler and its generator, cutting off all electricity. I knew where I was going to set charges to blow the water tank and water line.

I knew where I was going to set up to take out the radio and sat phone antenna. I knew a few bullets to the plane's engines would permanently ground it. And I knew if I no longer cared about collateral damage, we could stay in the hills and take out the staff from a mile away. But I am glad I didn't do that. Looking back, it would have doomed me, and all the girls, to a horrible death at the hands of government troops, who would have come in to quell the insurrection.

Q. Does it ever get better? Do you ever stop having nightmares?

The nightmares do stop, or at least they'll slow down a lot. It's the emotional pieces that stick with you. For me, they really started slowing down after I moved in with the man that is now my husband. He provided me with both structure and a safety net that allowed me to stop worrying so much. But I still occasionally have those nightmares.

Q. Can you talk about why the structure your then-boyfriend provided helped you worry less?

I was so used to having an authority figure give me the rules and structure that I couldn't provide it on my own. By and large, I still can't. While there were (and still are) rules he will punish me for breaking, by and large just having those rules to follow lets me handle a lot more of my own stuff than I could without them.

Q. Is this a kinky relationship? What part does that play?

Well, that's a can of worms! There are definitely significant power dynamics present in my relationship with my husband. My whole life I have felt a lot more comfortable in relationships with a very clear power dynamic. When I was in college, I did a lot better in classes where the teacher was an alpha personality. Those kinds of clear power dynamics are just far more comfortable to me.

Most of those I know who grew up in the troubled teen industry have the same preference for clear power dynamics. I think it's just easier for us, I think it's closer to what we're used to. I know more than a few people from the troubled teen industry who are very much attracted to kink because that's where these power dynamics are usually acceptable.

I wouldn't say all, but a very high percentage of those I know who came out of the troubled teen industry came out with significant fetishes revolving around power and control. Every single one of those can be traced back to a specific event or a series of specific events they suffered in the troubled teen industry.

Q. Do the commands still affect you today?

Yes, they do. If somebody I view is an authority figure, or even just somebody with a very authoritative tone of voice, was to tell me to mute, watch a wall, strip, nose-tits-n-toes, or just about any other island command, I go into a kind of autopilot where I automatically do the command without hesitation. When that happens, I can't even stop myself from following the command, it's that ingrained into me.

Q. So you feel you need to be "punished"?

Not exactly. But 'sometimes? It's more like, even if I don't know what I did to get in trouble, when I'm given a command, at least I know what I need to do not to get in more trouble and to have a path towards getting out of trouble.

When you grow up expecting serious punishments for everything, when you don't get them, it does kind of screw with your head. You end up punishing yourself and that's not ever healthy.

The other part to this is that if I'm in trouble, to this day I would rather take the punishment and have it over with than let it drag on, then let that person who has authority over me continue to be angry with me.

Q. Is this a common issue for those that have been through the troubled teen industry?

I am not an expert on this, but from the people I know who have been through the TTI, it is one of many common problems. I have talked about some of them already, but other problems commonly faced by those coming out of the TTI include:

- The need to be given permission and or rules.
- The persistent reaction to commands from the program.
- Issues with abnormal peer interaction, specifically due to learned behaviors.
- A much higher need for authority to be involved in social situations.
- Issues involved in trusting peers.
- Not understanding what they did to get in trouble but needing to have a path not to get in more.
- Food security issues.
- A whole litany of social skill deficiencies.

And yes, most find at least part of what they are looking for in the kink community. Who would have thought that TTI is a pipeline to kink, but it definitely is.

Q. How do you come to be grateful for something you hate, how do you deal with that?

I once had a very special teacher (hi Steven!) who famously told me that, taken in isolation, everything in this world is black and white. It's only when you mix them that you get shades of grey. But those shades of grey are where the most interesting things are.

When it comes to my time on the Island, there are definitely things I am grateful for, and definitely, things I hate. But when I look closely, the things I am grateful for and the things that I hate are not the same things.

I'm very thankful for some of the people I met. I'm not thankful for the beatings I took in Bunk 7. I'm thankful for all those storytimes I got sitting on Dad's lap. I'm not thankful for the psychological abuse of the groups I was in Bunk 7.

I'm thankful that Brother Mark protected Jess when he was at the groups. I'm not thankful for how he always blamed and punished me for Jess's potty accidents and parade meltdowns.

Here is an even more complex one: I am thankful that Brother Mark had a standard and never played sexually with the bodies of any girl sixteen and younger. I hate the fact that I was never chosen for that, that I was never good enough.

I think the trick is that it's OK to be thankful for the things that helped you, and it's OK to hate the things that hurt you. Even when those come from the same person or are the same thing.

Q. What was your aunt told? What did she know?

She was straight up lied to. She got these progress reports from the church that had nothing to do with life on the Island. I don't think the person writing them ever even saw the Island. The letters Jess's parents got were even less connected to reality than what my aunt got.

Jess's progress reports talked about her sailing and playing Polo!

Q. Were you scared of the real world?

When I was in Bunk 7, they constantly drilled into us that nobody outside the Island would ever understand us. They drilled it into us that nobody else would ever accept us.

Dad drilled into us the opposite, but most of the rest of the school still drilled into us that we were the outcasts. Mrs. Rawlings's message was the same as when I lived in Bunk 7, that none of us would survive without them.

The thought of the outside world both excited me and terrified me. I got such mixed messages I really didn't know what to expect. I think had I lived all those years in Bunk 7, I don't think I could have functioned in the world outside of the Island.

Q. Father Fred's letter said you were holding him accountable. But I don't see that in the book. What was that about?

In an early version of the book, the one he read, the letters from home section was made up of snippets of letters between Aunt Beth and me. One of those discussed how I resented Father Fred for not protecting all of us from Miss Rawlings but was also that I was thankful that he protected Jess and Jenna.

Part of me will always resent him for that, just like part of me will always be grateful he protected Jess and

Jenna, but reading his letter, it's harder, more complicated than I thought it was when I was seventeen.

Before you ask, we changed that section of the book when we found Jess and before we got the letter from Father Fred (we got the list of names from him seven weeks before we got the letter). Once Jess's letter was put in, the back and forth between Aunt Beth and I no longer fit and we went with all the other letters; we didn't change it for Father Fred.

Q. You seem to have "made it" in a way that's fairly rare for those from the troubled teen industry. How is it that you're able to function like you're not a kid that grew up in a gulag?

What makes you think I wasn't that kid? Did you read the part about my college physics class? What normal person thinks of yoked girls as a unit of measurement?

For a lot of my life, I was the outcast who grew up in a gulag. I was the social outcast. It was a lot easier to be with older people, though I can see now that it's because they made up for and bridged over my social deficiencies.

I was accepted in military circles because I had skills and followed orders. I was accepted in my job as a computer programmer because, at the time, so few people did what I found fascinating. Where I work accepted my lack of social skills as part of the trade for my getting done what I got done. But they hired a lot of us brainiacs with no social skills back then. Much less so today. I did find social skills classes helped a lot.

Q. The part about the physics of yoked girls, where did your numbers come from?

Experience! But my co-author actually was able to find numbers on this. The average teenage girl on the Island weighed 125lbs. Turns out that the average 125lbs girl can generate about 100lbs of pulling force for a short duration, about 65lbs ongoing, but that will wear them out fast. So, my numbers were spot on. On a cart, it could be moved a little by just 6 girls, and that's with the added weight of the cart!

Q. What advice would you give to a parent thinking of sending a child to a troubled teen program?

I have such mixed feelings about this. First, I am not an expert on selecting a program for your teenager that's going through a tough time. So, I can only share my thoughts with you.

On the one hand, I absolutely understand the need to find help. And I absolutely understand how few programs seem to offer any help, or more importantly any hope. So, I completely get the allure of these programs.

I, myself absolutely needed help to get off the booze, and twelve-year-old me absolutely needed somebody to get control of me. But where I went had far too much power over me. They literally had the power of life and death, and that's too much power.

Q. Can you talk about power issues in the TTI?

One of the big lessons I learned from Dad was that with power must come accountability. If you're looking at a program to help deal with issues you can't deal with, you really must think about and address the power issue. These places have so much power, you really must make sure the accountability is there. So, the first question I would ask is how they are held accountable?

Q. Can you talk about accountability in TTI programs?

If you are looking for a program, look locally. Find someplace that you can drive to, someplace where you can go and visit them whenever you choose to. And then make sure you visit them often. That's part of accountability.

Any way you cut it, you need to make sure the accountability is there. Some of that is licensing. Some of that is accountability through the parents. Some of that is having an office of civil rights or comparable office for investigating and dealing with complaints. Youth residents should have unrestricted 24-hour access to at least leave a message regarding abuse complaints. Parents or other representatives should be informed of these complaints at the outset of the investigation before staff is contacted about them.

And yes, some kids are going to abuse it. Sometimes you're going to have to take away the right to complain. That is sometimes part of life dealing with drug addiction and some of the other issues teenagers go through. But that's sometimes, it's definitely not anything approaching 100% of the time.

You also must realize that trends matter. If you get a dozen people complaining of the same staff person doing the same thing over a long period of time, chances are even if more than a few of the kids have truth-telling issues, you have a serious problem on your hands. So, make certain any place you send your child has this kind of a system of accountability in place. It's required of any mental health facility, and these places should be no different.

Some of that is making sure they are held accountable through their insurance policies. Ask to see their insurance policies. Ask to see what their insurance companies require them to do. If they are insured by a surplus lines carrier, like the Prime Insurance Syndicate (ISERA) or K and K insurance, it's a red flag. It means they couldn't get insurance from admitted marketplaces that specialize in insuring residential schools or medical programs and that says something (and not in a good way).

Ask to see their risk management plans. Ask to see their contingency plans. Ask to see what their insurance company requires in terms of reporting and accountability.

Q. Can you talk about communications restrictions in the TTI?

Before sending any child to one of these places, I think it's important to look at the communications restrictions they start with. "Phone calls are from 6:30 till bedtime" may be reasonable. "You have to earn a call home" is not ever reasonable.

Likewise, If they're censoring mail, or if they're monitoring your phone calls, those are probably the biggest red flags I see, as it directly limits what's probably the biggest source of oversight and accountability these places have—the parents.

If you are a parent with a kid in one of these programs, have a code word you can use to know if you have a problem. If you have a kid in a program and don't have a code word, on your next call, ask outright if the call is being monitored. If they say yes or if you get disconnected, you have a serious problem and go get the kid out right now.

Q. Can you talk about trust in the TTI?

That's a big topic. First, everyone lies to some degree. It's human nature. But by and large, teenagers will tell you the truth as they see it unless they have a reason not to, and that reason is usually that they don't trust you with whatever is going on.

If you have never really had an issue with your child lying to you, but these programs tell you to expect them to lie to you from the start, well that doesn't really track logically, and you need to think about who the one that's lying is. If your child doesn't have a history of lying to you, chances are they're not going to start now. Be especially wary of any program that tells you to expect your child to start lying to you.

Q. Can you talk more about earning basic communications?

This is common in the TTI, but it's not healthy. If the program requires children to initially "earn" the right to have normal social interactions, such as needing to be at a certain level in the program in order to have basic conversations with their peers, it's a program I would take my child out of right now if I were you.

Q. Can you talk about fear, shame, and humiliation in the TTI?

These were used a lot on the Island. We were always afraid of being punished. On the Island, shame and humiliation were used daily to control kids. This really screws you up, especially over the long term.

You must understand that fear, shame, humiliation, and feelings of intimidation are normal for teenagers. My teenagers are humiliated if I sing in the car, so you will never not have it present. On the Island, humiliation, fear, and intimidation were used all the time. It wasn't right then, and it isn't right now. Programs should never use it as a primary means of controlling kids. It should not be used as part of their behavioral modification practices.

Q. Can you talk about developing autonomy in these programs?

The teen years are all about developing autonomy, yet the way most TTI programs work, including the Island, is to take that completely away. If it wasn't for the Guardians, I don't know if I would have developed the autonomy I did. I can tell you that most girls on the Island never developed it at all.

As to programs today, maybe they have reason to do it, cultural shock can be an effective means of change. OK, fine, but even assuming they do have a valid reason to take it away to start with, what's the plan to help the kid develop normal teenage autonomy after breaking the old habits? This is something you really need to ask about. If they don't have a plan, and I mean a really good one, then it's going to royally screw up the kid.

The other issue you need to be aware of with these programs is known as social dwarfism. These places force weird versions of social skills on kids that really screw kids up in the long term.

For example, most TTI's (including the Island) teach 'I feel' statements as an attack, and not as a framework for resolution. When kids coming out of the TTI try to use these weird versions of the social skills they were taught, it alienates those closest to them, further isolating them and compounding the problems.

It wasn't until I was in my 30's and was accidentally put in a social skills class for middle schoolers that I learned how to fix these (not the teacher's fault, it was my first day, I was almost 2 hours early, I looked the part, Steven was expecting a new student and I didn't object…). That class was actually one of the best things ever to happen to me after the Island. I even paid another student $300 for her copy of the class packet and all of the magical social scripts it contained. Those made a major difference in my life.

Right along with this is culture. Is the program actually preparing your child to rejoin the culture of our country? If they are only preparing them for the whacked-out culture of their program (like was the case on the Island), then the program isn't doing them a service, and you really need to look someplace else.

Ask yourself how well you would function in that place, ask yourself if what these kids are learning would help you in your daily life. If the answer is no, then this is not the right place for your child.

Q. Can you talk about detox?

Detox is a multi-headed beast. I needed to detox when I got to the Island, and many girls needed to detox far more than I did. We had times when girls needed weeks in the cell to fully detox. And after they detox, then you need to break the cycle. Fortunately, we were on an island where you didn't have alcohol or really any drugs, so you had no real opportunity to relapse. But then, you never learned to resist it, you only didn't do it because you didn't have access. That's not a long-term solution.

Detox is seriously ugly. I had a hard time just seeing other girls I didn't know go through it on the Island, I don't think I could handle seeing my own daughters go through it. The reality is that some parents, many parents, can't handle that. OK I get that, as a parent maybe you can't participate in the detox process for your own reasons.

But that's your issue, that shouldn't be a program's blanket policy. And yes, that may be a tough week or two or more depending on the addiction. But when it goes on for weeks and months and longer, it's a real and serious problem on the program's side.

Q. Can you talk about the difference between kids earning privileges and being put on restrictions?

First, it's a mindset. Are you trusting first, or are you distrusting first? I think there's a big difference in restricting things from the start, then taking them away from the few, and it will be just a very few, that abuse them. There will be some kids that abuse the hell out of things, it is going to happen. Fine, you deal with the issues and maybe restrictions are part of it, fine. But it's not the majority that will abuse it.

Q. Can you talk about Educational Consultants?

I don't have a lot of personal experience with EdCon's, but let's apply some logic. How much can any consultant that does not consult heavily with your teen's current therapist, teachers, and other adults in their life really know enough about them to recommend a program? This is a big red flag. Likewise, any EdCon that doesn't spend the time to get to know your child before shipping them off someplace is a big red flag. You can't get that from a form.

Also, make sure to ask about how they are compensated, because most send kids to the highest bidder.

Another major issue I have with EdCon's is the pressure they put on parents. I find it unethical. Any place that puts a lot of pressure on parents to act now or uses other sleazy used-car-salesman tactics is a big red flag to me. If you get the sleazy used car salesman vibe, it's not going to be a good program.

Q. Can you talk about medications in the TTI?

On the Island, they basically took kids off everything, including things like epileptic medications. The only meds they didn't take kids off were antibiotics. They did this because the church didn't believe in medications. I think Molly would have done much better with proper neurological care. She didn't get it.

As for modern programs, ask about medications. Like the Island, many of these places just take kids off everything, often with questionable medical oversight. Make sure they are not taking your child off meds without their current pediatrician and psychiatrist being heavily involved.

Q. Can you talk about education?

Before Dad took over, education on the Island was a joke. They had 4 math packets, addition, subtraction, multiplication, and division. It didn't matter what you knew or didn't know, you did the 4 packets over and over again. Dad did a lot to give me an education, especially in how to think, but he also missed a lot. For example, how to write an essay. The sergeants did a lot as teachers, but they still missed a lot too.

Many modern programs are effectively no better. If you are a parent, check out the education. If you don't think a college will look favorably on the education your child gets there (such as self-study packets), don't send them. Ask your local high school if they will accept the transfer credits when your child comes back. Ask the local college. If you don't get satisfactory answers, find another option, because otherwise, you are just wasting time. If the program promises its credits will be accepted, get it in writing so you have recourse when you need to pay again for those credits.

Q. I went to both a religious TTI and a non-religious TTI. The level system doesn't look like the religious one. Why is that?

Because it's not. The Island had a much more complex level system that was based both on behavure and religious elements that would have outed the church. We felt strongly that readers needed to understand the pressure and importance of the level system, but we also knew we couldn't use the real level system without exposing the church. The solution to this issue, a brilliant idea from my second co-author, was to base the level system in the book off of the level system from Solstace East, where my second co-auther went, and then we added in Island specific elements. For the purposes of the book, it worked.

Q. How does it work with modern programs? Are they State funded? How do they get kids today?

I have been out of the TTI for a long time, so I am limited in what I can say about programs today. But my Co-author Noah is a recent survivor. So I will let Noah answer this question:

Hey, this is Noah, one of the collaborators on this book and a survivor of the modern TTI. Unlike the Island, modern TTI programs are mostly private pay, meaning that parents and health insurers pay thousands of dollars per month for their kids to be there. My family was one of those.

The people running these programs and talking with parents are incredibly good at their jobs. They find parents who are scared for their kids and feeling helpless and sell their program to them. They find families at the worst points in their lives and promise to help. Not only do they promise to help, but they encourage you to "act now," saying that if you don't send your kid away /right now/ that they will end up in jail/dead in a ditch/any other number of terrifying statements specifically designed to scare you and convince you that you're a bad parent if you don't send you kid there.

Q. How do TTI programs affect the parent-child relationship in the long run?

From what I have seen, they don't help. They promise to fix your kid and family's problems, but they can't and they won't, they just aren't built for it. My first set of parents died before I went, and Dad died while I was there, so it's hard for me to speak about the family impacts. However, Noah can talk about it:

Noah here again. My parents and I didn't have a good relationship before I went away. It was tedious, tense, and explosive at both ends. It was clear we needed a change, and sadly the way that it was answered was with the TTI. The TTI preyed upon my and my parents' vulnerability to convince them that wilderness & residential was the only option.

After I was sufficiently "broken in," it sort of looked like our relationship was improving. Instead of wanting to be away from my parents as much as possible, I was begging them not to leave every visit. I was so scared to go back and I knew that even if I told them what was really happening, they wouldn't believe me, and I would get in big trouble. Any time I saw my parents it meant I didn't have the full force of the program on me, and that was a relief. It was like I got Pavloved into associating happiness with my parents.

When I finally got home, I was so relieved to not be in the program that I followed every order. But as time went on, I realized that everything was just as bad as before, except now I had new C-PTSD and would break down crying if I thought I was "bad."

Once I went to college, our relationship was falling apart. I was upset when I was around them, but every time they dropped me off at college the trauma of them taking me back to the program had me crying and asking them to stay. Sometimes I even wondered if our relationship was worth it (cutting contact with parents after the TTI is common). Luckily, I stumbled my way into this book. Our other collaborator, Steven, convinced me to keep trying. It's been a lot of hard work since then, but my relationship with my parents is slowly but surely healing. It will never be the same as what it could have been if we were given proper help, but it's better than I once imagined it could be. If we had done that work from the beginning, it would be so different. But no matter how much work we do, there will always be a scar on our relationship from it.

I promise that sending your kid to "wilderness therapy," a "therapeutic boarding school" or a "residential treatment facility" is not the only option. You and your kid are stronger than you know. Tearing your family apart is not the answer.

Q. Why and how did the Island close? Letters from the book indicate something happened with a group of girls, what was it?

As much as I would like to tell you, answering that would reveal the church, and I just can't take that risk. I am just glad it did close.

Q. Any other suggestions for parents?

Yes, you need to check these sites out:
https://www. reddit. com/r/troubledteens/
https://www.breakingcodesilence.org/
https://www.unsilenced.org/

So, with a snip here and a stitch there, and a stitch here and a snip there, I have taken my time in the troubled teen industry and turned it into this story, something much bigger than myself, something much bigger than it ever was before.

Now that I have given you my story, please do something good with it. I ask you to remember my story when dealing with a troubled teen.

Be the teens Mr. S or Sergeant Davis or Richards or Sister Beth. Or better yet, be the one that cares and makes that connection. I promise you they are worth it. You may just save a life and that soul you save may just be your own.

~Vanessa White~